DEVIL'S CHORD

Devil's Chord

ANGELA M. HERRICK

Purple Dragon Press

Published by: Purple Dragon Press
Cover design by: 100Covers.com
Printed in the United States of America

To Danny who captured my imagination
and
to Jay who captured my heart.

Chapter 1

Jack walked down the long, ornate corridor of the Los Angeles Shrine Auditorium. He felt his nerves build. He tried to ignore the whispers.

"I heard he's a hummer," a white-haired man in a tuxedo murmured to his female companion.

She giggled at the term. "A what?"

"It's when a so-called composer can't write his own music. So, he hums a little tune to the orchestrator or the arranger, and they do the real work of writing it all down."

Jack heard every word. He felt as though he was on the outside -- like he didn't belong in this world. Hell, it never felt like he belonged in any world if he was honest. It didn't matter that he was nominated; the other film composers still thought he was a fake.

"I know you heard that I told you we shouldn't be here," Jack said to Tom.

"You earned this. We're staying," Tom insisted.

A long-time fan of Jack's band, Tom Price, had given him his first film scoring job. The quirky comedy was a hit, which led to more collaborations between the two. Now, the men were as close as brothers.

Their biggest project to date, a revival of a superhero franchise, had scored the Grammy nod for Jack. He was sure a win would force the other composers to take him seriously. However, winning an award meant getting up on stage and making a speech. His language was music - not words.

In an attempt to maintain a low profile amongst the bold, early nineties fashions, Jack had dressed in a vintage, pinstripe suit circa 1935. He topped off the look with a black fedora. Tom had teased him about his ensemble in the limo.

"At least lose the hat. No one will know who you are if they can't see your hair," Tom said as the car pulled up to the artist's entrance at the auditorium.

Jack took off the hat. His copper curls tumbled out from under it, covering his ears and dusting his suit's collar. He reluctantly left the fedora on the seat next to him, knowing there'd be no way to hide without it.

Blinded by flashbulbs, Jack and Tom made their way into the lavish theatre. Once they were past the gauntlet of reporters and paparazzi, they were able to enjoy themselves a bit. Especially when they realized that they were two feet away from Madonna. They were stunned when she approached them.

"Jack Herman! I'm a big fan!" she said as and took Jack's hands in hers.

"*You're* a big fan of *his*?" Tom asked, sounding surprised. Jack shot him a look.

"Yes, Jack just scored my latest movie. Let's do lunch soon, Darling," she said as she blew air kisses to Jack and walked away.

As the men made their way to their plush red velvet seats, they shook hands with Weird Al and David Byrne. Two of Jack's favorite musicians. The tension Jack had been carrying in his shoulders had just begun to ease when he saw fellow film composer nominees Enzio Marriazi and Anton Vogel seated near the aisle.

"Evening, gentlemen," Jack said as he attempted to stand tall and force a smile.

The two composers didn't respond, choosing to stare intently at their programs.

"Jack, we're over here," Tom said as he took Jack's arm and guided him to two seats directly across the aisle. Jack stared at the men again. Tom patted him on the back, "Hey, fuck them. They're just jealous. C'mon sit down."

Before Jack could take his seat, a young woman came running up to him.

"Oh, my God! It's you," she cried. "I've grown up on your band's music. I love you! Will you sign my ..." she stopped desperately rummaging through her evening bag for a pen and paper. She produced a pen and a parking garage ticket, "um parking ticket?"

"Sure, but you'll need this later," Jack said as he smiled and signed the little stub of paper.

"Screw it. I'll tell the garage I lost it. I don't care what they charge me!" She said excitedly. Then, she hugged Jack hard and ran off to find her seat.

Tom watched the girl as she went, "She was excited and um...perky," he observed.

Jack took a second look and muttered, "She's probably half my age."

"For a minute there, I thought she was going to ask you to sign her boobs," Tom said, only half-joking.

"Well, that would've been a first," Jack said. Tom raised his eyebrows as Jack added with a devilish grin, "at the Grammys."

From across the aisle, Enzio and Anton smirked at the scene. As Jack and Tom took their seats, Jack felt the tension return to his neck and shoulders.

It took an eternity to get to the award for Best Instrumental Composition of 1992. Most of the crowd was squirming in their seats, anxious to get to their after-parties. Jack sincerely hoped they were all asleep just in case he had to go up there and make a speech. As the nominees were announced, a cameraman ran up the aisle and crouched low with his camera locked on Jack's face. The next thing Jack heard was applause. He was momentarily blinded by the light of the camera shining in his face.

Tom elbowed him lightly in the ribs and said, "Hey man, you won. Get up there."

Jack felt as though he were walking in Jello. All at once, he was on stage, but he didn't remember climbing the steps. The award was lighter than he expected, and the lights were as bright as the ones at his concerts. His speech was a blur. He made sure to thank his family first. He thanked Tom, his manager, and dozens of others who worked on the film but was sure he'd forgotten someone. His undershirt was soaked in sweat. He felt the pretty blonde who had handed him the Grammy place her hand on the small of his back and usher him backstage to speak with the awaiting media.

As the lead singer of a rock band for the past decade, Jack had given many interviews. His answers were pretty static as he found that most reporters asked the same questions or some variation thereof most of the time. However, giving an interview about his new career as a film composer was something he was still getting used to.

The first reporter of the night stood up. A young, black man from MTV, "Hey Jack. You seem to have a lot of influences from 1930s jazz. I hear a lot of percussion and horns in some of your scores and lately in your band's sound. Any chance we'll hear more of that from you in the future?"

"I feel a strong connection with that decade and its music. Something about it feels familiar to me. I've often gone for long periods where I imagine that I live in 1930s Harlem. Limiting myself to listening only to music from 1938 and earlier. If a project comes along that's a fit for it, you can bet I'll use it," Jack said.

The next reporter was a middle-aged woman from Billboard Magazine, "It's nice that you're able to moonlight as a composer, Jack. But what your fans really want to know is when the next *Ah Ooga* album is coming out?"

The mere mention of his band prompted cheers from the crowd. They had a substantial following, especially in southern California.

"The band and I have several songs ready, but we're trying to choose which ones best fit on the album," he said.

"Do you have a release date?" she asked.

"No. As I said, we're just now recording -"

"With your composing work, how will you find the time to tour?" the reporter asked, cutting him off.

"I'm not sure we will," Jack said. He hated this question almost as much as he hated touring.

"But you have to tour to promote an album. At least do your Halloween show! It's a tradition."

"I don't have the answers you're looking for. Next question, please," Jack replied curtly, hoping the reporter would back off. Who was she to tell him what he had to do?

Another reporter stood up. He was an older gentleman who stood out in this young rock and roll crowd. The man introduced himself as Sterling Thorpe from Film Score Magazine. At last, a question about film scoring, Jack thought.

Thorpe said, "Mr. Herman, you say you're a self-taught musician. Any truth to the rumors that you don't write your compositions? Is that why you work so closely with your arranger Barry Stephens? Because you don't know how to write music."

Jack clenched his fists and felt his cheeks flush with anger. He took a deep breath to compose himself before answering, "I am self-taught, but I write all of my music down. Years ago, when I was in a musical theatre troupe called The Mysterious Order of the Ah Ooga, I transcribed jazz songs. That's how I learned to write and read music. Barry was a member of that group. He's been my arranger since, oh, about 1927," Jack added the last part in jest, trying desperately to contain his temper. The answer yielded a small chuckle from the crowd.

"Is that so?" Thorpe asked.

"You know, you can say that I'm terrible. That I can handle. Music is subjective, and not everybody's going to like what I do. Fine! But, don't stand there and tell me I didn't write my scores," Jack could feel himself getting angrier by the second. Knowing he would soon say something he'd regret, he stormed off the stage, cutting the press conference short.

One of the young men working the press room hopped on stage, "Um, I guess that's all for tonight. Thank you, Mr. Herman," he called after Jack.

The limo Jack had arrived in pulled up in front of Chasen's Restaurant. Musicians, celebrities, industry types, and, of course, reporters packed the after-party... A valet in a red jacket opened the car door. Jack took one look at the scene and decided that enough was enough. He needed to have some time to unwind before bed.

"Listen, Tom, I don't want to go in there tonight. Would you mind finding another way home? I could send the driver back for you."

Tom thought to protest, then said, "That's fine! Don't worry about it." As Tom slid out of the limo, he looked back at his friend with a big smile, "Congratulations, Jack."

"Thanks, man!" Jack said as he waved to Tom.

As the limo pulled away from the party, Jack told the driver, "I need to make an extra stop, please."

"Yes, sir," said the driver.

The car wound back and forth on the path near Wilshire that led to an older neighborhood full of well-kept homes. They parked outside of a yellow Craftsman-style house, Jack's childhood home. Jack quietly exited the limo and crept up to the house. He used his key and stepped into the front room. A sleepy voice echoed from down the hall.

"You won!" Jack's mother, Miriam, said.

"Now, how did you know that?" Jack asked.

"You keep all of your awards here. I figured you must have a Grammy for me," his mom said as she shuffled into the room wearing a fluffy pink bathrobe. She turned on the lamp and moved in for a closer look.

"You're one smart cookie!" Jack said.

"Also, I watched the show," she admitted.

"Oh, Mom, I told you not to!" Jack sighed as he went to hug her.

"You were fine. Let's see it," Miriam said as she made a bee-line for the statue instead, "It's lighter than you'd think!"

"Thanks for storing them for me," Jack said.

"Are you sure you don't want to keep this one at your place? Not many people know what the BMIs are, but a Grammy's a pretty big deal."

"It's not comfortable...I just can't," he said, avoiding her gaze.

"Having all these awards on your mantle would help you charm a special lady. Not that you need any help, of course," she said with a twinkle in her eye.

"Mom, not again," Jack moaned. His mom was always pushing for him to settle down.

"I know what you're going to say, 'I'm married to my work,' But life is nothing without relationships, Jack. Take it from a lonely widow," Miriam said, meeting his gaze.

"Ha! You're not lonely. You have more friends than me," Jack said, desperately trying to change the subject.

"That's what I'm saying."

"Are you sure you want me to take my Grammy home?" Jack asked.

"Are you kidding me? This thing gives me something to brag about when I host my book club. I love it. And I love you," she said as she finally hugged him.

"Love you, too! I want to take you to dinner soon."

"No, take a nice lady friend to dinner. You hear me?" Miriam said, putting her hands on her hips.

Jack flashed her a weary smile. "Night, Mom!" he said. He blew her a kiss as he walked out the door.

Chapter 2

Jack snoozed his alarm a few times, but he couldn't ignore the hungry Australian Shepherd licking his toes as they stuck out from under the covers. He rolled over and glanced at the time. Ten AM, he was already running behind. The meeting with director Howard Fritz was an early one by Jack's standards. Howard had insisted they meet at the movie studio to hear his demo of the film's score at noon. Jack reluctantly pulled on his black slacks and a dusty blue button-down shirt. He eased his ever-present suspenders over his muscular shoulders.

There was just enough time to run his fingers through his curls in an attempt to tame them and make his way downstairs to grab his breakfast - an apple. It wasn't much, but he promised himself a big lunch. The house was clean if a bit cluttered with take-out boxes on the counter and an overflowing trash can—the artifacts of a workaholic. At least the cleaning lady was coming today, he thought. Otherwise, Rufus might counter-surf for leftovers.

Just then, his dog's wet nose brushed his hand. Jack remembered that he'd have to feed and let Rufus out before he left. He resolved to be a little late as he filled the bowl with kibble. As soon the old boy was finished, Jack started for the door. Rufus began to whimper. Jack turned and saw that his favorite toy was stuck under the sofa. As he fished it out, he was greeted with grateful dog kisses.

Now he was not only late but covered in dog slobber and fur. Jack quickly cleaned up and jumped into his BMW. He zipped down the narrow, winding road through Topanga Canyon only to sit on the 101 in LA traffic inching his way toward Burbank. It was right at noon when he finally pulled onto the lot.

Jack typically had the directors over to his home studio. Using his equipment on his turf made him feel better. Howard had insisted on meeting at the studio. He had offered this job to Jack after the success of the superhero score. This was a massive production set just before World War II.

Jack tried to make up for the lost time by walking quickly. Just as he rounded the corner to meet Howard, he collided with a young woman who held a drink carrier full of smoothies. Jack glanced down to assess the damage. Thankfully, all but one of the drinks had stayed in their places. The fourth was askew and threatened to tumble from its perch. As he reached to set it right, he caught a glimpse of the startled woman's face. Her green eyes were wide open, staring at him. He could hear the music coming from her headphones.

"Hey!" he shouted in an attempt to be heard over the music," You have to be careful when you wear those. You can't hear what's coming." The woman was still staring at him like a deer in headlights. "Hey! Are you listening to me?" He asked, getting annoyed.

"Yes, I'm listening to you," she said as she untangled the headphones from her auburn curls, "I'm listening to Ah Ooga right now!" She blushed and looked away. Her gaze fell onto the precariously perched smoothie. As she reached to set it right onto the carrier, Jack saw that the straw had pierced the bottom of the cup.

"No! Wait!" he shouted as she moved the large cup dislodging the straw. It was too late. The slimy green contents fell from the opening at the bottom and covered Jack's dress shoes.

"Aw grits!" the woman said as she took in the damage.

"What!?" Jack asked.

"Something my grandmother used to say. I'm a huge fan. Of yours, I mean, and my grandmother, too. She's great. I mean, I'm so sorry about this! I have to go," she sputtered, turning to leave.

"No worries," Jack called after her. The young woman was awkward but adorable. He thought about catching up to her and asking her to lunch. No time. He was late, and he had to deal with his slimy shoes. He found a nearby restroom and had hoped for paper towels, but the bathroom only had air dryers. He did his best to clean up with the toilet paper, but whatever was in that green concoction dissolved it almost on contact. He would just have to make do with sticky, smelly dress shoes.

"Sorry I'm late," Jack said as he entered the scoring facility and attempted to explain his series of unfortunate events to Howard.

"There's no time for chit chat. I need to give this a quick listen and head for the airport," Howard said matter of factly.

Jack didn't like the sound of that. He was hoping to explain his choices for the tone of the score. Howard sat at the bay, ready to hear the music. Jack took a deep breath and played the first cue. Howard sat motionlessly. Jack desperately tried to read his face.

After the first track was over, Howard said, "Let's hear the next one."

This continued cue after cue until Jack had played everything he had for Howard's film up to that point. Howard then sat back in his chair and sighed.

"This isn't what I expected," Howard said.

"Oh?"

"The music doesn't set the tone I envisioned. It's an epic story of lovers in a dangerous time. The music you're playing is making my lead character seem like a stalker. He's not a stalker, Jack."

"I thought the tone was more whimsical than creepy -"

"It sounds like it takes place in some damn graveyard," Howard interrupted again.

"I wanted to capture the wonder he finds in meeting the love of his life and the sorrow of being separated by war, the light and the darkness," Jack quickly explained.

"This is not a Tom Price film! I don't want a standard Jack Herman score."

"I'm sorry, but I don't what that means," Jack said.
"You know, like a haunted music box. It's all tinkly and creepy, and you're sure someone's died. I thought you wanted to branch out." Howard took a breath, "I'll be back in a few weeks to hear what you've got. If I don't like it, we may have to go in another direction."

"I'm sorry that I was so far off, Howard. Let's play the scene one more time without my score. You tell me how the scene feels to you. I want to make this right."

Jack hated watching the rough cuts from the studio because they were usually scored with temporary music. The "temp music" was needed as a placeholder for the real score when the movie was shown to focus groups. Production had already taken two years. Time enough for Howard to become accustomed to the music that was already there instead of what Jack could create. As they watched, Howard leaned in closer to the screen with a smile on his face.

"Do you hear something you like?" Jack asked.
"Yes, I really like the music because I feel transported back to the era. There's quiet desperation in it. That mournful section right after the lovers part just pulls at my heartstrings."

Feeling deflated, Jack made a note of the cue Howard liked, and the two walked out together. This wasn't the first time someone had a problem with his work, but usually, it was the producers who didn't get it. The directors typically respected him as a fellow artist. Haunted music box? What did that mean? Was he becoming predictable?

He thought about lunch but wasn't hungry. He ambled to his car, hoping for another glimpse of the charming redhead with the smoothies. She was long gone.

As Jack drove home, he turned his attention to the work at hand. There was music in his head that had to get out. Back at his house, he hurried downstairs to the studio. He touched the keys on his piano and played through a possible theme for Howard's heroine. But, when he shut his eyes, "They Can't Take That Away From Me" was all that he heard. In his mind, Billie Holiday was singing along as he played. He could smell the sweat and whiskey of a nightclub. Jack felt transported to a dark, calm place in his soul.

Chapter 3

An Ooga ran like a well-oiled machine. Jack wrote the songs, and the musicians came in and recreated the demos. It worked this way nearly every time. Occasionally, one or two players would challenge a song or even the general direction of the group. Jack appreciated constructive criticism to a point. Still, the band had seen its fair share of personnel changes over the past decade and a half.

Lately, with the film score jobs coming in back to back and sometimes one on top of the other. The band had been neglected. A new album was way overdue.

While trying to rework Howard's score, Jack struggled to put aside the old jazz music he heard in his head. Every time he touched the keyboard, an old Django Reinhardt tune would tumble from his fingertips instead, and it would then morph into his own creation. He was stuck in that world. All he could see was 1930s Harlem. The music had begun to follow him constantly; so, following the path of least resistance, Jack had turned those pieces into songs. Two birds with one stone. He could give these new songs to the band and get the music out of his head.

The horn section was thrilled with their parts as they always were With Nirvana and Pearl Jam taking over the radio, there were relatively few rock and roll jobs for horn players. The new stuff Jack presented would show off their abilities quite well. The percussion section also dug their powerhouse parts. The bass player Andrew and guitarist Barry, however, did not look amused.

"What am I supposed to play?" Barry asked.

"I have you playing that little riff in the chorus," Jack said.

"This sounds really old," Andrew said.

"You've got a good ear. It's inspired by jazz music from the mid-30s. I riffed off some old Reinhardt and Ellington and came up with this smoky melody."

"This is a big shift in sound for us," Barry said, "I'm not sure our fans will dig it. We should try adding a little more of the rock sound back in. Like we usually do."

"I know what we usually do," Jack shot back at Barry. Then, seeing that his friend looked upset, he said, "I'm just so tired of doing the same old thing."

"Why mess with success?" Andrew asked.

"Why repeat ourselves?" Jack protested.

"To pay our bills, "Andrew replied, "Look, I play bass for this band, and that's it. I don't have a whole new career to fall back on. You and Barry might, but the rest of us are counting on the new album and tour to keep us going."

"That's not fair. I've been giving you half of what I make on each film, so you don't struggle while I compose. I need the creative freedom to write what I'm compelled to write," Jack said.

"You've had that freedom. We've given you so much freedom. But it's never enough. Is it? Do you want to record whatever you feel like on our albums, too? Take away our creative freedom?" Andrew said as he crossed closer to Jack.

"You don't understand," Jack lamented as he turned away from Andrew. He ran his fingers through his curls, trying to calm the storm inside him. He grasped for words to explain precisely how he felt, but the mounting frustration of the past few days wouldn't allow it.

"Listen, you might be fine, but the rest of us have wives and kids to feed. We have real responsibilities. You've never had to worry about anyone but yourself!" Andrew yelled at Jack's back.

That was it, Jack snapped and threw a beer bottle smashing it against the wall.

"Uh, that was mine," Barry said.

"Real mature. Call me when you're done with your tantrum," Andrew fired back. He turned to the rest of the band and said, "Let's get outta here." The other musicians began to pack up their instruments and follow the bass player out through the door that led to Jack's side yard.

"Wait. I'm sorry, guys," Jack called after them as all, but Barry filed out of the studio, "I'm just drained."

"If you're this drained recording, how are you going to manage to tour?" Andrew called back as he left.

Jack sat on the couch, ashamed that he had blown up at his bandmates. He buried his face in his hands. Barry sat down next to him.

"I hate touring," Jack muttered. He looked up at Barry, who nodded knowingly. "I wish we could just go back and play the Whiskey-A-Go-Go. Those were the days."

"Dude, you always get stage fright. No matter how big the crowd."

"But the small audience was worth it. I could see the faces in the crowd and connect to them. They were ready for any crazy thing we dished out. I miss playing the songs I would dig up from the old Cotton Club radio broadcasts and putting on my white tux with tails," Jack said.

"And your devil horns?" Barry smiled and elbowed him.

"Yes. It was so much easier in the Mysterious Order shows. Going out there as Satan, a clown, or in a gorilla suit, in costume, singing jazz," he turned away from Barry, " I could squint my eyes, and it would almost feel like I was there."

"What do you mean? You were there. We have the videos to prove it," chuckled Barry.

"I meant the Cotton Club, not the Whiskey," Jack said.

"Ha! Well, you'd definitely stick out there. Are you alright, Jack? You don't seem yourself," Barry asked.

"I'm just under a lot of pressure right now. I need to take the night off. Want to come upstairs and hang out? I owe you a beer." He added as he moved to clean up the broken bottle.

"Sorry, I'll have to take a rain check. I'm going to Back to School Night with the wife."

Jack replayed the day's events in his head. He wanted to make the band and their fans happy, but he didn't think he could do this much longer. He was used to having everything in order. Now, it felt out of control. He no longer felt comfortable in his own skin. Upstairs, the house felt cold and empty. Jack walked into one small cozy room that no one else was permitted to see. This was where he kept his old jazz records. It was an extensive collection full of Cab Calloway and Duke Ellington with their orchestras. There were some Gershwin and Stravinsky albums, as well. The one rule in this room was that no music recorded after 1938 could be played. It was Jack's retreat.

On a whim, he had bought some furnishings from the late 1920s and 30s. First, he put in a vintage piano circa 1927, so he could play along with greats. Next, came the brass bed and the minibar. Jack tended to avoid alcohol while composing, but today called for whiskey. He knew that listening to Duke Ellington while sipping it would calm his nerves. The warm sensation flowed through his body from the first sip. Jack shrugged off his suspenders and surrendered to the delicious feeling of dissolving as he sank onto the bed.

The next morning, Jack woke up with a slight headache. *I should have had some water after that whiskey.* Suddenly, there was a loud knock at the door. *Who's in my house?* He wondered. Where was Rufus? Why wasn't he barking? Just then, an older woman he'd never seen before barged into the room.

"Get up. It's check-out time," the lady said gruffly.

He was baffled! *Who is this woman? Did the cleaning service send her?*

"Did you hear me?" She said impatiently, "You need to leave now or pay for another day."

Intimidated, Jack reached for his wallet, which seemed an odd thing to do in his own home. Yet, his headache worsened, so he was willing to do anything to get some peace and quiet. To his surprise, his pockets were empty. He'd left his wallet downstairs in the studio. *The studio, that's it. I'll just hide away down there and work on Howard's score while she finishes up.* He grabbed his vintage coat from the back of the chair and headed for the door. There was a chill in the air, and he thought a brisk walk down to the outside entrance would help him locate Rufus and clear his head.

As he crossed the threshold of his room, the woman said, "Don't forget your paper."

"Uh, thanks," he said, taking the newspaper from her.

As Jack reached the hall, he realized that the room he had just left bore little resemblance to his own. He'd laid his coat beside him on the piano stool last night, but this morning it was on the back of a chair. A chair he'd never seen before. Where was the piano? The furniture was similar, but not his. The shelves of records and his turntable were gone.

That's when he realized he wasn't in his hallway. He was in a foyer of what looked like an old boarding house. Out of the open front door, he could see a bustling old city instead of Topanga Canyon and his lushly landscaped yard. He tried to pause in the entryway, hoping to get his bearings, but the old woman would have none of it. She ushered Jack swiftly out of the house and shoved him onto the sidewalk. The hills and Sycamore trees had been replaced with tall, dirty buildings stretching for miles in each direction. Jack stood out of the way and glanced at the newspaper. It was The New York Age, and the date was September 5, 1938.

Chapter 4

Terrified, Jack attempted to retreat back into the house. He didn't care whether it was his or not. He turned in a blind panic to bang on the door. Just then, Jack's body slammed into a brick wall where the door had been. He hit it hard and fell onto the sidewalk. Landing with a thud. It was clear he couldn't go back the way he came.

This is a dream, it has to be. No one just wakes up in the past. Jack reassured himself. He decided to wake himself up by splashing some water on his face. He crossed the street into Central Park and headed to the pond.

At the shore, he put his newspaper aside and stared at his reflection. It was the only thing that looked familiar. Jack cupped his hands and thrust them into the pond. He splashed cold water into his face. It felt like tiny needles on his cheeks and nose. He opened his eyes, hoping he would be back in Topanga, but all he saw was Central Park to his right and Harlem on his left.

Desperate, he immersed his entire head in the water. Not the cleanest water, he realized as he came back up. Before he could open his eyes, he heard the sounds of the city instead of the quiet seclusion of the canyon.

I must really be asleep. I know what'll work. Jack slapped his cheek hard. *Nope, still here. Dammit.* Then, he bit his hand violently. "Ow! That hurt," he said as he checked his hand. *But there's no blood. I must really be out. I'll just have to go bigger.*

Jack made a fist and tried to punch himself. He automatically ducked. "I can do this, I can do this." He said, but he dodged the second try. "Turns out, it's harder than you'd think to punch yourself in the face," he murmured.

As he readied his fist again. Two cars looked as if they'd collide on the street between the park and the city. Bam! Distracted, Jack had finally succeeded in hitting himself in the nose. A trickle of blood ran into his mouth. *I might not be dreaming*, he admitted as the hair on the back of his neck stood on end.

He took a look around. His first thought was that no one looked like him. There was a sea of brown faces in every direction. It threw him off at first, especially as a few of the passersby were regarding him with the same curiosity. Jack didn't like to stand out. Sure, he fronted a band, but he had some control over when he was on stage and being noticed. Concerts had a definite structure; this was chaos. He had no earthly idea of what was happening. No idea when this would end, if it would end.

He walked a couple of blocks regarding the scene from the sidewalk next to the park. The city was Harlem. That much he knew from the paper and the fact that he had visited back in 1986, but this wasn't Harlem six years older; it was Harlem about 50 years younger!

There were large, elegant automobiles, the likes of which he had not seen outside of classic car shows or black and white movies. Men and women dressed up in clothing that was considered vintage in 1992. Absolutely every adult man wore a button-down shirt, tie, and hat. All of the women were in dresses and dress shoes; most were in heels. There was a certain charm to it.

Jack took a deep breath and slowed down for a moment. Ashamed of his initial discomfort at being the only white man in sight. He'd grown up in Baldwin Hills, after all. A section of

LA known for its diversity. He and his brother were the only Jewish kids in the neighborhood, but that was okay most of the time. Not only that, but he had spent a year in West Africa when he was only a teenager. Surely, he could navigate this. Whatever in the hell this was.

He needed to know what was going on. To blend in, he found a bench on the border of the park and sat down to read the newspaper. Perhaps this was an elaborate practical joke or an incredibly realistic dream. The paper looked authentic enough. If it was a replica, it must have been an expensive one.

The headline was about an American victory in the Davis Cup, but the articles surrounding it were far more disturbing. There were whispers of the impending Second World War with the announcement of the Olympic committee changing the future site of the 1940 Olympics from Tokyo to Helsinki.

The article that really chilled him, however, was towards the bottom of the page with the headline, "Mussolini cancels Civil Rights of Italian Jews." An Op-ed piece buried further within the paper was written by an American minister who praised Mussolini's actions and said America should do the same. Jack reminded himself that, much like the time he visited West Africa, he would have to keep his heritage under wraps to stay safe.

He turned next to the Lifestyle section. There were ads with showtimes for the jazz clubs he'd always dreamt of visiting. The Lafayette Club, Club Hot-cha, and many others. But the one that really excited him was the announcement that Duke Ellington had made a brief return to the Cotton Club. The Cotton Club was the place where all the acts who were nationally famous would come to be heard.

Listening to classic jazz music had always made him feel like he was in this place and time. *But I am here*, Jack realized. *Why shouldn't I take the opportunity to actually enjoy being here?* He would go tonight, he decided. *If I'm stuck in a dream, I might as well make it a good one.*

Suddenly, he remembered his missing wallet. *Shit!* Back in 1992, he was a millionaire; but here he was in 1938 without a cent to his name. He decided to walk down Seventh Avenue, the beginning of the nightclub district. Not much would be going on as it was lunchtime. This area would really come to life when the dinner crowd arrived from Manhattan. He would need to figure out a way to make some money before then. As he made his way toward the border of the park, his stomach began to growl. He'd have to make enough money for lunch and his evening out.

As Jack made his way through the city, he tried to think of a way to make some cash. Several blocks down, he discovered a cathedral that housed a soup kitchen. This afternoon, he would survive as he had in Africa, by pretending to be a nice Christian boy.

The nun handling the line regarded his appearance and offered to let him skip to the front. It was an appealing proposition until he looked at all the hungry black families, most with small children waiting to eat. He said, "No, thanks. I can wait," and took his place at the end of the line.

Once it was his turn, the sister approached. "We don't get many of our own in here," she said with a thick Irish accent. She led him into the shabby old gathering hall. Heavy drapes in need of dusting blocked out the sunlight. The nuns had lined as many tables and benches as possible into the room. The hungry diners sat shoulder to shoulder, eating what was quite possibly their only meal of the day.

"Excuse me?" Jack asked.

"All the nice Irish Catholic families are moving out of Harlem, you know."

"Oh," Jack said, keeping his head down.

"It's nice to see a red-headed lad like yourself in here."

"Thanks," he said.

As she started to leave, she turned and added, "We had a lovely Irish lass in here earlier. Too bad you decided to wait in line."

That's the last thing I need, Jack thought.

His belly full, Jack headed back towards the night club district. The streets of Harlem were quiet until Jack heard the sound of a trumpet. The music led him to a street corner where a young, lanky street performer leaned his body back as he played his heart out. Consumed by the tune. Jack was drawn to the power of his performance. Passersby appeared from nowhere to watch, and soon the trumpeter had a decent crowd.

The scene brought Jack back to his early days as a musician. He'd played violin in a circus in Paris, percussion in West Africa, and, finally, picked up trombone in The Mysterious Order back in LA. All those gigs had one thing in common: Street performances were required to make ends meet. *I've played for my survival before I can do it again.* Jack said to himself, slightly amused to find that he was back where he started. However, he needed an instrument.

Jack continued his walk through the nightclub district as he considered where he might find one. He cut through the alley next to the Cotton Club and admired the jazz greats' posters that lined the exterior. Across the alley was a small grimy storefront with various items in the window, including a saxophone, a violin, and a snare drum with sticks. A faded wooden sign read, "Lenny's Pawn Shop and Repair."

Without thinking, Jack rushed into the store. The greasy, weathered man behind the counter barely looked up from his paper.

"Hi there, Lenny, I presume?" Jack asked. Without looking up, the man gave him a nod.

"How much for the snare and the sticks?" Jack asked as he reached instinctively for his missing wallet, "Er, I mean, could I interest you in a trade for it?"

"Got any jewelry or guns?" Lenny grunted.

"No guns, but I have a watch," Jack said. As he reached to remove the watch from his wrist, he remembered the time. Not the hour, but the year. It was 1938; he couldn't hand Lenny a digital Casio wristwatch. How could he explain its existence? He quickly covered the watch under the cuff of his shirt. "On second thought, it's an old family heirloom. I don't think I could part with it."

"Suit yourself," Lenny called over his shoulder as he retreated to the back of his shop. Jack bolted from the store to the rear of the Cotton Club. This was frustrating as hell. It had been a long time since Jack had been broke. Left with just the clothes on his back and a useless wristwatch from the future. Jack examined the Casio, wondering if it could be the cause of his predicament. He frantically mashed a few buttons. Nothing. Frustrated, he kicked a tin can down the alley and heard it hit something that stirred and moaned. The can had hit someone.

Jack rushed over to apologize. Covered in a mound of newspapers and scraps of a decrepit blanket was an old man. His hair and beard were a stark white against his dark skin. Jack bent down and asked, "Are you alright?" The man didn't wake but let out a deep sigh that was pickled in booze. He was plastered, and he was clutching a saxophone.

It was a little dinged up, but Jack knew it would still play. It was not an instrument he felt confident playing, but he was sure he could play it better than some passed out boozer. He started to reach for the horn then stopped. It made him sick to his stomach to think of stealing, especially from someone so down on their luck. This was the elderly man's only visible possession—likely, his only means of supporting himself. No, there had to be a better way.

As he walked on, a fluffy Australian Shepherd ran up to him.

"Hey Mister, can you hold onto my dog for me?" a little boy called to Jack, "I've been trying to catch up to him for three blocks."

Jack bent down to pick up the end of the dog's leash, and the pup greeted him with kisses. The dog looked so much like Rufus. It made his heartache. Poor old boy, I hope someone is taking care of you while I'm here.

"Thanks, Mister," The little boy said as he took the leash from Jack and walked away, "Come on, Monster. We gotta get home for supper."

Suddenly, Jack heard voices on the other side of the club and decided to investigate. A truck was parked on the side street, two men were loading their gear.

The tall one said, "Man, that was a wild crowd last night!"

"Don't I know it," said the smaller of the two. At that moment, the drummer tossed a mallet in the garbage.

"Hey, that was a perfectly good mallet," said the tall man.

"Well, now that I got myself a Sugar Mama, I can get a new mallet every night. She likes the way I bang things if you know what I mean," The smaller man boasted.

"That's wasteful, man."

"Just let it go. Will ya? We gotta head to Baltimore right now if we gonna make our showtime."

They finished loading their instruments into the truck and drove off in a hurry. Jack couldn't believe his luck. He hurried over to fish the mallet out of the garbage. As he made his way through the trash, he found a slightly rusted washboard and some spoons. Those can work together, but what will I hit with my mallet? He wondered. Finally, realizing that he had unloaded quite a few empty liquor bottles from the trash, a plan began to take hold.

He set up on Seventh Avenue in front of Club Hot-Cha. He found some twine and was wearing the washboard as a breast-plate. He would beat the spoons together like castanets and play the washboard. After that, Jack set up a small xylophone fashioned out of the liquor bottles of various sizes and tones. He would tap these carefully yet rhythmically. Jack placed his fedora upside down, assuming that the gesture meant the same now as it did in 1992. He began to perform on the street just as he had done so many years ago. To his relief, passersby began to watch and place coins in his hat. Maybe he would have his evening out after all.

As Jack played, he smiled at the children who danced along to the rhythm. It felt so good to perform like this again. This was the kind of audience connection he enjoyed the most. Then, he noticed a tall, young man in the back corner listening intently. It was the trumpeter he had seen earlier. As soon as he had finished playing, the man approached. Jack was nervous. He knew he was on the man's turf; he didn't want any trouble.

"Hey, you sure are a whiz with that mallet," The young man said, extending his hand to Jack, Name's Lowry Ringgold. I'm a musician, too. Wanna jam?"

"I know I was listening to you earlier. You're a solid horn player. I'm Jack Herman, by the way," he said as they shook hands.

Lowry took up his trumpet, and Jack played on his makeshift xylophone of booze bottles. Together they drew an even bigger crowd. He couldn't help but notice that the attrac-tive trumpeter attracted a sizable female following. *Ah, to be young again.*

A half an hour later, they had a decent amount of money in each of their hats. The men called it a day.

"You must be new here because I sure would have remembered if I'd seen your act before. Not too many red-headed percussionists in Harlem," Lowry said.

"Just got in today," Jack said, carefully hiding his watch.

"No kidding? Where from?" Lowry asked.

"I'm from Los Angeles," Jack answered. Sticking as close as possible to the truth seemed more manageable than trying to remember a bunch of lies.

"You came all that way? I thought I was nuts makin' the trip from N'awlins, but that's like a whole nother country! Did you work in the pictures?"

Jack almost told him he was a composer but stopped. *If I tell him I wrote music for movies, he'll want to know which ones.* "No, but I've always wanted to write music for movies," Jack said instead.

"You and me both. When I was a kid, my folks would take me to see the silent pictures. Those musicians would make up music on the fly to fit the action on the screen. It was aces! I always wanted to do that. Course, now all of em' are talkies, so I've had to dream me some new dreams."

"That would be a challenge. I'd be worried I'd fu- uh, I mean screw up their movie. Sorry," Jack said as he admired Lowry's pluck. *Imagine scoring a movie in front of a live audience!*

"It's alright. I'm 21," Lowry said with a chuckle, "these ain't exactly virgin ears."

Lowry had let him off the hook, but Jack resolved to watch his language moving forward. Desperate to change the subject, he said, "I've always been keen to visit New Orleans."

"It's the best, but if you wanna play with the big boys, this is the place to be! I'm parched after that set. You wanna come to my place and grab a drink?"

"That'd be nice. You could tell me some more about N'awlins," Jack said.

"I'd love to. Where ya staying, by the way?"

"That's a good question," Jack said. He hadn't thought about that, "I happen to be looking for a place to hang my hat while I'm here."

"Come with me, my man," Lowry insisted.

Chapter 5

Lowry's apartment was in a building that looked as if it had once been a grand turn-of-the-century home. Now, a shabby shell of what it once was, the place had been chopped up into several apartments. Jack and his new friend ascended a grand staircase that was in some state of disrepair. The stairs themselves were sturdy, but the once-elegant trim on the banister was broken and missing in places. At the top of the stairs was Lowry's place. It had high ceilings and tall thin floor-to-ceiling windows. The crown molding was broken in places; the wallpaper was peeling and more than a few layers thick.

"It ain't much, but it's home," Lowry said, showing Jack around the tiny studio. "You can sleep on my couch as long as you need."

"I don't have a job yet. It would be a bit before I could pay you," Jack said.

"Come down to the club with me. They're always looking for people."

"Where do you play?"

"Cotton Club, I play trumpet in the house orchestra," Lowry said proudly.

"You want me to come play with you at the Cotton Club?" Jack asked.

"Hold up. No one said anything about playing, but we've been looking for someone to maintain the instruments."

"Oh," Jack said as he felt the heat rise in his cheeks.

"The joint's been packed every night, and the boss added a midnight show, so the cats have kinda let that stuff slide. We're all pretty beat by two a.m."

Jack was taken aback. He was used to headlining stadiums and composing film music. *I pay people to maintain instruments for me.*

Breaking the awkward silence, Lowry added, "If you can't do maintenance, they're always hiring busboys."

In his youth, Jack had actually done both of these jobs, no way in hell was he going to back to cleaning after up other peoples' meals. "Oh, I can do maintenance. I build instruments, too. And of course, I play a bit." He offered again.

Lowry took a long look at Jack, "After jamming with you today, I think you just might have what to takes to sub in. Our regular skin tickler is frequently soused. One step at a time, though, okay?"

"Skin tickler? Oh, your drummer!"

"That's what I said."

"I play a few other instruments, too." Jack offered.

"Great. More opportunities to sub in that way. You do maintenance and play. Hmm, we may find a use for you, yet," Lowry said with a grin.

The pair walked up Lenox avenue at dusk. Jack's pulse quickened as he saw the famous marquee now fully lit. Until today, he'd only seen it in old black and white photographs. He was standing in front of the most famous jazz club of the Harlem Renaissance. The Cotton Club stood before him in full color. He was about to witness musical history in the making and participate in his own small way. Even if it was just maintenance.

Jack took his time walking into the club. The dinner crowd had started to arrive. He saw a large, muscular, white man working the door and noted that he was probably the bouncer. It was evident by their manner of dress that the patrons filing in were all white people of means. As he looked on, a well dressed black couple walked in with the crowd and took a seat in the middle of the club. A white, gray-haired man came out of the back office and pointed them out to the bouncer. Who made a beeline for the couple, quickly showing them the door. Jack noted that not only were there no black patrons, but the floor staff was also completely white. The only black people were the ones waiting backstage to entertain them. He found this fact all too disturbing and decided to catch up with Lowry backstage.

"Wow! Look at the red devil Lowry's drug in." Exclaimed an old man tuning an upright bass.

"This here's Jack Herman. He's a skin tickler," Lowry said.

"Among other things," Jack added.

"Red devil! Ha! Man's so pale, I thought we were being haunted," chortled the big guy holding a trombone.

Jack took the ribbing in stride. He knew it was good-natured, and he kind of dug the nickname.

"Hey, guys. It's swell to meet you," he said, "Lowry says you need someone to help with maintenance and to sub in occasionally. I'm here to help."

"Appreciate the help. Name's Moses, show me what you can do with this," he said, handing Jack his old trombone.

Jack spotted the maintenance closet and wasted no time cleaning and polishing the horn and tuning the slide. Then, he took a deep breath and began to play, hoping that the song he was about to play already existed in 1938. In his element, Jack began to relax. He danced over to the chair and picked up the mute. Using it at the end of the bell, Jack launched into a solo. When he finished, all the men were staring at him.

"That's not half bad," Moses said, genuinely impressed.

"Come with me," Lowry said as he and Moses led Jack to the piano in the rehearsal room, "Show us what you can do on the keys."

Jack wasted no time. He sat down and launched into "Take the A Train."

"Very nice," Lowry said. He and Moses looked impressed, but another young man in the doorway smirked.

Jack went to the club with Lowry every night that week. He felt out of place in 1938; who wouldn't in his position? But, the instruments' vibrations through his body felt the same now as they had in his time. Playing them soothed him, if only for a moment.

Then there were the shows. Seeing Duke Ellington play live was better than he'd ever imagined. The bouncer would allow Jack to sit in the back and take in the early show before sending him on his way. He wasn't allowed to sit too close; the bouncer had made that clear. On more than one occasion, Jack overheard the large man refer to him as a "coonlover" to others as they came and went from the club.

He wasn't wholly welcome backstage either. While Moses and Lowry had been friendly, some of the other musicians refused to acknowledge his presence. Others would talk in hushed tones, suddenly going silent when Jack appeared. Never feeling quite at home in the club, he adopted a routine of getting there early, fixing what needed to be fixed, and taking his seat at the back of the hall. Being extra careful to leave before overstaying his welcome.

Weeks of not really fitting in anywhere began to weigh on him. Jack had always been a reserved man, but he'd had a few close friends and family members to reach out to. Now, it was impossible to reach any of them. Maybe his family, friends, and even Rufus were lost to him forever.

One foggy late September evening, Jack was lying on the couch reading the paper. In the top right corner of the page was a review of the Duke's triumphant return to the club. The headline read "The Duke's Return Brings Other Talent to the Court." The article by a reviewer named Beck Taylor discussed the many talented musicians in Duke Ellington's orchestra. He praised the talent and energy with which they played. Also, singling out many of the men in the house orchestra. It all sounded so exciting. But it wasn't, not for Jack. He was once again on the outside looking in.

He looked up from his paper in time to meet Lowry's disappointed gaze, "Why ain't you dressed? We gotta split soon."

"I think I need to look for another gig, man. Being around music and never getting to play is really frustrating me."

"Tonight is not the night for you to decide to quit. Come on," Lowry said as he playfully pulled Jack off the couch. Jack noticed that Lowry was grinning to himself and trying hard to conceal it as they walked to the club.

Moses met them as they entered through the backstage door. When he greeted Jack and Lowry, Lowry's grin reached its full Cheshire Cat potential. Whatever was going on, Jack was sure Lowry was in on it.

"Would you like to sub in? I've got a missing second chair. He's probably still blotto from last night," Moses explained.

Would he like to sub in? Jack couldn't believe it. He was once again worried this might be a dream. Was he really about to play with Duke Ellington? If it was a dream, he didn't want to wake up!

As he entered the backstage area, many of the performers stared at him. There were a few welcoming smiles, while others regarded him with annoyance and outright disgust. As he made his way to the men's dressing room, he heard Lowry arguing with another man.

"Lowry, I don't care how good he is, he's got no business sharing the stage with us," a young man with dark brown skin said as they entered the room, "If we're not good enough to sit out there with the whites then they don't belong on our stage!" He protested.

Lowry noticed Jack in the doorway. He cleared his throat and said, "Isaac, if we tell talented musicians they can't play with us because of their race then we're no better than them."

"Can't we have something of our own? Something they ain't got a say in?" Isaac asked Lowry.

"Maybe I shouldn't be here," Jack muttered.

"That's nuts! You've got the chops. Now get ready, cause we're on in ten," Lowry reassured him.

"I've got my eye on you. We've worked too damn hard to get here. Don't you mess it up," Isaac said to Jack as he brushed past him.

As the room started to empty, Jack dressed for the performance and sat down in front of the mirror. *What in the hell am I doing? This is crazy, I don't even like being on stage all that much. That guy's not the only one who doesn't want me here. I saw the looks I got walking backstage. What if Duke Ellington doesn't want me up there?* He began to get a sick feeling in his stomach, sweat gathered on his brow.

"It's almost showtime. Places everyone," A woman called out from the hall.

"Thank you, places," Jack replied.

After a moment, the woman called from outside the door. "Places are at the back of the stage, not in the dressing room. Everything all right in there?"

"Yea," Jack said weakly.

"You don't sound alright. Can I come in?" asked the voice in the hall. The woman's voice sounded sweet and calm. He wanted to hear more.

"Please," he said as he tried to conceal his anxiety.

A cute redhead walked into the room. Jack's heartbeat even faster.

"Oh, what are you doing here?" She asked, "Did someone break an instrument?"

"What?" Jack asked.

"You're the guy who fixes the instruments, right?" she asked.

"Yeah. I'm supposed to be subbing in on trombone, but now I'm choking," Jack admitted. As he said it out loud, his body gave up all pretense. The color drained from his face, and his shoulders slumped as he slid down in the chair a bit.

"Sounds like stage fright. Here, take this towel and wipe off your brow. Want me to grab you some water?"

"Yes please," Jack said.

As he patted his brow with the towel. He noticed his hand was trembling slightly. Jack watched the woman as she turned to get him a glass of water from the sink. He couldn't take his eyes off of her. As she approached, he found comfort in her kind smile.

"Hey, Rebecca!" Moses called out from the hall, "You see my second?"

"The red-headed guy?" the woman asked.

"That's the one. Come on, Red Devil," Moses said.

"He's on the move," Rebecca said as she gently took Jack's arm and led him down the hall, "Come on, take some slow deep breaths. You're gonna be great."

The hall was long and dark. For a moment, it felt as though the walls were drawing closer as if to crush him in between. He tried slowing his breath as Rebecca had told him to do. "I always get so nervous before I go on," Jack explained sheepishly.

"Do you need a bucket? Leroy gets sick before every show. So, we have extras."

"It's not that bad," Jack said.

"Good, because you're on," Rebecca said as she gave him a gentle nudge up the stairs to the stage.

Chapter 6

Once the lights came up, and the adrenaline took hold, Jack was able to play. The show was a blur! Seeing Duke Ellington live on stage was phenomenal even if it was mostly looking at his back while trying to play a horn. It had been a while since Jack played trombone. The last time he played was with The Mysterious Order of the Ah Ooga, a musical troupe his brother Robert founded.

He was no longer accustomed to the facial vibrations, and it made his nose itch. He knew that the performance was far from his best, but he hoped it was good enough for him to be invited back. As he walked down the hall, the clarinet player purposely tripped him. Jack grabbed onto a pipe on the wall and caught himself, "Hey, what's wrong with you?" he asked.

"Ain't nothing wrong with me. I know my place. You need to find yours and stop taking jobs from our people."

Lowry was waiting for him in the dressing, "Well, that was a good start, Jack. You were a little rough, but you'll catch on soon enough."

"I don't know about that," Jack said as he glanced across the hall at Isaac and the clarinet player. The two were engaged in a hushed conversation and occasionally paused to look over at him, "Some of the guys have made it clear that I'm not welcome."

"You really going to listen to them?"

"They're pretty hard to ignore," Jack protested.

"You think all of us have had an easy time finding a place that would let us perform? We all worked hard to get here. No one hands someone who looks like us a job—especially one where we're on stage in front of white folks. We have to be twice as good as other musicians for them to listen to us. If this gig means as much as you say it does then stay and earn your right to be here."

Lowry was right. Jack knew that nothing worth having comes without some kind of fight. He would stay and do the midnight show. Prove to them that he deserved to be there. At this point, what did he have to lose?

"How we doing tonight, boys?" asked a tall man with a British accent. All eyes turned to see an older, smartly dressed man enter the room. Jack recognized him as the big boss. They'd never met face to face. After all, the boss spent most of his time barking orders from his office. Finally getting a closer look, the man reminded Jack of a movie star. He wasn't brawny like his bouncer, but he carried himself with an air of absolute authority.

All of the men looked a bit apprehensive as they murmured greetings to their boss. He turned and noticed Jack.

"And who might you be?" he asked.

"Jack Herman," Jack said, offering his hand. The man shook it with a firm grip.

"Name's Owney. Owney Madden, this is my club. I heard you hired on for maintenance. Didn't realize you were a performer. You planning to do it again?" he asked.

As Owney stared at him with piercing blue eyes, Jack chose his words carefully, "If you and the orchestra will have me. It would be an honor."

"We don't have too many performers like you here. Most people come down here from their high rises just to see how animalistic these jungle boys can be. They take that primitive energy back uptown if you know what I mean."

"Mr. Madden?" Jack began.

"Owney, please."

"Owney, do you have a moment to come up on stage with me before the house opens for the late show? I'd be happy to show you what I can do."

The two men headed back up the stairs. Stage fright had always manifested in unusual ways for Jack. He was nervous playing in front of crowds, but he could use that nervous energy to push through and even enjoy the rest of the show. However, playing for one person, auditioning no less, was torture.

Fortunately, he wasn't alone with Owney for long, as most of the musicians followed them. He played a bit on the piano, then borrowed Dusty's violin and showed off by performing Stephen Grappelli's part in "Minor Swing" by Django Reinhardt. Owney and boys were tapping their toes to the bouncy melody. Then, Jack took a seat in front of the main drum kit, letting loose on the skins. It felt so good to hit something.

As Jack struck the drums, the tension loosened in his shoulders and neck. Where it had gathered into tight knots underneath the skin. Sweat poured gloriously down his back. He finished his solo with a flourish and grinned expectantly at Owney.

"Not bad, Mister...what was your name again?"

"It's Herman, Jack Herman."

"Let's give it a shot, Jack. Work hard and don't make any trouble. Unless I ask you to," Owney said with a wink. He turned and called out, "Pipes!"

"Yeah, Boss?" The bouncer answered from across the hall.

"Jack Herman works up here now. Tell Rebecca to take care of the paperwork."

"You got it," Pipes said as he lumbered off in the direction of Owney's office.

"Pipes? Is he a singer, too?" Jack asked.

"Ha! He's got a voice like a frog. The name's from squeezing other people's pipes. He keeps the riff-raff out of this joint."

A little unnerved, Jack headed backstage to freshen up for the midnight show. He turned the name Owney Madden over in his mind. He'd heard the name before. Connected to the Cotton Club, but somewhere else, too. As he changed his shirt, Moses came over to him.

"Bossman give you any trouble?" Moses asked in a low voice.

"No, I just needed to prove that I had the chops to play with you fellas."

"Be careful around him. They don't call him "The Killer" for nothing. He's got that fancy accent, but he was in the pen not long ago for plugging some other hood over a dame. Best to keep a low profile."

"Got it," Jack said as he tried to sound nonchalant. That's where he'd heard the name before. Owney was not only the owner of the Cotton Club, he was also an infamous gangster. *Great. I haven't even been here that long, and now I'm working for a gangster.* A knock at the dressing room door interrupted his thoughts.

"Hey, fellas. I have fresh undershirts, everyone decent?" Rebecca called out.

"Yes," the men said.

Rebecca entered, weighed down by a towering stack of shirts. Jack reached out and took them from her. Their arms briefly brushed against one another. Jack felt a spark; he wanted to touch her again. Distracted, he nearly dropped the shirts. Rebecca reached out to help steady the stack. Both of her arms pressed against his as they struggled to gain control of the laundry. Together they set the shirts on a nearby chair for the men to go through.

"Thanks for the help," she said as she smiled shyly at him.

"My pleasure," he said.

"Are you feeling better? Do you need anything?" she asked.

"I'm feeling much better. Thanks," Jack said with a big grin. Why couldn't he stop smiling at her?

"Hey, Rebecca," Lowry called out "Leroy's gonna need that bucket."

"Be right back," she said, dashing down the hall.

Jack was disappointed to see her go. He turned and looked at Leroy, who wasn't a bit green. Lowry came up and handed him a clean undershirt. Jack realized he was even sweatier than he had been during the drum solo. He started to change.

"Cute as a bug's ear, isn't she?" Lowry said.

"Uh-huh," Jack said.

"I knew it!" Moses said as he laughed, "Didn't I tell you the ole Rusty here would be sweet on our little gingersnap?"

"Wait, I didn't say I was sweet on her. I don't even know the girl. She's probably too young for me. Besides, I prefer sophisticated women," Jack said as he grew more agitated. It was none of their business.

All eyes were staring past Jack. He turned around and was face to face with Rebecca - and he was shirtless. She stared directly at his torso and blushed. Then, her gaze shifted to Leroy. She remembered her mission and ran past Jack handing the bucket to Leroy. She turned as if to say something to Jack, but stopped and left the room so quickly that she hit the door frame hard with her shoulder.

"Aw grits!" she exclaimed out in the hall.

Jack felt terrible, but at the same time, he was trying to remember where he'd heard that phrase before.

"You okay, Miss Rebecca?" Moses called after her, but all they heard was the clicking of her heels as she took off down the hall.

"Well, well, well, aren't you the ladies man," Lowry said as the rest of the room erupted in laughter.

"Gentleman, we have a show to play," Jack said as he tried to recover some dignity. *It's good to know that I am just as awkward with the ladies in 1938 as I am back in the 90s*, he mused as he walked up the stage steps. He was ready to have a stage and an audience. *Time to regain some control of my surroundings, even if it's only for a little while.*

The midnight crowd was much more fun than the dinner audience. The patrons were loud and tipsy, just the way he preferred them. Moses let him take the solo, which was a tremendous surprise, and Jack played like he was on fire. Most of the audience was encouraging, but he caught that a few stares and whispers were exchanged. He decided to use their rejection as fuel to continue; he would keep showing up, determined to win them over.

After the show, Jack tended to a few of the horns. He could still hear the crowd ringing in his ears but noted that it was not nearly as loud as playing in front of a rock band. His thoughts turned to the hearing test he'd had weeks before he arrived in Harlem. After reviewing the results, the audiologist told him to retire. Fronting a rock band for so many years was costing him his hearing.

Rebecca walked in front of the stage, then into Owney's empty office. Jack saw her gather up the night's earnings and place them in a deposit bag.

"Pipes? The deposit's ready," she said.

Pipes appeared from behind the bar. "Thanks. I was just having a bite. Boss said to remind you that you can eat dinner out here with us before we open if you want."

"I'm fine eating backstage," she said defiantly.

"Suit yourself. I gotta scram," Pipes said as he wiped his mouth with his sleeve, then left with the money in tow.

"So, is Owney your daddy?" Jack asked her as she exited Owney's office.

Rebecca turned startled by his voice. With some confusion, she said, "No, we're not related."

"Not that kind of daddy, " Jack said with a smirk.

"Oh. No! He's just my boss," she said.

"Sounds like he wants to be more," Jack said.

"Why would you say that?" she asked, looking even more puzzled.

"He invited you to dinner."

"Owney's dating a gorgeous actress. He only wants me to eat out here because that's where the white people are supposed to eat," she explained. As she went past him, he could see that she was obviously annoyed, but he wasn't sure if it was with him or the topic at hand. Then, she called back over her shoulder, "He'll ask you; next, you'll see."

"Well, then I'm glad we cleared that up before he offered," Jack joked as he followed her through the maze of tables and chairs. Rebecca let out a little chuckle as she continued toward backstage. There was music in her laughter. He could listen to it forever.

"Hey! If you could eat dinner with anyone. Who would it be?" He called after her.

After a long pause, she turned to Jack and answered, "James Cagney."

"So, you do like redheaded men." he teased, noting that her cheeks had turned crimson.

"Well...who said it was the hair? Maybe I just like men who are... great dancers," Rebecca said, playfully.

"You mean like this?" Jack offered as he went into a wild dance from his musical theatre days. It was far from the sophisticated dance moves of Cagney. Rebecca laughed, and to his astonishment, she joined him. Rebecca stopped abruptly.

"Well, that wasn't very sophisticated," she said, looking away.

"Listen, I'm sorry about earlier. It was just that the guys were, uh. I mean, I'm just not -"

"Rebecca? You out there, honey?" a woman's voice called from backstage.

"Yes, Mama Esther," Rebecca called back to her.

"Let's go home," Mrs. Esther said as she came around to the front of the house. She was one of the older solo singers from the house orchestra. A powerful performer with a big soulful voice.

"You live with Mrs. Esther?" he asked.

"She's a widow, so she takes in boarders. Mostly, girls who work at the club," Rebecca said. Her guard was up again, her arms folded protectively in front of her.

"Then I guess you don't need me to walk you home," Jack said, disappointed.

"No, she doesn't," said Mrs. Esther as she grabbed Rebecca's arm and led her toward the exit.

"Goodnight, Jack," Rebecca said as she looked back over her shoulder.

As they neared the door, Esther said, "Watch out for those musicians, you hear?"

"You can walk me home," said Lowry in a feminine voice, as he sauntered over to Jack.

"Thanks," Jack said as Lowry laughed at his own joke.

Chapter 7

Jack woke up and rolled off Lowry's couch onto the hardwood floor. He'd dreamt he was back in his king-sized bed in his home in the hills. Instead, he was smacked in the face by 1938.

"Mornin', watch that first step, it's a doozy," Lowry said, "And so is the review from last night."

"They actually gave Duke Ellington a bad review?!"

"No, just you."

"Let me see that," Jack said, grabbing the paper from Lowry. The headline read "Strange happenings at the Cotton Club" by Beck Taylor. The article went on:

"Since its inception, the Cotton Club's been supporting black talent. Mr. Madden has taken great pains to host and promote through national, bi-weekly radio broadcasts the gold standard in jazz and vaudeville. Including giving a start to the now world-famous Duke Ellington and his orchestra." Mr. Taylor went onto praise the Duke and noted several outstanding performers and musicians before adding, "That being said, I didn't care for the inclusion of trombone player Jack Herrmann in last night's show. He was a decent musician, but why keep the dining room of the Cotton Club segregated and include white performers onstage? The jazz district is one of the few places in New York City for black performers to earn a living. Someone like Mr. Herrmann could surely find an audience almost anywhere else in the city."

Jack threw down the paper and pulled on his coat.

"Where are you going?" Lowry asked.

"I'm going down to The New York Age office to give that Beck Taylor a piece of my mind," he said.

The office was several blocks away. Jack was so angry he almost mowed into several people on the sidewalk. Nearly collided with two moms walking side by side pushing baby buggies. Almost punted a tiny dachshund, he didn't see walking next to his humongous and imposing owner.

Still, he tore up the street as fast as his legs would carry him. When he reached the building on Seventh Avenue, he was surprised to see that the newspaper occupied only a small storefront. Still furious, he stormed into the newspaper's office and demanded to speak to Mr. Taylor.

"He has no right to tell me where I can or can't play! Tell that coward to come out here and face me like a man," Jack demanded.

Just then, a small, Jewish man close to Jack's age entered the reception area, "I'm Virgil Gellar, the editor. May I help you?"

"Where's Beck Taylor?"

"Mr. Taylor is not employed by the paper," Virgil explained, "We're a small publication. As with most of our writers, he is paid per review."

"How can I find him?" Jack asked.

"Casey, do we have an address on file for Mr. Taylor?" the man asked his receptionist.

"No, sir, we don't," she said as she looked through Beck Taylor's file, "He's new."

"We need to get his contact information next time he's in."

"It's just that I've never seen him. He always sends his assistant," Casey explained.

"His assistant?" Virgil asked.

"Yeah, a redheaded lady. She works nights at the Cotton Club. I think her name is Rebecca."

"Thanks!" Jack said as he took off.

When he arrived at the club. Rebecca was already running around backstage, preparing the dressing rooms for the performers' arrivals.

"Evening, Jack."

"We need to talk," he said.

Rebecca said, "Oh. Okay. We can use Owney's office. He's not in yet."

Rebecca tried to engage Jack in small talk on the way, but he was so angry he answered only in little grunts and scoffs. By the time Rebecca shut the office door, he could barely contain his anger.

"Where the hell is Beck Taylor?" he demanded.

"How would I know?" Rebecca asked, looking at her feet.

"Don't play coy with me. The lady at the newspaper said you were his assistant. I need to speak to him."

"Why?"

"I'm sure you read his column. He blasted me last night. He could cost me my job!"

"Owney's not going to fire you," she said as she smiled and walked toward Jack, "Beck wasn't talking about you specifically. It was more about segregation. A talented man like you could play anywhere."

"Wait. Are you defending him? Why would you do that? Is *he* your fella or something?"

No answer. Rebecca backed away until Owney's large desk was between them.

"Great. That's just great," Jack said.

After a long silence, Rebecca met Jack's gaze and said in a low voice, "If I tell you where you can find Beck Taylor, will you promise not to tell anyone?"

"Fine. Where is the bastard?"

"Right here. I'm Beck Taylor. It's my pen name," she said.

Jack felt like he'd been punched in the gut. He was so furious he couldn't speak.

Beck explained, "Back home, I always went by Beck, never Rebecca. One of my first tasks here was to call and invite the reviewer to see the show. I forgot. I was so desperate to keep this job that I wrote the review myself. I used the name Beck to throw Owney off. When I turned in that first article, everyone at the paper assumed Beck Taylor was a man, and that I was his assistant. I had a feeling that if I corrected them, Owney would fire me or worse, and my reviews would never see the light of day."

Jack was livid, "RIght now, I wish they hadn't!" As he moved for the door, he added, "If you were going to screw me over, you could have at least spelled my name right."

"Jack, we both know that wouldn't be safe for you," she said in a hushed voice.

Rebecca had a point, it was a dangerous time to be Jewish. She'd purposely changed the spelling from "Herman" to the German spelling, "Herrmann." Having no idea what to do with her care and concern, he stormed backstage. Lowry was just coming in.

"Do you need help burying the body?" Lowry asked.

"What body?"

"I figured you done killed you a newspaperman the way you stormed out this morning. Did you find him?"

"It's...complicated," Jack said. Wondering why he bothered protecting Rebecca or Beck when she didn't deserve it. *She protected you.* He immediately tried to dismiss it. He wasn't ready to think nice things about her.

The two of them managed to avoid each other most of the evening. Jack grabbed his own towel and water. Beck busied herself with Leroy, who was sicker than usual due to nerves and some bad seafood he ate. Jack checked the board and found out he was subbing on drums. Good, he needed to hit something instead of someone. He looked forward to the release.

Chapter 8

Beck's review had emboldened those who felt Jack didn't belong at the Cotton Club; they were even more vocal about his presence. He responded by drawing into himself, like a wounded turtle in its shell. For the past week, he did his job, came home, and slept. Interacting with others only when he absolutely had to. Jack had gone as far as to learn Lowry's schedule and feign sleep until the apartment was empty.

He picked up the newspaper dated October 1st. *My favorite month, and I'm stuck here.* As he sat at the table, he saw a note on the table with his name on it. The handwriting was bubbly, with large loops. The cream-colored envelope had purple roses on the flap. It smelled vaguely of vanilla. He opened it to find a single sheet of stationery, it too was cream-colored with purple roses climbing down the left-hand side of the paper. It read:

"Dear Jack,

I'm sorry about the review. It was wrong of me to criticize you for performing at the club, based on the color of your skin. I write my articles to promote the talented black performers there because I want others to see them for the artists they are and not solely for the novelty of their appearance and origins. You are so much more than a 'decent' musician. You're truly gifted, and that should have been all that I said about you in my review. I have submitted a retraction to the newspaper. Please let me know if there's anything else I can do to mend this rift between us.

Yours,
Beck"

In his mind, Jack forgave her immediately. Her note made him dizzy. Rebecca admired his music. She wanted to fix things between them. Why was he so giddy? Why was he still smelling her letter? "Uh, oh! I'm crazy about her," he said to himself. Starting something with Beck was a bad idea for many reasons. They worked together. She was a lot younger than him. He would be forty soon, and she was only in her mid-twenties. *I guess technically she's about forty years older than me*, he thought, half amused.

Then, he thought about the big question, whether or not he'd ever return to 1992. Jack had no understanding of how he'd come to be here. Originally, he'd suspected his Casio watch since it traveled with him, but he'd pushed every button on the damn thing in every combination. Eventually, he gave up and hid it in the top of Lowry's closet.

At any rate, I'd have to leave at some point, right? But there's been no indication of that. I might never return to my own time. Maybe, I'm overthinking it. Death is just as unpredictable. Maybe I should take a few chances. After all, no one lives forever.

The matter settled, Jack headed to the Cotton Club with a grin on his face. Lowry greeted him backstage.

"I see someone got their fan mail," Lowry said.

"Evening, Lowry," Jack said. He patted his buddy on the back.

"Glad to see you're finally in a better mood."

"Much better," Jack said.

He walked all over the club and backstage. He couldn't manage to find Rebecca. Finally, she peeked her head out of the ladies' dressing room and upon seeing him went right back inside. When she came to announce ten minutes to places and bring Leroy his bucket, Jack approached her.

"Do you need something?" she asked, avoiding his gaze.

"Can we chat after the show?"

"Okay," she said as she turned to leave.

Jack was subbing in for the horn section again. Mr. Ellington had resumed his tour, and Cab Calloway wouldn't return for a few weeks. This meant that the club was left with the smaller house orchestra, and there'd be more filler from lesser-known singers, even some comic skits to lead into the songs. The guys asked Jack if he wanted to go from his trombone solo into singing "St. James Infirmary". He was thrilled.

"Since you call me the Red Devil, maybe I should dress up," he suggested.

His song was after the last skit, so he ran back to the dressing room and put on a black vest, red bow tie, and glued a pair of fake horns to his head. Recreating his favorite costume from his Mystic Order days. Renewed, Jack played and sang his heart out. At last, the whole crowd was with him.

Out of the corner of his eye, he caught a glimpse of Rebecca. She looked as if she'd seen a ghost. She didn't move for the entire song. After he took a bow, he gave her a little wink as he ran past. The color returned to her cheeks. She followed the band down the hall and waited for him outside the dressing room. He quickly toweled off and grabbed a drink of water. Then, he took her hand and led her into the alley.

"I got your letter," he said.

"Good," Rebecca said. After a moment of awkward silence, she looked at him, "Are we okay?"

"I don't think I'd ever want you as an enemy. If that's what you mean," Jack said as he grinned at her.

Rebecca laughed then asked, "Does that mean you'd like to be friends?"

"I don't know. If I take you to dinner, will you continue giving me bad reviews?"

"That depends, are you bribing me with dinner so I won't?"

"Maybe," Jack said playfully.

"Oh, really?"

"You're an intriguing person, Rebecca. I'd like to get to know you better," Jack said in earnest.

"Back at ya," she said. Then she glanced around to make sure they were really alone and added, "Please call me Beck. When it's just us. I mean."

"But I will feel the sting of your words every time I say it," he said melodramatically.

"I think you'll rally - eventually."

"The club's dark tomorrow night. Is it a date?"

"As long as you wear the horns," Beck said under her breath.

"What was that?" he asked, knowing full well what she'd said.

"Nevermind," she said, blushing once more.

"Be careful what you wish for, Beck," he said, touching her arm and giving her a mischievous grin.

Chapter 9

Mrs. Esther lived on the opposite end of the nightclub district on a street with stately old homes that had once been occupied by wealthy Jewish families. Once the black families moved into Harlem, most Jewish families moved out, dividing their homes into rental apartments.

Esther's place was different. She was the only black person in 1930s Harlem Jack knew of who owned her own home. Unlike the buildings with absentee landlords, Esther's grown sons maintained the house for her. Her husband, who had been one of the city's first black doctors, died several years earlier, leaving her the sole owner.

The woman was incredibly independent and no-nonsense. Jack hated to admit it, but he was more than a bit intimidated by her. Nonetheless, she was fiercely devoted to the women who lived under her roof. If he wanted to take Beck out, he had to go through Mama Esther.

"What do you want?" she asked as she swung the door open.

"Evening, Mrs. Esther. I'm here to take Beck to dinner. Didn't she tell you?"

"Don't be coy with me, Jack Herman," she said as she narrowed her eyes at him.

"Excuse me?"

"What are your intentions toward my Rebecca?"

"To show her a good time," Jack said.

Mama Esther slammed the door in Jack's face.

"I didn't mean it like that. I just want us to have fun and get to know each other better," Jack called through the closed door. *The last time I had to work this hard for a date, I was in high school.* The door didn't open, but Jack could hear that Mrs. Esther was having a conversation on the other side of the door.

"That red devil is only after one thing. I know these musician types, why do you think I married a doctor instead?"

"I don't know if I even want to get married, Mama Esther," Beck said, "I'm only twenty-five, I have plenty of time to think about settling down later."

"Are you crazy?! Twenty-five is entering old maid territory. We've got to find you a fella fast."

"Well, you could start by letting the one in that's already here take me to dinner. Unless you've already scared the man off."

"I don't scare that easily," Jack called out from the other side of the door.

The door flew open. Mama Esther did not look amused.

"No one asked you!" she said.

He didn't dare make eye contact with her. His eyes drifted behind her, and he caught a glimpse of Beck. She was all dolled up for their night on the town. One side of her wavy, red hair was secured with a gold comb, and the wave on the other side framed her face. Her silk, green dress clung nicely to her hourglass figure and matched her eyes.

"Do you hear me, Jack Herman?" asked Mrs. Esther, "You may take my Rebecca to dinner, but that's it. Don't go thinking that if you buy her dinner, that gets you everything else."

"Mama Esther, please!" Beck pleaded.

"I'm telling you that's all these musicians are after, especially his type."

"What's my type?" Jack asked.

"You're a confirmed bachelor. How old are you?" Mrs. Esther asked, "Have you ever been married before?"

"I m thirty-nine, and no, I haven't," he admitted.

"Told you he's only out for one thing. He ain't bought no cows cause he been getting all the milk for free!"

Now Jack and Beck were both embarrassed.

"Mama Esther! As much fun as it is to stay here and be compared to cattle, we need to go," Beck said, brushing past her and Jack.

Jack turned to go, Mrs. Esther grabbed his sleeve.

"You listen to me, Jack Herman," she whispered furiously, "I found that precious girl scared and hurt in a hospital bed not long ago. She had no family or friends to comfort her. I spent most of my volunteer shifts holding her while she cried. Then, I brought that sweet child into my home. She needs somebody, and I am pretty sure it's not you. Don't you dare hurt her."

"I would never." Jack protested.

"We'll see," said Mrs. Esther.

He wanted so badly to ask her why Beck had been in the hospital, but he had a feeling she might not tell him. He would figure out a way to ask Beck soon.

"Are we ready?" Beck called Jack from the sidewalk. She was trying her best to smile and act casual. As Jack walked up to her, she asked, "Where are you taking me?"

"After that bit of excitement, I thought we'd start the night off slow. Do you like cabarets? We could have dinner at the Sugar Cane Club. Then we could visit some of the other night-clubs in the district."

"It sounds like fun. Listen, Jack, Mama Esther means well. She's just very protective of me and all the ladies who live with her. She and her husband had four sons, and now that they're grown and her husband's passed she says we're her daughters. She means it, too. It's kind of a blessing and a curse," Beck explained.

"It's fine, Beck. I didn't take it personally," Jack said. Offering Beck his arm, they crossed the street and headed into the district.

The Sugar Cane Club was busy, but the two managed to find a small table in the corner. Jack went to pull out Beck's chair, and she flinched.

"Are you alright?" he asked.

"Oh, I have two younger brothers, and they used to do that and then pull the chair out from under me. I'm sorry. You were only being polite. Thanks."

"Tell me more about your family," Jack said.

"Not much to tell, I am the oldest, then there's my brothers, Steven and James. My mom is a decorator, and my dad builds houses."

"That must be a tough business right now. Your mom works, too?" Jack was intrigued. Not many women worked in the 1930s.

"My parents are divorced. She has to work," Beck explained.

"I didn't know people would hire decorators."

"They don't much anymore, another tough business. What about your family?" Beck asked. She seemed anxious to turn the tables.

"They're both teachers, I mean they were. My dad died a few years ago."

"A male teacher?"

"Um yeah, for the military," Jack needed to change the subject, "I have a brother, he's older. His name is Robert. He makes ...pictures."

"In Hollywood?" Beck's eyes lit up as she asked.

"Yeah, that's where I'm from."

"I love it there," she said wistfully.

"You've been to California?"

"I lived there, I mean we moved around a bit with my mom. I'm originally from Louisiana."

"You must have heard some great jazz," Jack said.

"Yes, but what I really miss is the food."

"Oh, let me order you some gumbo," Jack offered.

"No, thanks, it wouldn't be the same."

Beck seemed nervous. Jack was on edge. *I'm trying to connect with this cute girl without telling I'm from the future. But why is she anxious?*

"Excuse me, I have to go to the restroom," she said suddenly.

"Of course," Jack said, standing up.

"Oh, I can see where it is. You don't have to get up," Beck said.

Something is definitely odd here, Jack thought. This was not what he expected dating to be like in the 1930s. Why was his chivalry making her nervous? Beck returned, and Jack stood again.

"The waiter came by with our drinks, and he said the food will be here shortly."

"Great. I'm starved," Beck said with a smile, "I was wondering, how many instruments do you play?"

"Well, I started out as a skin tickler."

"A what?" she asked, blushing.

"You know, a drummer," Jack explained.

"I've never heard it called that before."

"Really? Not even at the club?"

"I haven't worked there very long."

The waiter brought the entrees. That's when Jack realized they were still standing.

"Uh, Beck? Shall we sit now?"

"Oh yeah, go ahead."

"No, you're supposed to sit first."

"Oh," she said and sat down, not meeting his gaze.

My date must be a bumpkin, but she's a pretty one. Manners can be learned, after all. He reasoned.

They ate for a while in silence when Beck said: "You were telling me about the instruments you play."

"Oh yes, I also play piano, trombone, and guitar. I'm more of a writer, though."

"Really? I write, too."

"You're a songwriter, too?" he asked excitedly.

"No, I write scripts for plays and movies. A different kind of writing."

"I write music for movies," Jack said.

"Then, why are you in Harlem?"

"I'm... expanding my...repertoire. The more I expose myself to different kinds of music, the better I am at my job."

Jack felt a little disappointed, and remained silent. *How can I get to know this girl when I'm hiding a huge secret?*

They headed up Lenox Avenue past the Cotton Club, which was dark on Monday nights. It was strange to see the marquee lights out. They continued past the club to the Savoy Ballroom.

"What are we doing here?" Beck asked.

"We need to loosen up. I'd like to take you dancing."

"I don't know, Jack. Neither one of us really knows how."

"What do you mean? We danced together, just the other night."

"Not in a structured way. We were being silly," Beck protested.

"Come on. They have a new dance called the Snakehips, it sounds like fun."

As they walked in, Jack realized they were out of their depth. All of these dancers were doing an expert version of the Lindy Hop. To his modern brain, they all looked like professionals.

"I tell you what," Jack said, "I'll buy us some drinks to take the edge off. What do you like?"

"I don't really drink."

"Suit yourself," he said, then he turned to the bartender, "One whiskey neat, please."

"And for the lady?" asked the bartender.

"I'll have a glass of red wine," Beck said.

She wasn't kidding about not drinking. A flush came over her nose and cheeks as she took her last sip. The band announced the Snakehips dance by Earl Tucker, and before Jack knew what was happening, she had dragged him out on the floor.

Mr. Tucker's dance was a good deal more complicated than either of them had bargained for. Jack had never felt so utterly white as he attempted to undulate his hips. Beck alternated between an almost indecent bump and grind and circus clown moves. They looked ridiculous, but they were tipsy enough not to care. At the end of the song, they dissolved into giggles and had danced their way into a dark corner.

"Thank you! We're gonna slow it down to a sweet, simple waltz, dedicated to the poor firetops over there in the corner," said the bandleader.

"I think he means us," Beck giggled, "I've never been called a firetop before. I dig it!"

Just then, the lights lowered, and the band started playing "But Not For Me." Jack and Beck realized that to waltz, their bodies would have to touch. He took her hand, and it felt like a jolt of electricity. He put his arm around her waist and held her close. She smelled like vanilla, and Jack was dizzy again. To his surprise, she put her head on his shoulder. The song was over much too soon, and Jack felt lost when he had to let her go.

After several more songs, Beck said, "Let's go to Gladys' Clam House next. I'm hungry again."

The pair walked into Gladys' and immediately realized that they were not going to be served seafood here. Most of the couples in the joint were same-sex with only a few heterosexual pairs. Jack didn't think a lot of it until he remembered that they were in 1938. He quickly looked to Beck, expecting she'd want to leave.

Instead, Beck said, "The only table I see is right there close to the stage. Let's grab it."

The two sat down and were treated to one of the most unforgettable cabarets Jack had ever seen. It reminded him of the Mysterious Order's shows. *Nice to see we weren't too far off from the period.* Instead of a "red devil," the band leader of this show was the incomparable Gladys a voluptuous black woman clad in a tuxedo and a top hat. She was so much fun!

The pair ordered a piece of cheesecake to share, and it arrived with a stein full of champagne compliments of Gladys herself. As they polished it off, Jack realized that he had had very little. Apparently, they'd found Beck's drink of choice.

"Was it good? Because I hardly had any," Jack teased.

"Oh please, she sent it to me," Beck said as she waved to Gladys, "Thank you!"

"You betcha, Darlin'," Gladys said, winking at Beck. Then to Jack, she said, "That's one wild filly, you got there. Better hang on for the ride."

"I intend to," Jack said.

Beck giggled and said, "Neigh, neigh."

"Whoa! That was too much champagne," Jack said, "Let's go for a walk."

Walking seemed to help. Beck was still a bit giggly, but she was no longer neighing and weaving around on the sidewalk.

"Are you feeling better?" he asked.

"Yes, the fresh air helps. Are we going anywhere else, because I think I need some water."

"I saw a sign at Club Hot-Cha's, they serve breakfast."

"I'm only thirsty. I don't want you to spend too much. You'd have to do a lot of skin ticklin' to make up for two meals out," she said as she attempted to tickle him.

"I think we should keep walking," Jack said, moving her hands away from him.

"I think you should kiss me," she said, pressing her body against his.

"Beck, we need to walk," he said as he moved away from her embrace.

"Oh. Okay," Beck said. She frowned and walked away from Jack a little too quickly. She stumbled. "Aw grits!" she exclaimed as he caught her.

There it was again, that saying. Jack suddenly remembered where he'd heard it before. Beck had said it, but so had the cute redhead at the movie studio back in 1992. She had told him it was a saying of her grandmother's. Could this be her grandmother? Beck did say she'd lived in California. By courting Beck, he might be putting that poor girl's very existence in jeopardy! He walked a few steps ahead in an attempt to put some distance between them.

"I need to get you home."

As Beck caught up with Jack, she touched his arm and seductively gazed up at him, "Don't you want to kiss me?" she asked.

Jack stopped and smiled at her. Of course, he wanted to kiss her. He caught her as she swayed again. "I don't kiss drunk girls," he said as gently as he could. That was only one reason in a long list of reasons not to embrace her but he hoped it was explanation enough. He could tell from the pained expression on Beck's face that his rejection had stung.

After a long silence, she said, "I'm sorry. It was good champagne and I needed to unwind. It was the first time I'd felt relaxed since I got here, but now I'm so out of it."

Suddenly, Jack remembered what Mrs. Esther had said, *"I found that precious girl scared and hurt in a hospital bed not long ago."* What if drinking had put Beck at risk? "Beck? Why were you in the hospital?" he asked.

"Who told you I was in the hospital?" she asked defensively.

"Mrs. Esther, she said that's where she met you. She said you were hurt."

"I had a head injury, but I'm better now," she said, turning away from him.

"That sounds serious. What happened?"

"It's dumb. I wasn't paying attention and crossed the street right in front of a car. They tried to stop but knocked me down. I hit my head pretty hard."

"Jeez, Beck!" Jack said. He placed his hand on her shoulder.

"It's alright, I met Mama Esther. She was my advocate or something like that. She's been wonderful to me. I'm fine now. Really. Can we talk about anything else, please," she said, turning back to face him with a sheepish grin.

"I hate to think of you all alone in there," Jack said.

"Well, I'm not anymore. Okay? Tell me more about you. What did you do before you came to Harlem? How did you get into writing music?"

"My parents gave me a guitar for my eighteenth birthday, and music has been my life ever since."

"Were you ever in a band?"

"Yes," Jack said.

"What was the name of your band?"

"At first, we called it The Mysterious Order of the Ah Ooga," he answered truthfully.

A smile spread wide across her face. Then she said, "I wish I could have seen it."

"We were crazy, more of a musical theatre troupe. But, I think you would have liked it. I wore my horns a lot, he said with a wink. Beck's cheeks were pink again. "I like making you blush."

"You're very good at it."

"You feeling better?"

"Much better," she said as she took his hand and pulled him into the alley, "I'm not drunk anymore," she declared as she touched his cheek and moved her face toward his. Jack turned away. He adored her, but it just wouldn't work. For all, he knew he could vanish from 1938 as quickly as he had arrived, leaving her future forever altered.

Chapter 10

"I need to go home," Beck said in a cracked voice. She started to walk in the direction of Mrs. Esther's.

Jack followed close behind. He felt trapped in the middle of a big tornado of emotions. *Why in the hell am I here? How do I get home? What is it about her that makes me want to stay? There's no resolution in sight for being stuck here, but I can end whatever this is with Beck before it begins. Maybe then I could finally figure out how to leave.*

"Beck, listen. You don't want to get mixed up with me. I've never been good at relationships. Music always comes first and no woman has ever been able to tolerate that. Nor do I think they should."

Beck swiveled around to face him, raising her voice, she said, "I didn't ask you for anything! You're the one who asked me for a date. Remember?"

"I know. I'm sorry."

"For what? I only asked you for a kiss. If you think I'm being too forward, or you've changed your mind about me, that's fine," Beck said, her eyes were welling up with tears.

Jack offered her his handkerchief, fighting an almost irresistible urge to wrap his arms around her. Beck shook her head and walked away. People were messy, music was ordered. Only twelve major chords. This was so much more complicated. His attraction to Beck resonated through him like the dissonance of the dreaded tritone. The "Devil's Chord" as it was often called. Its sinister combination of notes made all who heard it long for resolution—oh God, how he needed something to feel settled right now.

I'll tell her the truth now and she'll think I'm crazy. She'll reject me. Better for both of us to hurt a little now than to set ourselves up for a big heartbreak later.

He stopped and took a deep breath. Then, catching up to her, he said, "Beck, I need you to tell you something about me, and when I do, you're not going to want to be with me anymore."

"I won't?" she asked, as she turned back to him.

Jack softened under her gaze, and stepped closer to her. He really didn't want to run her off, but reminded himself that this was best for both of them. Reluctantly, he said, "You're going to think I'm crazy, and I won't blame you. It's best that I say it now. So, you can walk away before this...before we..."

"Try me," She said confidently, taking his hands in hers. Then she looked him in the eye and said, "I'm strong enough to hear anything you have to tell me."

If only, he thought as he savored her touch for the last time, "Beck, there's no easy way to say this. I'm from the future. The year 1992, to be exact. I don't really understand how I got here. There's no time machine, I just went to sleep in 1992 and woke up here. I don't know when or if I'm ever going back," He braced himself for her reaction.

She smiled and said, "I know."

"What? How do you know?"

"Because I am too," she said.

"Excuse me?"

"I'm from 1992, just like you."

"Now, I think you're crazy," he said, letting go of her hands.

"I'm not, I can prove it," she insisted, "You're Jack Herman band leader of The Mysterious Order of the Ah Ooga --"

"I just told you that," Jack protested.

"The group was founded in 1972 by Robert Herman your big brother, you were the Musical Director. After he left you decided you wanted to be in a ska band, and you shortened the name to Ah Ooga. You wrote a song called "Don't You Go." The music video was set in the 1930s. I've loved that song and this decade ever since. The first time I heard it was in high school. I've had a crush on the lead singer--you--ever since. And you really do write music for the movies. At first, for Tom Price, but now you write for lots of other directors. Which is probably why you were at the studio that day when I accidentally spilled a smoothie on your shoes."

"That was you?" Jack asked, astonished.

"I'm sorry," she said.

"So, you're saying I am stuck in 1938 with a crazed fan from 1992?"

"Well, I wouldn't go that far."

"You sound like a stalker."

"I'm not! I just happen to know and appreciate you and your work."

"Wait a minute. Did you bring me here?" Jack asked.

"I don't think so. I'm just as confused about how I came to be here as you are. You said you fell asleep?"

"Yeah, I have a room in my house furnished exclusively in antiques, nothing newer than the 1930s. It's where I keep my jazz records. I go in there when I need to unwind. I'd had a rough few days, so I drank some whiskey while listening to Django Reinhardt. I fell asleep and woke up here. I thought maybe I was dreaming."

The two were quiet for a long time. Neither one was quite able to look the other in the eye. They stole little glances at one another until he asked, "Beck, how was it for you? Did you just go to sleep and wake up here, too?"

"No. It was the day after we met. I kept thinking about you and how much I love your music. I had lost my favorite song of yours. "Don't You Go" for a long time."

"Lost it? How?" Jack asked.

"Because I couldn't remember the name. Meeting you jogged my memory. So, I went over to the used record store on my lunch hour that day and bought all of the Ah Ooga tapes they had. I had my Walkman on when I was walking back to the studio, blasting the song. I remember that a car hit me in 1992, and I woke up in a hospital in 1938."

"Oh, Beck," Jack said, pulling her closer to him.

"I know you warned me. I should have listened. I was pretty sure I'd died, and that this was some sort of afterlife. When you showed up at the club, I thought I was in heaven. But, I have to admit, I was kind of scared when you first came onstage in your devil costume!"

Now it was Jack's turn to laugh.

"What?" Beck asked.

"I never considered that we might be dead."

"Thanks, that's very reassuring."

The two had made it back to Mrs. Esther's house.

"Goodnight, Jack."

"Beck, I'm sorry. This evening didn't go as well as I had hoped."

"It's not your fault," she said, looking at the ground.

"I don't think I handled all of that as well as I should have," Jack said.

"Hey, it not like there's a handbook for telling your date you're from the future. We did our best under the circumstances. I only wish I'd told you sooner."

"Why?"

"I figured out who you were pretty fast. I saw you in your devil costume. Before that, I pissed you off with my review..."

"Is that why you wrote it?" he asked.

"In part, I knew that the real Jack Herman would be pissed and call me out. Boy did you! I wasn't entirely sure until you told me your band name tonight. Something I knew no one else in 1938 would know. For weeks now, I've known that I might not be alone. I'm so sorry I didn't approach you sooner."

"Now that I'm over the shock, it's nice to know I'm not alone. I've felt connected to you from the first moment I saw you. Now I know why," Jack embraced Beck, "Can I kiss you now?"

"Do you think dead people kiss?" she asked.

"Let's find out," Jack said as he pressed his lips against Beck's. Feeling her soft lips melt into his. He kissed her slowly at first, then with a building intensity. Jack wasn't dead; in fact, he'd never felt more alive!

Chapter 11

In the park the following day, the air felt crisp. All the leaves were changing colors. New York had never seemed so vibrant to him. Until now, Harlem had been a sea of dirty blues and grays. But all of that had changed. He was no longer alone in this mess. His time-traveling companion was a breath of fresh air and not hard to look at either. Beck had brought a picnic lunch and a blanket. The pair were resting, watching the city go by.

"What did you do back in 1992, Beck?"

"A lot of different things. I earned my Cosmetology license and did makeup on movie sets. I was hoping to make connections for acting jobs," she explained.

"Did it work?"

"Not really. I was an extra in a couple of movies, but that was boring. I was used to doing live theatre, but Hollywood is all about film."

Jack nodded and said, "Yeah, New York is a much better place for stage actors. What else did you do?"

"I wrote. When I was in middle school, my family life was a mess. Things were so bad that I almost failed seventh grade. Then one day, my English teacher called me a writer. I'd never been referred to that way before. It was like she spoke this truth about me into existence. I've been writing ever since, but I haven't sold anything yet," she explained.

"That's great. I like to write, too."

"I know. I heard that you had sold a couple of screenplays. I don't know how you find the time."

"Like I said, I have no social life," Jack said, only half-joking, "So far, you've only named two things. Tell me what else you do?"

"In 1992, I worked as a production assistant so I could learn how to direct films. I directed plays in my drama class back in high school and realized that I liked being in charge of telling the whole story," Beck stopped suddenly and grew silent. She frowned, then said, "When I say all this out loud, I sound so flaky," she said.

"No, you don't. You're a generalist."

"A what?" she asked.

"Someone good at and interested in multiple things. I'm the same. It's hard because the world prefers specialists. Take jazz, for instance. Django is a great guitarist, Louis Armstrong plays the trumpet amazingly well, and Cab is a phenomenal band leader. They all specialize. But I'm all over the place writing, composing, playing different instruments or trying to at least. People don't understand when you keep reinventing yourself."

"But, you're extremely talented and successful at everything you do. I can't seem to get anything to happen. I worry that I'm just not good enough."

"I have that same worry about myself all the time. Every award I win, I keep at my mom's house because I feel like I'm one score or album away from everyone figuring out that I'm a fraud. It's crazy! I'm not, I work very hard at what I do. I just never feel worthy of the accolades. You're young and talented. You have time."

"You're being sweet," Beck said, smiling back at him.

"Have you ever heard about my "SIlver Dollar" film scores?" Jack asked.

"No. What's that?"

"I try and do one every couple of years or so. I only charge a silver dollar to write a score for a small, independent film. Some directors get creative with their payment and give me rare coins. It's fun to encourage people who are just starting out."

"Well, if we get back, I'll have to keep these and take you up on that," she said, brandishing two 1938 silver dollars. "Look, one for each eye," she laughed as she laid on her back and placed the coins over her eyes.

"You're never going to let me live down that 'maybe we're dead' comment, are you?"

"Nope!" Beck said, giggling.

"I need to head to the club early. We only have the house orchestra for two weeks while we wait for Cab's orchestra to return. Lowry and I were messing around with some songs and sketches to introduce them. Why don't you help us with the script?"

"I'd love to," she said, sitting up bolt right on the blanket.

Lowry and Esther were already working on staging when Jack and Beck arrived at the club.

"You gonna wear your horns for us tonight, Red Devil?" Mrs. Esther asked.

"Yes, ma'am, Mrs. Esther," Jack said as he noted she had softened just a little toward him.

"We're just trying to work out a lead into St. James Infirmary, but we're stuck," Lowry explained.

"Let's ask a writer for help. Rebecca, can you give us some assistance, please?" Jack asked.

"Sure. Let's see, you want a reason for the devil to be sad. That's tough because the devil usually just takes what he wants. Give me a second," Beck said.

Jack and Lowry checked the instruments and order of the sheet music on the stands while Beck scribbled down notes in the little notebook she'd produced from her handbag.

"I've got it," Beck said.

"Great. Come on over," Jack said.

He was cleaning his trombone as she climbed the steps.

"I forgot to ask, do you play any instruments?"

"Not well," she said, "I took piano for a while as a kid, but I didn't practice it enough. I joined the band class in middle school, I wanted to play percussion, but my mom told me I couldn't because drums are a boy's instrument."

"Hmm, I wasn't aware that instruments were divided up by gender," Jack said.

"I know it was dumb. I went to my first band class, and I needed to pick an instrument. I saw all the girls in the wood-wind section. I remembered that my mom had played the clarinet. No way in hell was I going to play any of those instruments. I wouldn't give her the satisfaction. So, I looked at the brass section. It was almost all boys. The trombone section, in particular, was full of cute boys, including one with curly red hair. So, that's the instrument I chose. So, I could sit with all the cute boys."

Jack laughed, then said, "Wait! You play trombone? I want to hear this," he said as he grabbed his horn and thrust it into her hands.

"No, you don't! I'm terrible. So terrible that my mom would beg me not to practice, so I never got any better," she warned him.

"Please, Beck?" Jack pleaded.

"Don't say I didn't warn you," Beck sighed as she held the mouthpiece to her lips. The sound that emerged from the trombone sounded like a combination of a cow dying in agony and someone strangling a duck. Beck was right.

"Nevermind, I see what you mean," Jack admitted.

"That was awful!" Lowry said, "I hope you're a better writer than you are horn player."

Beck chuckled then said, "Here's the idea, do any of you remember the Greek myth about Persephone? She was the daughter of Demeter, Goddess of Agriculture. The king of the Underworld, Hades, fell in love with her. He kidnapped Persephone and convinced her to marry him. Grief-stricken, her mother, refused to produce any crops or flowers until Persephone returned.

Hades was forced to strike a deal with Demeter that Persephone could join her each spring. But she had to return to the Underworld at the end of the season. She is both the Goddess of Spring and the Queen of the Underworld. What if Jack is Hades, and he loses his Persephone to Mama Esther? One of the dancers or Adelaide could play Persephone."

"Great idea, but Adelaide's not here tonight, sugar. She got a singing gig down in Atlantic City," said Mrs. Esther.

"I'm sure one of the dancers could do it," Beck said.

"They're not actors," Lowry said.

"You need to do it, dollface. You can be my Persephone," Jack said.

"I don't know about that," Beck said, "The dancers are prettier."

"Stop that! You're a looker, too. Besides, all those dancers are the same height as I am. We can't have Persephone towering over Hades."

"Jack, I really don't think I'm the right choice..."

Jack melodramatically dropped to one knee, "Please be my queen, and we can rule the Underworld together!"

"Jack, don't do that," she said.

"Is that a no?" he asked.

"I'm just not sure about this."

"Then I must take you as my hostage!" he said, jumping to his feet and picking her up. Beck squealed.

"Okay, okay. I guess I have no choice," Beck said, laughing as he set her down.

Mrs. Esther had been observing the scene. She said to Jack, "You do know that Demeter went to hell and back for her baby girl."

"That's why you're perfect for the part," Jack said to her, smiling. Before Esther could help herself, she smiled back.

"Jack, we need a sweet song for Mama Esther to sing," Beck said.

"I'll find one, and if I can't, then I'll write one."

They were off and running with their plans. Before long, it had evolved into a full-blown revue. Jack was having the time of his life. Writing and choosing songs was much more fun than singing the same old ones over and over again. The orchestra planned to perform jazz standards with an original song or two added into the mix. Lowry proved to be invaluable as an arranger. They would write and rehearse overnight while the club was closed.

"I've adjusted the tempo on your new song, and I'm working on the harmonies for the horns," Lowry told Jack.

"I'm so glad you know how to do this. I had a good friend back home who helped me with that part. I would be completely overwhelmed without an arranger."

"Hey man, I was wondering if you'd listen to some of my songs?" Lowry asked as he shifted his weight and fidgeted with the pencil in his hands.

"You write songs, too?" Jack asked as he smiled up at his friend.

"Yeah, my momma, loved classical music, French composers mostly. I first learned to play the piano for her. I write my own stuff on piano now whenever I can sneak a few moments on it at the club."

"You play classical piano?"

"Well, that's how I was trained. I dig that stuff, but the other kids in our ward made fun of me. I felt kinda shy about my music until I snuck out to the French Quarter one night in high school, and visited some of the clubs. That's where I fell in love with jazz. I started teaching myself to play those songs on our church's piano after services. Later, I switched to trumpet as my instrument of choice."

"Why did you switch?"Jack asked.

"Chicks dig horn players."

"True," Jack said, chuckling, "Lay one on me."

"You got it," Lowry said as he bounded over to the piano.

Lowry began to play a fast-paced swing song. His fingers flying over the keys. It needed a little polishing, but the bones of the piece were solid.

"I've written out parts for all the sections," Lowry said as he demonstrated the parts for the different instruments on the keys. What'd ya think?"

"Lowry, that was aces! I have some suggestions for the bridge and the percussion used. Please say you'll let us use it in the show. The world deserves to hear from a talented composer like yourself. "

Jack had never seen Lowry speechless before. He was worried he'd overstepped offering suggestions.

"You alright? Did I say something wrong?"

"No, I've just never been called a composer before."

"It feels weird the first time someone says that to you. I remember the feeling. But you need to embrace it, You are a composer, Lowry. Don't let anyone tell you different. You can't let other people's expectations define you."

"I found some soup in the kitchen. I thought it would help us keep warm." Rebecca said.

"Thanks, I'd love some. October is a lot colder here than it is back west. How about you, Lowry?"

"I'm gonna keep working. You go sit with your dame." Lowry said.

"Thanks, I was beginning to forget what he looks like," Beck said.

"Look in a mirror, kitten. All y'all gingers look the same," Lowry kidded before diving back into his work.

"Were you missing me? Why didn't you say so?" Jack asked Beck.

"You've been having so much fun up there. I didn't want to interrupt."

"I love working like this. I can't remember the last time I felt so alive."

"You're burning out on Ah Ooga, aren't you?" she asked.

"That's part of it," Jack admitted.

"Do you like composing better than performing?"

"You see how nervous I get before going on stage, Beck. And, this is a nightclub. It's so much worse when it's a stadium full of people. I can't see past the first few rows. I'm okay once I connect with the audience out here, and I am typically in character. It's tough to be myself in that larger space, trying to connect with so many people."

"You shouldn't let fear keep you from doing what you love, but it sounds like you might not love it anymore," Beck said.

"It's not only that, Beck. I had a hearing test right before we ended up here, and the doctor said that I've really damaged my ears with all of those rock concerts."

"Oh, Jack!"

"The doctor said if I continue fronting the band. I'll lose my hearing. So, I can't keep doing what I'm doing, and if I lose my hearing, I won't be able to be a composer either. It'll all be over."

"That sucks!" Beck said.

"Shh!! That's a pretty crass thing to say here, dollface," Jack reminded her.

"Oops. You know what I mean. Wait, doesn't it hurt your ears to play up there?" Beck asked, pointing to the stage.

"No, orchestras are softer, much easier on my ears. Besides, I'm pretty comfortable staying right here," Jack said as he held her hand.

Beck protested, "We can't stay here forever, Jack."

"We may not have a choice. But, if we do go home, I'll have to tell the guys in the band the truth. I'm scared. I don't know who I am without music, Beck."

"Well, if that ever happens, and it won't. I'll just have to saw the legs off of your piano so you can lay on the ground and write by feeling the vibrations through the floor."

"You mean like Beethoven?"

"Exactly," Beck said, kissing him on the cheek.

"Hey, I need your help with a song I've written for the show."

"You need my help with music?" she asked.

"I need a tempo. May I put my hand on your heart?" Jack asked.

"Why?"

"You're going to set the tempo for my song," he explained.

"Um," Beck glanced at the stage. She saw that Lowry was wholly engrossed in his writing, "Okay."

Jack carefully placed his hand just above Beck's breasts. Her heart began to race, and so did his. Not the tempo he had in mind. So he said, "Tell you what, I'll take it from your wrist, okay?"

Beck nodded. Her heart was still racing.

"Take some deep breaths for me, okay?"

"I'm sorry!" she said.

"It's okay. You're just not used to me," Jack said, smiling. He sat there gently, holding her wrist for a few minutes, "That's it, Beck. Relax."

"I'd like to get used to you," Beck murmured. Her eyes were closed. This was the first time since Jack met her that Beck looked entirely at peace. He studied her oval face and her long eyelashes. Her top lip was a perfect cupid's bow. He wanted to kiss her again, but his mission was to memorize her heartbeat at rest. He closed his eyes and felt the rhythm etch itself into his soul.

Chapter 12

"Do I need to bring in two buckets? You don't look so good," Beck asked Jack as she handed him a towel.

Jack was incredibly anxious. Owney had insisted on a preview of the new revue on Tuesday afternoon, before their opening show later that evening. He was worried that Owney might hate it and pull the plug on the project after they'd all worked so hard.

"No, but I could use some water and fresh air."

"Go ahead. I'll grab you some water and meet you out back," Beck said.

Jack didn't feel very steady on his feet. The crisp autumn air was a slap in his face as he opened the door. It reminded him to breathe.

"Here's your water. Do you need help putting on your horns?"

"Not for the preview. I'll wait until the show. When are you going to put on your costume?"

"I don't come on until later in the revue. I'll have one of the dancers help me get ready after the show starts. I won't bother dressing up for the preview. The costume makes it difficult for me to move around backstage. Speaking of which we need to head in now."

The preview ran through about two minutes of each song, and Beck talked Owney through the scripted parts. He did not look pleased.

"We've got a formula at the Cotton Club. I book nationally famous bandleaders. When I can't book them back to back, my house orchestra plays jazz standards on those evenings. We don't do Negro Revues. The clientele ain't used to 'em. You've got songs in there no one's ever heard of before," Owney said.

"They're original songs written by Lowry and myself," Jack explained proudly.

"People don't want to hear anything new. They want what's familiar. Toss out the skits and your songs. Keep the standards and the dancing girls."

"Owney, please hear me out. I know there's risk involved with trying something new, but this could take your club to the next level. None of the other clubs you compete with offer a house orchestra that writes their own material. This could be good for you. Especially, when the Duke and Cab are on tour. I'll make a deal with you. Let us play the revue in its entirety tonight. If your audience doesn't like it, we'll move forward with the changes you want tomorrow night. Besides, Tuesday is our least busy night of the week. What have you got to lose?"

Jack paced and busied himself with instrument maintenance. Owney sat at his table, thinking and making notes on a pad of paper. After a while, Owney looked up at Jack.

"Alright, I'll let you do it your way tonight, but if my customers don't love it, we do it my way from now on."

Excited, Jack embraced Beck, he lifted her off the ground and spun her around. A gesture that would have been perfectly acceptable in 1992. But not in 1938, at least not in front of their boss. A hush fell over the cast.

"Rebecca, get over here," Owney barked, "The rest of you are dismissed."

Rebecca slowly moved down the steps to his table. Concerned for her, Jack busied himself onstage, trying to listen in.

"So, is Jack your fella now?" Owney asked.

"Well, we've been out a few times," she said as she glanced up at Jack and then quickly back to her boss. She was fidgeting with her fingernails.

"I don't like my employees dating each other. It's bad for business. You have a lot of responsibilities here, and I don't want your head getting muddled over some fling. And, if I *ever* see you throwing yourself at another one of my performers. You'll be out on your sweet derriere. Do we understand one another?"

"Yes, sir," Beck muttered as she looked down at her feet.

"Back to work, then," Owney ordered.

Jack came down the steps. "Hey, Rebecca didn't throw herself at me. I took her by surprise. If you have beef with anyone, it should be with me."

"Boys will be boys, Jack. It's her job to be above it. I've no beef with anyone. Just reminding my assistant of her place. You have a show to do. Go on," Owney said, dismissing them.

Rebecca and Jack walked backstage together. It took all the restraint in the world not to turn around and throttle Owney. *But, he's our boss and a dangerous man. If I had attacked him, Pipes would have dispatched me quickly and easily. Dammit! I should have never put her in that position.* Safely backstage, he turned to look at her. Beck was trying to be strong, but he could see the tears glistening in her eyes.

"I'm so sorry, Beck!"

"It's okay. That's just how Owney is. I can deal with it," she said as she started to walk away.

"Why didn't you tell Owney I was your daddy?" Jack asked.

Beck turned back to him. She said forcefully, "I'm *never* going to refer to you as my 'daddy' because that's gross! Besides, we haven't actually talked about what we are to each other."

"C'mon, Beck. I think it's sexy, and around here, everyone says it," he pleaded.

"I know, but it sounds wrong to me," Beck protested.

"But I could be your daddy, and you could come sit here on my knee," Jack said provocatively.

"Not funny!"

"If I can't be your daddy --"

"Ugh! Will you please stop saying that?"

"Okay, If I can't, then can I be your fella?"

"Is that like a boyfriend?" Beck asked, hopefully.

"That's exactly what it means. Can I be yours?"

"Of course," Beck said. A grin lit up her face, "Now I want to kiss you, and I can't!"

"Check," he said.

"What does that mean?"

"'Cash or check is something the couples say here. It means 'Do we kiss now or save it for later?'. Your answer would either be cash for now or check for later."

"I always feel like I'm playing catch up with the slang and etiquette. You're always ahead of me. But, even I know that public displays of affection are off-limits in the 1930s, Jack. Especially, in front of your boss. You got me in some serious trouble just now."

"I'm so sorry," Jack said again.

"You're forgiven. Now come on, we've got a show to do."

"That's right, we get to do our show," Jack said as butterflies gathered in his stomach. Sweat began to bead on his brow. "Beck, I need more water."

"Check." Beck said with a wink, "be right back."

Chapter 13

Jack peeked out at the crowd at the Cotton Club. As usual, the customers were almost exclusively white. Rare exceptions had been made but only for certain black people of influence. Owney knew if he was seen sharing a table with famous writers and artists like Langston Hughes or Aaron Douglas that his customers would be impressed. This crowd hungered for something new and different. The white men and women who traveled to Harlem sought novelty. They hungered for the animalistic rhythm of the music. Yet, they still regarded black people as "dirty" and "inferior." They feared that dining with them was unsanitary. So Owney instructed his busboys to make a show of throwing away any plates, glasses, or utensils touched by his black guests.

"Ever feel like we're working in the wrong place?" Jack asked Beck as he pulled her into a private corner near the stage.

"I don't like it either, but we have the luxury of options. We could work almost anywhere, but our friends are stuck here. This is the most famous club in Harlem. It's the one place that pays a decent wage and gives them a shot at becoming nationally well known."

"That doesn't make it okay."

"Of course it doesn't, Jack. I'm just saying that, instead of walking away, we should stand by them and help whenever we can. Remember, we both know how this ends. Their perseverance helps them gain respect, and it sets the stage for equal rights later on."

Jack nodded and said, "Then we'll start by helping them put on one hell of a show."

The revue opened with a few jazz standards to warm up the crowd showcasing the orchestra. Then, they debuted Lowry's swing song. With its solid backbeat, the audience simply couldn't sit still. The dance floor writhed with bodies, as Lowry launched into his trumpet solo, improvising over the melody. The orchestra followed his song with several more swing tunes.

The final part of the show featured Beck's Persephone story. Jack had not seen Beck's costume before she took the stage. Her gown was half olive green matching her eyes and accented with gold and purple flowers. Its hemline was short in front with a small train in the back. The green part was at the moment pointed downstage towards the audience while the half she had hidden upstage was copper with gold flame accents that matched her hair. She took his breath away.

He launched into Hades' abduction song, a modified version of "Minnie the Moocher." Next, Esther took command of the stage in an elegant hunter green evening gown. She belted out "Demeter's Song," which Jack had written as promised. Her voice captivated the audience. She was indeed a force of nature.

Finally, as Hades allowed Demeter to lead Persephone away, Jack picked up his violin and introduced the last song. "This is an original, it's called "Rebecca's Theme." It was a haunting violin piece reminiscent of a Grappelli song; filled with longing. There wasn't a dry eye in the house, including Beck's, as Esther sent her back across the stage to Jack. Where he handed off the violin and embraced her. Thankful that it was allowed within the context of the show. The revue ended with thunderous applause.

Owney jumped up on the stage and accepted the accolades from the audience. "You cats dig that? This revue is exclusive to the Cotton Club. Tell your mates, they can only see it here!" Then, he turned to Jack and shook his hand, "Congrats, old boy. You got your two weeks."

Backstage, Rebecca was struggling to balance between her acting role and her talent management duties. "Gentleman, please throw your underclothes in the laundry bin. Remember to hang up your costumes," she said as she moved to rinse out Leroy's bucket. Jack watched her catch a glimpse of herself in the mirror and pause.

"Let me grab that for you, darlin'. I don't have as much to do to change, and it would be a shame to mess up that pretty dress," Jack said.

"Thanks, I'll run and change," she said as she headed to the ladies' dressing room.

"You know, Leroy. You could do this yourself," Jack said.

"Why, I gonna do that when Miss Rebecca does it for me?" Leroy asked.

Jack sighed as he picked up the bucket and noticed that none of the men had put their shirts in the laundry bin. *How does she do this night after night?*

Since she needed to make sure everything was set for the following evening, Rebecca was always the last to leave. The only time Jack could manage to be alone with her was when he walked her home from the club. So he'd started helping her clean up each night. The faster she finished, the more time they were able to spend together. As they met in the alley, Beck looked around and then threw her arms around Jack. "Cash," she whispered in his ear. He smiled then kissed her passionately.

"You wrote that song for me?" she asked.

"Of course I did."

"Jack, it's beautiful."

"You think so?" he asked.

"Of course, I do! It's a work of art. No one's ever created art for me before."

"You inspire me," he said as he took her arm in his.

"You inspire me, too. You always have," Beck said.

"It's strange to think that you knew me before I knew you."

"Correction," she said, looking up at him, "I didn't know you. I knew *of* you. I'm getting to know you now."

"Are you disappointed yet?"

"Not yet," she said with a grin.

"Good, because I feel like myself for the first time since I don't know when. I have so much music running through my head right now."

"That's wonderful. When we get back, you can record it all."

"Beck, I don't know if I ever want to go back. My life before Harlem was a pressure cooker," Jack said as Beck looked away. "What?"

"I have a feeling that being here won't last forever. That it's not supposed to last forever," Beck said.

"You can't possibly know that. We have a new life here and no idea how to get home. Let's make this our new home. Just go with it. I have."

Beck took her arm away and said, "It just seems wrong to me, Jack. I don't think we're meant to stay here."

"Don't you trust me?" he asked.

"This isn't about trusting you. This is about whether or not I trust the situation, which I don't."

They had reached Mrs. Esther's. Jack didn't want to fight, so he embraced her instead of continuing the conversation. *In time, Beck will learn to love it here as much as I do. She just needs a win. Once people realize that she's so much more than the laundry lady, the vomit bucket cleaner. Beck will be as happy here as I am.* As he held her, the tempo of her heartbeat penetrated his soul. *Don't worry, darlin'.* Jack thought as he held her. *Soon everyone will know how great you are. I'll make sure you get what you deserve.* He kissed the top of her head softly, then saw her safely to the door.

Chapter 14

The revue continued to draw bigger and bigger audiences over its first week. This was thanks in part to the good word of mouth that had circulated through the theatre district. The balance came from a glowing review of the show by none other than Beck Taylor in The New York Age. Beck highlighted Lowry's composition skills and the orchestra's delivery of his song as "a dance number that makes one leap out of one's seat with its irresistible rhythm." Also, the reviewer praised Mrs. Esther's powerful voice saying, "This writer feels blessed to be alive and in Harlem at this point in time if only to witness a voice so dynamic." Beck also mentioned that "back up musician Jack Herrmann composed two of the songs, and very handily played multiple instruments in the show. "While I had some initial concerns about adding a white musician to the Cotton Club stage, this talented musician complements the orchestra quite well."

The Cotton Club had a hit on its hands. The weekend shows all sold out, and the weeknights sales were climbing. After the last performance on Sunday night, Rebecca announced that all performers were called to the stage for a meeting with Owney. As soon as they were all assembled, Owney said, "Ladies and gents, rest up tomorrow cause you're going live on the radio Tuesday night." Cheers filled the club. It was routine for the Cotton Club to host bi-weekly broadcasts on NBC radio. But Owney had always put them on hold in the absence of Duke

Ellington and Cab Calloway's orchestras. This was big, the entire nation would hear The Cotton Club Revue!

Once they were all backstage, Lowry called out, "This calls for a celebration. I'll see y'all at Club Hot-cha's!" There were whoops and hollers backstage. The group invaded Club Hot-cha around 1:30 a.m. The cast tipped their hats to the small house band.

"Looks like they might be finishing up for the night," Jack said.

"Shows what you know, Devil Man, nothing much happens here before 2 a.m. They're just getting started," Lowry said with a chuckle.

Jack took in his surroundings, which were not nearly as big as his Malibu living room. There were at least twenty-five souls from the Cotton Club, all smashed into the small venue. The smell of sweat, gin, and tobacco hung in the air, punctuated by the distinct smell of marijuana. Through the smoke, Jack traced the scent of reefer to an ancient black man with curly white hair. He was dressed modestly in a cream button-down with suspenders and brown tweed slacks. The man was affectionately greeting the influx of patrons. Through the greetings, Jack was able to deduce that this was Clarence, owner of Club Hot-cha.

As the small yet mighty band began to play, the Cotton Club performers packed the dance floor, gyrating to the primitive beat that pulsed through each of them. Jack was standing near Rebecca, but when the music started, the two were pushed forcibly up against each other. He could feel the backbeat of the song resonating through her and into him. They attempted to dance but didn't exactly have room to move. Finding themselves pushed together in the darker recesses of the club, a sly grin spread across Rebecca's lips. She pulled him toward her and kissed him hard. At the end of the song, she asked him to join her in the alley. Jack was intrigued.

In the seclusion of the alley, it was Jack who grabbed Beck and gave her a long, lustful kiss. He was excited to see where this would lead when Beck murmured, "We need to talk."

"No, kissing's much more fun," Jack insisted, moving to kiss her again.

"Jack, this can't wait. I'm worried."

"Yeah, this is not the most private or cleanest of places..."

Beck did a quick survey of the trash-strewn alleyway, "Ew! I mean, this place is gross, not you. You're dreamy. Wait, that's not the point. I'm worried about the broadcast," she said as she regained her composure.

"Is that all? It's going to be great. After last week, the show runs like clockwork. Are you worried about how you sound? Because your sweet voice will carry just fine. You're ready for this. We all are."

"Dammit, Jack. Stop guessing what I want or about what's worrying me when I am trying to tell you something. I need you to close your head and hear me out for a change."

"Hey. You learned some slang," Jack said, desperately trying to lighten the mood. He could tell by the look on her face that it was indeed time to "close his head."

"Are you done?" she asked. After a moment, she said, "I'm concerned that if we do this, participate in a recording, that we'll cause some sort of Butterfly Effect."

"Who cares? We live here now. It's foolish to sit around and do nothing," Jack said.

"I'm not suggesting that we do nothing. I am suggesting that we not leave records of ourselves in 1938," Beck protested.

"It's a bit late for that little miss reporter. You know as well as I do that all your columns will be on microfiche forever."

"So you're saying since we're already doomed? That we should just keep on risking it?" she asked.

"I don't believe in the Butterfly Effect, and I wish you would learn to savor a victory when it's staring you straight in the face. Have a little faith, will you? Not just in me, but in your-self. We are killing it here, and we deserve this. No one is calling me up and bugging me for the same old thing. You're earning respect for your writing and your acting. When you came here, you were stuck in a menial job struggling to be no-ticed. Here you're not only noticed, but you're also appreci-ated, Beck. What more could you want?"

"I just want to be with you and to know that it's all going to be okay."

Jack pulled her close and wrapped her in his arms, "This broadcast is a good thing, darlin'. You'll see. You know you're my girl, I'm not going anywhere." He moved in for another kiss; Beck sighed as she surrendered, and their lips met.

As they walked home in hand in hand. Jack spoke excitedly about the upcoming show, "Every night we go out there, I can feel that the audience is with us. I think the other perform-ers feel it too. Lowry's getting braver with his improvisations. Man, someone is going to hear that kid and snatch him up, I just know it! Beck?" He could tell from her tense shoulders and the lack of eye contact that she was still not entirely on board. *Why couldn't she just enjoy their success?*

By the time the performers arrived on Tuesday evening, NBC had already set up their equipment and was ready to go. The excitement was electric, the house orchestra members knew that if this went well, it could open doors to bigger and better things for them. It could lead to an invitation to join a jazz ensemble, to get a recording contract, or, for some of them, to be picked up by Cab Calloway or the Duke's touring orchestras. They'd be paid to see the country.

Lowry was particularly excited because he and Jack had just polished a new opening number that Owney had approved. It was another original song of Lowry's that would be featured in the show. Jack was incredibly proud of the kid and impressed with Lowry's composition skills. He loved watching his passion for writing music blossom, it reminded Jack of when he first started composing. He knew that was what he truly wanted to do. Helping out his young friend inspired him to write more and more of his own compositions.

After checking their instruments for the show, they went backstage to prepare. Jack was concerned when he didn't see Beck. So he returned to the dining room; she wasn't there either. Finally, he located Beck alone in Owney's office. She was seated at the desk and had fallen fast asleep on a pile of paperwork. Her light auburn hair fell around her, hiding her face. Jack gently brushed the wavy locks away from her cheeks. *Poor doll, she had to come in hours before us and coordinate all of this. She's exhausted.* Looking at the clock on the dingy wall, he realized that he couldn't let her sleep anymore. It was time for everyone to get ready, they'd need her help backstage, and she would still need time to pour herself into that gorgeous Persephone gown.

He kissed her forehead, then her cheek, and finally her lips. She woke with a start but smiled when she looked up and saw him standing there. "Did you get a little rest?" he asked her. Beck nodded, and they headed backstage. Before they could chat, Moses grabbed Jack to help him with an issue with his trombone. Beck was needed to treat a minor injury that one of the dancers had sustained.

The frenzied pace continued as the performers took the stage. Jack felt a combination of excitement and nausea come over him as he waited to make his entrance. He fought hard against the stage fright. Determined that his girlfriend would not see him throw up. He noticed that Lowry was trembling, too.

"Hey man, we're going to be fine. We just need to treat this like any other night," Jack said, attempting to comfort his friend.

"I've done so many of these broadcasts, but I've never done one that featured my own music. This could change our lives, Jack. Lots of people are going to hear us. If the right ones like us, it could lead to big things, really big things," Lowry said.

"Oh, I'm aware! That's why I pushed Owney to add "Because She's Mine" as our intro. You're one talented cat; you deserve to be heard."

"I can't thank you enough for what you've done for me."

"Sure, you can. Go on out there and play the best you've ever played, kid," Jack said as he patted Lowry on the back.

The band took its nervous energy and channeled it into their performance. Jack had never heard them sound as polished as they did that night. They played to a packed house of enthusiastic fans who responded to the new songs as enthusiastically as they responded to the hits. He hoped the folks at home would hear the fun they'd had tonight coming through radios. The Persephone skits and songs played very well. Jack performed "St. James Infirmary" in his devil costume as Esther left the Underworld with her daughter Persephone in tow.

He played "Come Home," which was the name he gave "Beck's Theme" for the show on the violin as his queen returned to him. The closing number worked in solos for as many members of the orchestra as they could fit in before the end of the broadcast. Jack had a blast but did wish if only for a moment, that crowd surfing had already been invented.

Despite the enormous victory he and the rest of the performers had enjoyed, Jack felt a tad homesick. *I wish Mom and Robert were here to see this.* All at once, it hit him. *That's why Beck hasn't felt settled. She misses 1992.* He had just started to form a plan to help her when Owney approached him.

"Not bad, old boy. Not bad, at all. Slip me five." Owney said as he reached out to shake Jack's hand. As they shook hands, Owney palmed Jack some cash.

"Thank you, sir," Jack said, pocketing the money.

"A bonus, you've earned it. You're still carrying on with my assistant, I see,"

"We're still dating," Jack said, hoping that this did not mean more trouble for Rebecca.

"Well, do me a favor and let her down gently when one of these touring acts snatches you up." Jack wasn't quite sure where Owney was going with this. So he didn't respond.

Owney stared for a moment, narrowing his eyes, "Unless this is more serious than I thought, and you're planning to settle down and make a bunch of red-headed babies. In that case, I want you to consider staying on as a songwriter for me. The hours are much more favorable for a family man, and you could sit in with the band from time to time. Rebecca could stay on until the first little ankle-biter shows up."

Typically a private man, this conversation was extremely personal and uncomfortable for Jack. He knew he would never leave Rebecca here in Harlem and take off on tour. But he hadn't thought of things like weddings and babies either. Their relationship was less than two months old. He reminded himself that things moved faster in the 1930s. As Owney spoke, Jack realized he had just been standing there in silence.

"I see you've thought this out real careful like," Owney laughed, "Poor girl, she ain't getting any younger."

"What?" Jack asked.

"Rebecca don't get married soon; it's not going to happen. That's the trouble with dating at her age and your age. It comes with certain expectations. You ain't exactly no spring chicken, but she can't be picky now, can she?"

"May I be excused?" Jack hadn't asked that of another person since getting up from the dinner table as a child. *Still, when talking with one's boss, whose nickname was "The Killer," manners are important.*

"Sure, sure!" Owney said as he walked past Jack and into the dining room.

Jack found Beck backstage and helped her finish the cleanup. They were quiet during their work as Jack pondered how to make Beck feel more at home and aggressively tried to push thoughts of marriage and babies out of his head. As hard as he tried, he couldn't help sorting through the questions Owney posed.

There was one crucial question that Owney had not explicitly asked. *Do I love Beck?* If not, then the answers to all the other questions were quite simple. If he loved her, well, then that's where things would get messy. *Isn't it always messy to love someone? My mom and dad loved each other madly until his heart stopped suddenly.* But he wasn't thinking only of the inevitable emotional mess and grief that typically walks hand in hand with loving somebody. Ever practical, Jack was also thinking of the confusion of how the two of them came to be here, and whether or not they were going back. *That's what Beck's been saying all along.*

Before going to her, he had peeked at the cash Owney had slipped him. A fifty dollar bonus! That's what he made in a week. Now, he had a mission and the means with which to carry it out. He found Beck waiting for him at the backstage exit. As usual, they were the last ones to leave.

"Hey darlin', what do you miss most about 1992?"

"That's easy, two things that start with a P," she said playfully.

"Oh my," Jack said, his mind going straight to the gutter.

"That's not what I meant! Pizza and pants, Silly."

"Pants, huh?"

"Yes, I miss my jeans! I love 1930s fashion, but it's a pain in the ass to be expected to wear a dress and stockings every day. Did you know that these are stockings?" she said, pointing at her legs, "They're not pantyhose. They're seamed thigh-high stockings held up by a garter belt. I have very complicated underwear, and I am not particularly gifted at putting it on," Beck complained.

"I'm sorry," Jack said, trying not to laugh, "I never thought about it that way."

"It's not funny! Mama Esther chases me around every morning, grabbing at my legs because I never can get the seams straight," Beck said as she started to laugh with Jack.

"Well, for what it's worth, you look beautiful. Sorry about your intricate but sexy-sounding underwear," Jack said as they started to laugh again.

"I'm just not equipped to be this fancy all the time. It looked like so much fun in the movies," Beck sighed.

"All of this looked like so much fun in the movies," Jack agreed.

"Why does real life have to be so complicated?"

"Listen, I don't know where I could find you pants, but I do know where we can find pizza," Jack said.

Chapter 15

Jack hailed a big yellow taxi and relished the look of surprise on Beck's face. The back of the car was spacious with what looked like a large sofa for a backseat. It reminded him more of a limo. Although there was plenty of room on the plush rear seat, Beck snuggled right up next to him. Her nose felt like an ice cube on his neck, and he had to fight the urge to flinch. "Poor Beck, you're always so cold," he said, rubbing her arms and back to warm her.

"I grew up in the south, and then I moved to California. My thin blood isn't used to this weather. I'm worried I'll freeze to death after Halloween. Wait. Please tell me they celebrate Halloween here."

"Yes, darlin'. They celebrate Halloween, not much different about it than where we're from," he said as he indicated the driver.

Beck lowered her voice a little, "Oh good. Halloween is my favorite holiday."

"Is that so? It's always been my favorite, too. My family was the only one in the neighborhood that didn't celebrate Christmas, and I always felt left out. But, we all celebrated Halloween together. It's been my favorite holiday ever since. Did you ever see one of the band's Halloween shows?"

"I've always wanted to see one of your Halloween shows, but you only do them in California. When I finally moved there, the tickets sold out so fast I didn't stand a chance."

"Back in 19--," he looked at the driver again and corrected himself," I mean back "home," I'm working on songs for a musical Tom came up with that's all about Halloween."

"A Halloween musical?" Beck asked excitedly.

"Yeah, it's supposed to be an animated movie. I was going to voice the lead."

"I love everything you've said. You, Tom Price, Halloween, and animation? This has to happen. Even if I have to build a freakin' time machine myself."

"Shh. I don't think I'm doing a good job of helping with your homesickness," Jack said.

"No, this is good. I need to talk about home, and you're absolutely the only person I can talk to about it. I get that you don't miss it, but it just feels so good to be heard." Beck explained.

"I miss things, too, Beck."

"Really? Like what ...or who?" She said, suddenly serious.

"I don't have another girl back home, Beck. I'm not a cad."

"I didn't mean that. I'm just surprised that someone like you is still single. Haven't you ever been in love?"

"I thought I was a few times, but it never lasts. I'm different offstage; I'm reserved. That disappointed a few of them, and the ones that weren't disappointed complained that I work all the time."

"I've noticed. You are devoted to your work. It's who you are."

"Well, it's hard for people who are close to me," Jack explained.

"Like who? Who are you missing?"

"I have a sweet old Australian Shepherd named Rufus and some great friends, I didn't see them as much as I should have, but I still miss them. I miss my mom and crowd surfing."

Beck started to giggle. "Your mom and crowd surfing? That's an odd combo. Does your mom crowd surf?" Beck asked, with a grin.

"I didn't want you to think that I was some sort of mama's boy, so I sandwiched her in there," Jack explained.

"I find that how a man treats his mom is a pretty good indicator of how he'll treat his girlfriend," she said, smiling up at him.

"Oh really? Have you seen this with *your* many boyfriends?" Jack teased.

"I was speaking in generalities. I haven't actually had a serious boyfriend."

"I find that hard to believe."

"I've dated a couple of guys, but not for very long. I tend to scare them off or run when things get too serious. My parents had a very messy divorce, so I honestly think I might be better off single and living with a cat," Beck said as she laughed nervously.

"Well, I don't scare so easily. I just hope I don't run you off," Jack said as he pulled Beck closer.

"You won't; you're too busy," Beck quipped. Then, squeezed him tight.

The pair cuddled and kissed on the comfy rear seat as they rode across Harlem until the taxi came to a stop at Patsy's Pizzeria. It was a small but stately storefront. The smell of mozzarella and tomato sauce was intoxicating. Inside, the restaurant was long and narrow, with bistro tables along one wall and large booths on the other. The walls were brick with wood wainscotting. Jack was surprised at how similar it looked to when he had visited in the 1980s. The soda cooler was missing, the pictures on the walls were different; other than that, the place looked the same. Older Italian men with much younger female companions occupied many of the tables. The men were elegantly dressed and exuded a zest for life. Yet, at the same time, there was a distinct air of authority. They were not to be messed with.

"I feel like I just stepped into one of the Godfather movies," Beck whispered.

"With good reason, we're surrounded by Italian mobsters. Coppola was a regular here. He said that his time at Patsy's inspired his direction for the movies."

"You always take me to the most interesting places," Beck said.

"You wanted pizza. This is the only place I know that has pizza," Jack said as he found a quiet table for two.

He pulled out Beck's chair and was surprised that she didn't flinch this time. She was learning to trust him, at least a little.

"I wonder why you ended up here with me." Jack said, "Were you a fan of this time, too?"

"I love the 30s and 40s. While you're more into the 20s and 30s. I guess this is the decade where we overlap. I love the movies from the era and the jazz and big band orchestras. In high school, I would wear dresses like this from time to time."

"But not the stockings, right?"

"Oh God, no," Beck laughed. "Not the seamed stockings. I wanted to learn to swing dance and would daydream about being a nightclub singer. My friends didn't know what to make of it. I would daydream about dancing with James Cagney."

"Hey! It's not nice to talk about other men you're sweet for when you're on a date." Jack teased.

"I was just going to remind you that what first drew me to this period was you."

"Me?" he asked.

"I told you I loved the "Don't You Go" video. The first time I saw it, I loved all the costumes, the band, and the audience were wearing. You all looked so elegant. I wanted to look like that, too. Most of all, I was smitten with the handsome, redheaded lead singer with the seductive grin and the suspenders. They drove me wild."

"Suspenders? My suspenders drove you wild?"

"Ever since I saw you in your suspenders, I've found myself drawn to any man wearing them. It's all your fault," Beck said.

"Wow," Jack said suddenly, pleased he was wearing suspenders, "You must be going crazy because most men wear them here."

"I don't notice because when you're here wearing them, you're the only one I see."

"Beck, who do you miss back home?"

"Like you, I have some great friends, but most of them live in the south. My move to California was pretty recent. I was just getting to know the area and my coworkers. My family drama is ongoing, and we've been kind of distant from one another. I guess I was pretty lonely, actually. Maybe I should embrace this new normal. I mean, I like my work here, and I love you."

The look on Beck's face at that moment showed that her words had betrayed her. Jack noticed that it was not the face of a woman who had planned to say those three words out loud. At the same time, he could tell that she meant them. Beck looked anxious. She also looked so beautiful to him. He decided to tell the truth both to her and to himself.

"And, I love you, Beck. This is all so crazy, but this is the one thing that makes sense to me, "Jack admitted.

Beck reached across the table and took Jack's hand. A smile slowly spread across her face, and her eyes sparkled, "That makes things complicated. We don't know how long we have here."

"You're pizza's ready, Mr. Jack." their server interrupted.

Jack and Beck were pretty hungry, and the pizza was delicious. They had entirely forgotten that they were rubbing elbows with the mob until one of the older gentlemen approached their table.

"Good evening, name's Tony Firelli," he said as he shook Jack's hand.

"Hi, Jack Herman."

"I know I saw you at the Cotton Club last weekend. What are you doing in this part of Harlem?" Tony asked.

"We just wanted pizza," Jack said, motioning towards Beck and their food.

"There's no pizza in the Jazz district?"

"Not any worth eating," Jack said. Tony's men had joined him just in time to hear this, they chuckled.

"Clearly, the man's got good taste," Tony said to his associates.

"Speaking of which, this is my girl, Rebecca Taylor," Jack said. He was just thinking how happy it made him to be able to introduce Beck as his girl when he caught her eye from across the table. She was noticeably worried.

"Taylor, huh? What's a nice boy like you doing with an Irish dame?" Tony asked, bluntly.

A younger man in Tony's party added, "Irish ain't welcome in here."

"What my associate means is that there are certain Irish that we have a problem with. I hope your dame ain't one of them," Tony said, moving closer to Rebecca's side of the table.

"The club's just a paycheck for us. Our dealings are strictly with the talent," Jack explained. Feeling his pulse quicken, his muscles tensed as his body prepared to protect Beck.

"I hope that's true. Owney and his goons are bad news. You're a very talented man. I'd hate to see things go bad for you," Tony said, still staring at Beck.

"Thanks. We'll be careful," Jack said.

"I still don't understand why a nice Jewish man would choose an Irish girl. I'm sure you have lots of choices," Tony said, shaking his head.

"When a sweet mama like this waltzes into your life, you don't care where she's from," Jack said. He hoped this would improve things with Tony and at the same time, knowing he had probably just made Beck angry with his slang. But at the moment, she was the least likely of the two to be armed. How did this guy guess he was Jewish? Tony was taking an uncomfortably long look at Rebecca, then he suddenly laughed.

"I see, a tomato's a tomato. Don't matter where the vine grows," Tony said. Then, he leaned in, "Listen, you take care, capisce? I got Jews in my family on my ma's side, and there are nasty things happening back home and here in New York. It will probably get worse before it gets better."

Tony doesn't know the half of it! Jack was surprised and moved by Tony's words. "Thanks, Mr.Firelli. I will." Jack said as he reached out and shook Tony's hand again.

"Don't forget what I said about your boss," Tony said to Jack and Beck as he and the rest of his party headed out the door.

"Sweet mama, huh?" Beck said to Jack.

"Sorry, "tomato" was more fitting. Sad Tony thought of it before me," Jack said. He flashed her an impish grin.

"You're going to pay for that," Beck said.

"I thought so. What's my punishment?" Jack sighed.

"I'm eating the last piece," Beck said with a smile as she grabbed the last piece of pizza.

"Go ahead, I deserve it," he said, relieved that, while the pizza was "to die for," they hadn't actually died for it!

Chapter 16

The next day, Jack kept replaying the evening at Patsy's in his mind. He was recognized as a musician for the first time outside of the club. He had been so proud to introduce Beck as his girl. Their conversation was effortless, and Beck had been so happy. The sadness and fear ever-present in her eyes had disappeared. A definite shift had occurred in both of them. It felt important; it felt right. Jack opened the rear door of the club and walked right into Otis and his saxophone.

"Hey!" Otis cried out as he fell hard on his bottom while protecting his horn.

"I'm sorry!" Jack said, rushing to help Otis up. Once he helped the man to his feet, he asked, "Where you going?"

"One of the keys is stuck on my gobble pipe. I was going to run down to Lenny's to see if he could fix it."

"Here, let me take a look," Jack said, reaching out for the horn.

"I thought you was too big a deal to fix the instruments now."

"No, it's still part of my job," Jack said as he inspected the key," Hand me a damp towel, will you?"

"Why?" Otis asked, handing Jack the cloth.

"You spilled booze on your horn. That's why it's stuck. Be more careful." Jack said.

"You're one cool cat, man. I'm gonna be able to say I was there when it all started." Otis said.

"When what started?" Jack asked as Lowry entered.

"You mean, you don't know?" Lowry asked.

"What?"

"Guess who called Mr. Madden up after he heard the broadcast. None other than Mr. Cab Calloway himself. He loved our revue. He wants to sing our songs when he comes next week, and he wants you to perform your version of Minnie the Moocher onstage with him!"

"That's incredible! I love Cab Calloway. Hey Congrats, Lowry. Those songs deserve to be heard. Slip me five, my man," Jack said as he shook Lowry's hand.

"That's not all. Mr. Calloway wants to discuss 'our futures' with us after he finishes up his run here," Lowry said. He grinned that Cheshire Cat grin of his and bounced up and down. He was such a brilliant musician, but his giddiness reminded Jack of just how young his friend was. Lowry was only 20, and Jack was excited to see that there were big things in his future.

He couldn't believe his own luck either. *I've always looked up to Cab Calloway. He's not only a talented musician but a marvelous showman. And, I'm going to be able to perform with him. I was worried that Cab would be put off by my interpretation of his song. I never thought that he'd want to sing it with me. What did he mean about 'our futures'? I can't think about that right now; it's too much. I'm creating music, sharing the stage with one of my heroes, and dizzy with a dame. Beck. I have to tell her!*

He went looking for Beck and found her in Owney's office. The two of them were discussing Calloway's return.

"So, you're up for the task, Love?" Owney asked.

"Absolutely! Mr. Calloway was very specific about the scenes. I'll message him the first drafts tomorrow afternoon." Beck said.

"Tomorrow? You sure?" Owney asked.

"Yes, Sir. The sooner we finalize the script, the better. We only have a week until Halloween, and I want to be able to get his orchestra, our performers, and the tech all on the same page as soon as possible."

Owney noticed Jack in the doorway, "Well, well, if it isn't the man of the hour. Did the boys in the band give you the low-down, then?"

"I think so. I know that Mr. Calloway wants to play Lowry's songs, my two songs, and they said that he would like me to join him for the parody of "Minnie Moocher," Jack said.

"Yea, he wants all the original music you and Lowry wrote for the revue, and he'll have his own songs and standards to fill out the rest of the music. He wants Rebecca to rewrite the scenes to better fit the transitions from the revue songs to his songs."

"That's not all," Beck said, smiling.

"Mr. Calloway's show director has to cool his heels in the big house for a couple of months, so he has requested that our Rebecca fill in for him. Pretty good opportunity for a dame," Owney explained.

"I appreciate the opportunity, Mr. Madden," Beck said.

Jack had not witnessed this side of Beck. *She's so confident in her element. It's sexy! Just like her Persephone costume.* "Wait. How will you be my Persephone if you're directing the show?"

"The Persephone storyline is out. I'm reworking the lead into the song. You'll have to flirt with a lucky audience member instead."

"I'll miss you up there," Jack protested.

"Hey, Loverboy. You'll see her after the shows." Owney said.

"But not tonight. I have a lot of work to do," Beck said as she walked hurriedly out of the office.

Shit. I deserve this. Jack felt a little deflated, but he remembered all the times he had to forego being with family and friends. The sacrifices he had made to get the music out of his head and onto the page. *She's an artist, too. Beck needs the time and space to create, just like me.*

After he helped Beck close up the club, Jack and Lowry went for a drink at the tiny Log Cabin Club. The music was terrific, which came as no surprise to Jack. The musicians were not as polished as the Cotton Club performers. Still, there was a primitive charm in the raw, simplistic tunes they played. The venue allowed for much more opportunity for improvisation than Lowry and Jack were used to. They chatted with the musicians on their break.

"You the guys that played at the Cotton Club, ain't ya?" the tall, skinny bass player asked.

"Yea, how'd you know?" Lowry asked.

"We heard it on the radio. Not surprised, this one got songs on the radio," the squatty, little drummer said, indicating Jack, "But, it's nice to hear a brother can catch a break."

"Hey, don't knock the ole Red Devil here. He fought hard to make sure my songs were played. Jack's always got my back." Lowry said.

"Thanks, Lowry. I do what I can. You deserve to be heard," Jack said, "You all do."

"You may have good intentions, Face, but you ain't doin' us no favors." the bass player said.

"Yea, just you wait. As soon as white folks like you show you can play as good as us, they'll jump at the chance to put a white face on jazz," the drummer explained.

The bass player added, "Back in January, Benny Goodman played Carnegie Hall, and the newspaper said it was 'the single most important jazz concert in history.' That it made jazz 'respectable' music. If that ain't some malarkey, I don't know what is."

"Goodman's a bandleader, I'm rarely out front. I don't like performing all that much. Besides, I've learned so much from Lowry and the others. At the same time, I feel like I bring something to the table in my own way. Surely, there's a place for me, too," Jack argued.

"You a white man, there's a place for you at every table," the bass player retorted, "You can't know what it's like; you don't wear our shoes."

"I can never know exactly what it's like, but I want to understand. I want to help."

"Ain't nobody asked for your help, Face. You Jews are all the same, trying to own everything. Jazz is ours!" the drummer yelled.

"We're gonna make tracks," Lowry said. He took Jack's arm and steered him toward the exit.

The drummer followed them, continuing his tirade, "Don't you understand? These people are ruining Harlem. They gutted their fine homes, carved em into slums for us to live in. All so they can get rich off our backs."

Lowry turned to face the man, "You really think the answer to hate is more hate? You obviously got a problem with your landlord, but Jack here ain't done nothing to you."

"That's where you're wrong. Jews ain't nothing but thieves. Including this man who's taking what's ours. Now get the hell out of here you dirty Shylock!" the drummer exclaimed as he reached past Lowry in an attempt to push Jack.

Lowry blocked the man's attack with his body and said, "I'm not one to start a fight, but I will finish one. You best step off, Pally."

As the drummer sized up the young man, his boss emerged from his office, "I ain't paying you to run off your mouth. Get back to playing."

Seizing the opportunity, Lowry and Jack left the Log Cabin Club.

"Let's head home," Lowry said.

"You still want to put me up after what you found out tonight?"

"I don't follow you, Jack," Lowry said.

"Now that you know I'm Jewish," Jack explained.

"What? You're Jewish?" Lowry said, feigning surprise, "I don't give the price of biscuits what you are, now come on."

The two walked along in silence. Then, Lowry said, "I do need to know one thing. Level with me, Jack, are my songs solid, or are you just helping me to make yourself feel better?"

"What do you mean? I take music very seriously," Jack said. Lowry's words had cut him deeply.

"Yea, but do you take me seriously?" Lowry asked.

"Of course, I do. My entire adult life has revolved around music. I never had lessons or any interest in playing until I went to Africa and fell in love with their percussion. I learned from the musicians of West Africa. They let me play on street corners with them. They housed me in their huts and tiny shacks and shared their meals with me. Most of all, they taught me their music. I didn't learn to play as a child like you. I learned from experiences. All I've ever wanted was to learn from all of you and help you in any way I can. If me being white gets Owney to finally listen to how talented you are, then I going to use whatever power I have to help you. Not because I'm feeding you a line, but because you and all the other talented musicians deserve to be heard."

Lowry was speechless for a bit. Jack's heart hurt. How could Lowry doubt him? He was worried that perhaps his speech was a little too impassioned. He certainly didn't want to come off as the "Great White Savior" of Jazz musicians. He just wanted to do the right thing, whatever that was. He wanted his friend to believe him and for Lowry to believe in himself. As they started into the apartment building, Lowry said, "I get it now."

"You do?" Jack asked, hopefully.

"Yea, you've gotta long history of getting my people to take care of your pale ass."

"Oh, Lowry," Jack said, defeated.

"Man, I'm just teasing you. It's so easy," Lowry said as he started up the stairs laughing as he went. "Come on, *Africa*, we can't let you sleep on the street."

Chapter 17

"Let's run that lead in one more time. Mama Esther, I need to see a bit more tension in Demeter's confrontation with Hades," Beck instructed, "Great job on the final notes of your solo. You sure know how to let it smolder."

"You got it, Baby girl," Mrs. Esther said.

"Aces! Let's take it take from the top,"

The days leading up to Halloween were incredibly busy at the Cotton Club. The entire cast was coming in to rehearse the new show early in the evening and still performing two shows of their own revue at night. Beck was a good director, but Jack could tell she was exhausted as she rubbed her eyes.

As soon as rehearsal was over, she ran backstage to take care of the talent. She delivered and collected laundry, helped with makeup, and made sure all ran well during the Cotton Club Revue. Only to run backstage at intermission to dress and come on one last time as Persephone.

The two of them tried to steal moments together whenever they could, but Beck could barely keep her eyes open on their walks home.

After the final show, Jack and Mrs. Esther pitched in to help get her home faster. When Jack was done, he went looking for Beck. Instead, he found Mrs. Esther in the backstage hallway right outside the ladies' dressing room.

"Shhh, our girl is having a little rest," Mrs. Esther said as she opened the door a bit wider; Jack could see that Beck had fallen asleep on a purple chaise lounge chair. From the looks of it, she fell asleep while attempting to unknot a lace in one of the other actress's shoes as it still dangled from her hand. Esther went over to her and gently removed the pump. She took care of the knot herself and placed the shoe by its mate on the rack.

"You ready for the big day tomorrow?" Mrs. Esther asked.

"As ready as I'll ever be. I wish I'd had a chance to run through "Minnie" with Mr. Calloway. I hope he's happy with me." Jack said.

"Cab's one of the sweetest men I've ever met. I'm sure it'll be fine. You're very talented."

"Thank you, ma'am," Jack said. He was honored to receive praise from such an accomplished singer.

"I had my doubts about you at first."

"You don't say," Jack smiled at Mrs. Esther.

"I love this little lady as though she were one of my own. I couldn't be too careful," Mrs. Esther explained.

"I love her, too, Mrs. Esther."

"I believe you do, Jack. Say, the room's clear, come on in and wake our girl for me, will you? I need to get her home. She should rest in her own bed, not on some smelly, old couch."

"Of course," Jack said as he moved toward Beck.

"I'm going to surprise her with breakfast in bed tomorrow. What do you have planned?" Mrs. Esther asked.

"What do you mean?" Jack asked.

"Are you two doing something special. Maybe you're giving her something special?"

"Oh, you mean something like a director's gift?"

"No, Jack Herman! I do not! Are you so wrapped up in this show that you forgot your girl's birthday?"

"Birthday?" Jack said, stunned, "I didn't forget. I can't forget something she never told me in the first place." Jack said defensively, "Rebecca told me that she loved Halloween. She didn't tell she was born on Halloween!"

"Maybe she doesn't want you to know she's another year older. Forget I said anything," Ms.Esther said.

"I already feel strange about our age difference. Why would I mind if she was another year older?"

"Women around here are old maid's at twenty-six, the men tend to pass em by. You know Rebecca loves you. Maybe she didn't want to lose you over something as silly as not getting a ring," Mrs. Esther explained.

"You mean she thinks I'm going to propose?" Jack asked, still shell-shocked.

"I'm sure she wants you to, but I doubt she expects anything. Especially since she didn't tell you about her birthday."

"I can't believe this. It's after midnight. It's already Rebecca's birthday. What am I going to do?"

Mrs. Esther wasted no time. She said, "Well, Rebecca loves opals, that's her birthstone, and I know a good a jeweler over near the hospital."

Beck started to roll onto the floor, and Jack caught her in the nick of time.

"Hey there, Darlin'," Jack said, "We're all set here. Let's get you home so you can get a bit of rest."

"I'm sorry I didn't mean to fall asleep." Beck moaned.

"You've been working too hard," Mrs. Esther said, "Jack's going to help us get you home."

Jack carefully helped Beck stand up and draped her arm across his shoulders. As they reached the sidewalk, she was able to take his arm. They walked along in silence for a while. Jack wasn't sure if he should bring up her birthday, especially without having a plan as to how to celebrate it. They were almost to Mrs. Esther's when she suddenly said, "Rebecca, did you know it's after midnight already?"

"Oh? I'm sorry I kept you both out so late. You have to rest up for the show tomorrow," Beck said.

"I wasn't complaining, Honey. Do you know what day it is?" Mrs. Esther asked.

"Yeah, it's Halloween," Beck said as she turned and looked up at Jack with a big grin on her face. He gently kissed her, and as he hugged her, he shot a pleading look over her shoulder to Mrs. Esther.

"That's right, Happy Halloween," Mrs. Esther said to her. Then to Jack, she said quietly, "That's the place I was telling you about," indicating Fulton's Fine Jewelry across the street. Jack nodded. Thinking that if he decided to get a ring, it would more likely have to come from the pawnshop on his side of town. After a block and a half, they reached the house. He said goodnight to Mrs. Esther, and with her looking on, gave Beck a very chaste goodnight kiss.

The next day, Jack stood outside Lenny's Pawn Shop and Repair when it opened, his best guitar in hand. He wished that there was some sort of sign that he was doing the right thing. *Maybe Lenny won't trade the guitar for a ring. Maybe he won't even have an opal ring.* As he started to peruse the jewelry section, Lenny approached.

"Are you bringing in the guitar, or did you finally decide to part with that old family heirloom?" he asked.

"Family heirloom?" Jack asked.

"Yea, the watch," Lenny reminded him.

"No, the watch is in a safe place," Jack replied. He wasn't lying. Jack had stashed it in the inner pocket of the coat he'd arrived in. The coat was rarely worn now that he had acquired other clothes. It had been relegated to the back of the closet. "How much will the guitar bring?" Jack asked.

"I see you looking at the rings. Maybe we could work something out," Lenny suggested.

Jack took a closer look at the rings, and almost hidden in the very back of the case was a delicate, heart-shaped opal with a tiny diamond chip on each side. It was perfect.

"How about a trade for the heart-shaped opal in the back?"

"Oh, a nice ring like that? You sure you don't want to bring in that heirloom? That would bring an even trade. For this, I'd need the guitar and a five-spot."

"No way the guitar is worth at least $20," Jack protested.

"Maybe when it was new, but you've played the hell out of that thing."

Just then, the bell on the door clanged, and Moses walked in, "Hey Lenny, good to see the aliens didn't get you."

"What that's?" Lenny asked, perplexed.

"The broadcast last night," Moses explained.

"Oh yeah, that Orson Welles knows how to stir things up," Lenny said, "You got the five-spot you owe me?"

"Yeah, I need to pick up my mouth organ," he said.

"Hold up. I got another customer," Lenny said. Then, he turned back to Jack," Like I said, that guitar ain't exactly in mint condition. I'll give you the ring for it and $3."

Before Jack could answer, Moses said, "Wait a minute. Aren't you Jack 'The Red Devil' Herman? he grabbed Jack's hand and shook it, "It's an honor to meet you. Lenny, I didn't know you had a famous jazz musician in the store. I heard this guy on the radio last week. He's a whiz!" Jack looked at Moses, confused. His friend gave him a quick wink.

"Is that so? Well, I'll tell you what I'll do, Red Devil. I'll trade you the ring for the guitar as long as you sign it first. Have we got a deal?" Lenny asked.

"Sounds fair. Thanks," Jack said as he traded the signed guitar for the ring. He turned and smiled at Moses, returning the wink.

As Jack left the shop, he hid the ring in his front pants pocket. He was still very nervous, but at least he had a plan.

Chapter 18

Beck had been at the club for hours when Jack walked in. She was running a cue to cue rehearsal of the lights with James, the club's electrician. Pipes entered, carrying a large package. Beck turned and saw them.

"Hi guys!" she called, "Pipes? Is that my dry ice?"

"Sure is," he said.

"Great. Please put some in each of the buckets I preset on either side of the stage. Thanks!"

"You got it," Pipes said as he left.

A woman so charming she's got a hitman running her errands. Jack mused as he watched her work.

"It's for the fog effect during your big number," She explained proudly, then to James, she said, "Ok, show me the sequence for the finale, please."

Jack came up behind her as she sat alone in the back of the empty club and gently kissed the side of her neck. She drew in a quick breath. There wasn't much light, but he could feel that he gave her goosebumps. He slid a hand down her arm to her wrist. Her pulse was up. "Just breathe, Darlin'. You've got this," he whispered. She slowed her breathing, and in a minute, he felt the rhythm, her rhythm under his hand. To his surprise, she moved his hand to just above her breasts. She kept her hand on top of his, and he rested his chin on the top of her head.

"Thanks, James. Looks like we're all set," she said. She stood up and pushed Jack's curls back away from his face with her hands. She said," We need to get you ready. Want me to do your makeup?"

"Sure," he said, wanting any excuse for Beck to keep touching him. Backstage he sat in a makeup chair while she worked. He felt so comfortable with her touch. *She's never felt like a stranger to me.* His uncertainty was not about whether or not he wanted to commit to being with her, although it did seem a bit soon. It was the instability of their situation that bothered him.

Not knowing exactly how they came to be here and whether or not they would ever return to their present time was beginning to gnaw at him. *How will I find Beck again if we go back? If I marry her here, we'll have to get married all over again if we return. That would be okay. I mean, I'd want my mom there. She would never forgive me for eloping. Mom's still mad at Robert for marrying his first wife while he lived in Paris.* She'd brought it up on Mother's Day, and Robert had said, "Mom, would you give it a rest? That was two wives ago," As Jack recalled his big brother's antics, Beck turned him to face the mirror.

"Voila!" she said proudly.

"Wow, this look takes me back," Jack said, surveying his devil makeup. Beck had arched his eyebrows over his eyes and extended them with burnt sienna eyeshadow out towards his temples. There was a line of the same color eyeshadow going just above the corner of his eyes, reaching towards the tops of his ears. She added heavy brown eyeliner with a dramatic wing on the upper lids and a thin brown line under his hazel eyes. She'd finished the look off with a Devil Red lip. "How did you know to...Wait! Did you see my first movie?"

"Don't be silly. I couldn't bear to watch the whole thing. I ended up fast-forwarding to your scene, and then I watched it over and over until the tape wore thin," The couple laughed.

Then, it hit Jack, what he was about to do, and the butterflies returned.

"I'm going to step out while the men get dressed and check on the ladies. Do you need anything before I go?" Beck asked.

"I'll be fine. I'm going to get dressed and see you in about ten minutes."

Beck left, and Jack told the men about his birthday surprise for her. Not about the ring, only Moses knew about that, and he'd been sworn to secrecy. They only knew about the part he needed them to play. He had already clued Mrs. Esther in earlier, so the ladies could help.

Once they were dressed. Jack had a stagehand tell Beck that she was needed in the dining area quickly before it opened.

The band came in playing "When the Saints go Marching In" with Jack on trombone and the singers right there with him. Many of them were dressed in costumes for the Halloween show, but as Jack surveyed the group, they looked and sounded like a rogue Mardi Gras Crewe.

He was pleasantly surprised to find Beck in her Persephone gown. She looked happy but shocked at the spectacle. Then, the crowd parted, and Lowry traded Jack his horn for his violin, he played "Beck's theme" on it, and then he sang "Happy Birthday" to her. Jack started to go to one knee and was surprised when Beck met him on the floor. She hugged him close and said quietly, "That's beautiful, but it's not really my birthday."

"What? But Mrs. Esther said..." Jack whispered.

"When I was when in the hospital, I thought I was dreaming, dying, or both. So, I decided to have a little fun and give myself a new birthday. Halloween is my favorite day, so..."

"Are we anywhere close to your actual birthday?" Jack asked.

"No, I turned twenty-five back in July," she answered sheepishly.

"Oh, Rebecca," Jack sighed. As they stood up, he realized the crowd had moved on. He decided the moment had passed. The ring would live in his pocket awhile longer. "Nice costume. Are you joining me tonight?"

"You know I can't. I didn't mean to get your hopes up; I just wanted to dress up for my favorite holiday. You need to head back now. Can I get you anything?"

"A kiss for luck?" Jack asked.

Beck took a quick look around and then gave Jack a kiss.

"Your heart is pounding, Sweetie. Do I need to stay backstage tonight?" Beck asked.

"Absolutely not. You deserve to sit back here and see how all your hard work comes together, Madame Director."

"Jack," Lowry called out, "Mr. Calloway's looking for you."

Jack's leg felt wobbly as he walked through the dining room backstage. He could hear the dinner show patrons flooding in behind him and the unmistakable laugh of Cab Calloway ahead of him.

Cab was standing backstage in a bright red zoot suit with red devil horns on his forehead; it made a nice contrast with Jack's new costume, which was a white tux with tails and matching white devil horns. Cab took one look at Jack and laughed again, "Evenin' old scratch, woo wee, someone did a number on your face."

"Says the man in the big red suit," Jack said as both men chuckled, "Mr.Calloway, it's an honor."

"Right back at ya, Jack. Please call me Cab," he said as he shook Jack's hand.

Jack started to feel butterflies in his stomach again. *This is going to happen.* Cab noticed Jack's nervousness. "Don't worry, my man. You're with me now just follow my lead, and when the time comes, don't screw up my song," Jack grew even paler than usual, "I'm just kidding, you're going to be just fine," Cab reassured him.

As Cab walked away, Leroy came up to Jack," Hey, Red, you need my bucket?" Jack grabbed the white bucket and heaved up the entire contents of his stomach into it. He was thankful that Beck wasn't backstage to see that.

Like most of the best moments in life, Jack saw the show fly by. Before he knew it, it was time for the big finale. The stage was awash with reds and subtle purple hues. Sammy and his stage crew made the dry ice fog, which hovered just above the stage floor. The orchestra entered first and began their intro. Simultaneously, the Cotton Club dancers overtook the dance floor dressed as demons in sequined bikinis and coordinating horned headpieces.

Jack and Cab entered the stage from opposite sides with a spotlight trained on each of them. The crowd went wild as the men danced out to the first few notes of "Minnie the Moocher." Cab introduced them to Jack "The Red Devil" Herman, and he conducted the orchestra as Jack began to sing. He was sweating under the hot spotlight. His undershirt clung to him as it ran down his back. The singing sounded like it was coming from another place. He allowed himself to fully inhabit the character Beck had recreated for him. It was exhilarating!

Cab joined him for one last chorus and unleashed some of his famous moves while Jack did his best to keep up with his hero. He knew it wasn't perfect, but that didn't matter. He was dancing and singing with Cab Calloway.

It was over all too soon. Jack was grateful that he'd get to do the show with Cab a few more times. The crowd went crazy as they took their bows. He couldn't see Beck, but he knew that she was out there in the darkness. He couldn't explain it, but somehow he knew that she was proud and happy.

Chapter 19

"Let's give it up to the cool cats of the Cotton Club Orchestra!" Cab said, raising a glass to the performers who had joined him across the street at the Theatrical Grill. The place was packed for the club's annual Halloween Party. Almost everyone wore elaborate costumes as the crowd was primarily made up of casts from different Harlem revues.

A swinging band was playing, strolling magicians were doing table-side magic, and onstage belly dancers and circus performers took turns entertaining the crowd. The decorations made the place look like a voodoo sanctuary straight out of New Orleans.

The walls had bones, feathers, animal skulls, and creepy dolls hung about them. From the ceiling, there were sequined voodoo flags. Jack and Beck wore their Satan and Persephone costumes. They were delighted that the whole community turned out to celebrate in such a big way. "This is my kind of party," Jack said as they walked around.

"Very authentic decorations," Beck observed.

"I'm pretty some of the skulls and shrunken heads are real," Jack said as he moved in for a closer look.

"Oh?" Beck looked puzzled.

"I collect stuff like this. Bones, skulls, voodoo artifacts, creepy dolls," Jack stopped himself as he realized Beck looked more concerned than impressed. "What's wrong?"

"Oh, nothing. My boyfriend just said that he 'collects bones,' I'm wondering if I should be worried about that statement."

"When I was a kid, things like that used to scare me. I resented that it had that kind of power over me. So, I exposed myself to as much of it as possible, and now it only makes me laugh. Except for the dolls, there's a lot of creepy juju in dolls."

"I love dolls," Beck said.

"Were some of yours passed down to you?" Jack asked.

"Of course, I was the only girl grandchild. I had dolls from my mom and both of my grandmothers."

"So, those dolls have juju from you, your mom, and your grandmothers. Maybe you'll pass them down one day. That's why they're interesting."

"Sounds like you think about death and the supernatural a lot."

"I don't want to be afraid of death. It keeps us from doing things we should while we're alive."

"Were you afraid when you got here?" Beck asked.

"Of course, I was. At first, but playing with Cab and the Duke, falling in love. Those things wouldn't have happened in 1992. At least two of them wouldn't."

"I wasn't afraid when I got here because I thought I was dead. I woke up in the hospital and thought, 'I might as well act as if there's nothing to lose' because there wasn't. I used to fear failure, but it was so freeing to know that no one here knew me. There was nobody to impress. Then, I met you. I realized that this wasn't a dream. I have something to lose again," Beck explained.

"Oh, Beck, you always make me proud. I'm not going anywhere...if I can help it."

"You were right, though. I need to go back to living like there's nothing to lose. I can't keep looking over my shoulder anymore. I'm tired of running from time. Wondering if it's going to jump forward or end completely. I'm happy here with you and everyone else right now."

"Beck, I love you so much," Jack said as he remembered that the ring was still in his pocket. As he reached in to grab it, a beautiful belly dancer dressed in purple and gold grabbed his other arm and pulled him onto the stage for an impromptu lesson. Jack thought to protest, but he remembered what Beck said about living in the moment. So he gave the most ridiculous belly dance performance stripping off his gloves, jacket, and shirt for added effect. He had lost Beck's face in the crowd, but he could hear the unmistakable melody of her laughter. He surveyed the stage and saw some of the circus performers' equipment. Jack had an idea.

"May I?" he asked as he took the torch and dipped it in the paraffin oil.

"You sure you know what you're doing, Devil Man?" the magician asked.

"I promise it's not my first time or even my fiftieth. I have plenty of experience with fire," Jack assured him, "Got a light?"

"You best be telling the truth," The magician said as he lit up the torch while Jack took a swig of the oil.

He took the blazing torch from the magician and brought it up to his mouth. As he forcefully expelled the fuel from his mouth, the space above him filled flames as the audience gasped. He hadn't done this in almost 20 years but found that he still loved it. He launched flames from his mouth a few more times as he strutted around the stage. The crowd went crazy as he handed the torch off to the magician and took a bow.

Just as the magician extinguished the torch, a big crash came from outside the club. All the lights went out inside, plunging the club into complete darkness. Someone was soon able to find and open the door to the outside. There was only a sliver of the moon; its light revealed a car that had smashed into the light pole. The patrons began slowly lumbering through the darkness of the club and emptying onto the street. They were feeling their way through the house, knocking into tables as they drunkenly stumbled to the exit. The sound of bottles and glasses smashing was heard over and over again. Jack finally made it from the stage through the house and out onto the sidewalk. He saw a very inebriated young, white man being helped out of the car by Otis and Lowry.

"He'll need stitches for that gash in his head," Mrs. Esther said as she passed Jack and went to help the driver.

Seeing her reminded Jack that he had come out here to find Beck. She was nowhere to be found, and half his outfit was still inside the club. He walked against the stream of people still emerging from the exit. He felt his way through the building, bones, and all. As he neared the stage, he heard a small voice, almost a whisper.

"Jack?"

"Beck, what's wrong?"

"Please get me out of here," She pleaded.

"Of course, I will. Are you okay? You didn't get hurt trying to find your way out, did you?" He took her hand and pulled her to him, relishing the feel of her against his bare chest. That's when he noticed she was trembling, not out of excitement but fear.

"I'm not hurt. I couldn't move. I'm afraid of the dark."

"Really?" Jack asked.

"Do you think I would tell you something like that if it wasn't true? It's totally embarrassing."

"It's just unusual for someone...," Jack said as he tried to find the rights words.

"I know, I know it's weird for a grown-ass woman to be afraid of the dark, yet here we are. Can you please get me out of here?"

"I need to go back up to the stage and grab my clothes. I'm naked from the waist up, remember? Should I come back for you?" he asked.

"Don't leave me alone; take me with you," Beck pleaded.

Jack and Beck made their way up onto the stage. He found his clothes on top of the piano and began to dress. Then, remembering how little material Beck had in her Persephone costume, Jack took his tuxedo jacket and wrapped it around her shoulders.

They made their way back through the club to the sidewalk. There was still a crowd gathered around the wreckage. The young driver was being loaded into an ambulance. As the group began to disperse, an old woman turned to leave and ran right into Jack and Beck. They each caught one of her arms to keep her from falling. She recovered her balance but held on tightly to their hands. The ancient woman wore a turban of an elegant woven cloth, a long dress, large elaborate earrings, and a long necklace of small bones. She gazed intently at the couple.

"You're not supposed to be here," she said.

"We live in Harlem," Jack explained.

"No, I speak not of the physical; you are not of this age. Neither of you," the voodoo woman declared as Jack and Beck exchanged a quick look of astonishment," You are untethered to time, yet strongly tethered to one another. Beware the shifting sands of the hourglass. Cling to each other," she said as she joined their hands and slowly walked away.

"What was that about!?" Jack said.

"I don't know! You're the one with the voodoo collection."

"Well, You're the one from the south."

"Yes, where we were taught to have a healthy fear of this kind of stuff in nursery school. You were just going on about your understanding of 'juju.' You tell me." Beck said.

"We're fine. It's not like the woman hexed us. She just told us what we already knew." Jack said.

She leaned in to kiss him, but he stopped her, "Paraffin oil tastes awful, Darlin'. Here," he said, offering his forehead to Beck instead. She gasped then giggled.

"What?" Jack asked.

"You're missing an eyebrow," she said, unable to stop laughing.

"Well, it has been a while since I'd breathed fire."

"I didn't know you could do that. You scared me to death. It was very sexy but terrifying."

"Well, what do you expect from Satan?" Jack asked with a devilish grin.

Chapter 20

Owney appeared in the dining room right as the sound-check ended. Since the return of Cab Calloway had been so triumphant, he was around quite a bit. Soaking up the accolades for bringing such gifted musicians together.

"I have a bad feeling about this, Jack," Beck told him for what seemed like the hundredth time, "Owney changes the entire dynamic when he's here. Don't you feel it?"

"We just have to be patient. Owney will get bored of the club again soon until then we need just need to keep to ourselves," Jack reassured her. He hoped he was right, but he couldn't shake an uneasy feeling that it would only be a matter of time before one of the boss' many endeavors would require their attention.

"Jack, Rebecca come over here," Owney said, calling the pair over to one of the best tables in the dining room.

"Yes, sir?" Beck asked as she and Jack made their way slowly over to him.

"Have a seat. Don't look at me like that, Doll. You ain't in trouble," Owney said as he and Jack waited for Beck to take a seat. Once she was seated, the men took their seats, and he continued, "Listen, we're having lots of new press and showbiz types here with the live broadcast tonight. There's been lots of buzz around the show, as you know. We had a hell of a write up in the New York Age. Beck Taylor loves us."

Beck and Jack exchanged a quick look.

"Anyway, I've invited Cab Calloway to join me in the dining room for dinner before the show, and I want you two to dine with us as well. It's good exposure for you both, and I get to tell em' I discovered you. Like I said, we have a lot of influential people on their way. People that could change your lives. What do you say?"

Beck and Jack were silent for a moment. Jack knew this was a big deal. He would get his name and face in front of many influential people if he accepted Owney's invitation. They'd have no choice but to accept him as a Jazz musician and composer. Then, he'd have the freedom to choose to stay in Harlem to write jazz, or he could head back to California and get in on the ground floor of film composing. He'd have a chance to be a pioneer in the field that he loved so much. Beck would have plenty of opportunities to write and direct after tonight. They could even open their own movie studio. They could make musicals together.

All we have to do is put up with Owney for one lousy meal. How bad could it be? Cab will be there, too. Isn't it progress that Owney is allowing a black patron in the dining room. Well, isn't it? He started to reply, but Beck spoke first.

"Are you planning to extend this invitation to the rest of the cast?" she asked quietly.

"Rebecca, that's not practical. There's no room. You know that as well as I do," Owney said.

"Not even Lowry? He contributed just as much to the show as Jack did," she protested.

"The invitation is for Jack, Mr. Calloway, and yourself," Owney said. He was beginning to sound annoyed with her.

"Then, we'll pass. No, thank you," Beck said. As she stood to leave, the men stood as well. She looked expectantly towards Jack.

"Well, actually," Jack said, "I'd be happy to join you and Mr. Calloway. I'll go freshen up and see you in about ten minutes."

"Well now, at least someone's making sense. Come on, doll-face. Won't you pretty up our table? Let me show off my director. Besides, you don't want your man to look available with all those starlets around, now do you?" Owney said.

"I gave you my answer," Beck said. Her voice was steady, but her flushed cheeks and clenched fists betrayed her true feelings. She stormed off as fast as her heels could carry her.

Jack hurried after her. She needed to see how crucial it was to be seen at this dinner. "Darlin', I don't think you've thought this through."

"I am not the one who needs to think. You are," Beck snapped as she turned to face him. "How could you? After all, the performers here have done to support you?"

"This will be good for all of us. Cab and I will talk up Lowry and the others, you'll see."

"No, I won't, because I'm not going anywhere near that dining room," Beck said.

"If you ever want to make it in showbiz, Rebecca. You'll have to learn to sit down with people you don't like and humor them. It's all a part of how the game is played."

"Is that all this is to you, Jack, a game? There are real people back there, and you're stepping on them to get what you want."

"It's not like that, Darlin'. I'll take all of you with me. I promise," Jack said. He lowered his voice and pleaded, "Look, this could be our ticket out, a chance to move beyond the Cotton Club and Owney's backward thinking. We just need to use him to make the right connections."

"You know, Jack, when I first realized who you were, I was so excited that you were here. I had always been inspired by you, but then I thought maybe I shouldn't meet you. You'd been a hero of mine for so long that I was worried I would meet you and find out that you were some pampered brat. I didn't think my heart could take the disappointment."

"That's you're flawed thinking. I never asked to be put on a pedestal. Stop being so dramatic," Jack sighed.

"Except for when it suits you, right? You love when I fawn all over you, but when my principles get in the way of your ambition. Then, I'm just supposed to fall in line. Isn't that right?" Beck asked. He had never seen her so furious.

Determined to make her see how much he cared for her and their future, he tried again to plead his case, "Beck, I'm not doing this just for me. It's for us. I want you to be able to write and direct bigger and better projects. This is a good opportunity for both of us. Let's dream big. You can do whatever you want after this one simple dinner."

"I don't see it that way at all. How could you ask me to betray our friends? Mama Esther has done so much for me. How do you think she'd feel if I went out there?" Beck asked as her eyes filled with tears.

"She'd want what's best for you. Besides, It's not a whites-only thing, Doll. Cab will be there. He's already said he would be. It's integrated dining. You should be happy," Jack said, hoping he's finally talked her into it.

"Don't you dare tell me how I should feel! Is that what you're going to say to Lowry later? 'I went to this dinner you weren't allowed to go to, but don't worry, I mentioned your name' That's bullshit, and you know it," Beck shouted at him.

"Don't tell me what I know. I've been hustling to make a living at this since you were in diapers. I know the ins and out of this business, and I'm not going to let some...," Jack searched for the right words, but Beck chose her own.

"Fling?" she supplied.

"I was going to say emotional entanglement. I won't let what's happening between us stop me from doing what I need to do to secure our future."

"You're really going through with this, aren't you?" Beck asked. The whites of her eyes were pink, which caused the irises to appear intensely green. Tears flowed freely down her cheeks.

"I already gave you my answer," Jack said quietly. Hoping against hope that she would understand. *We can't both be idealists. One of us has to be practical.*

"Well then, there's no need to concern yourself with 'our future,'" Beck said, "WE no longer have one."

He reached for her, but she turned and walked away.

Chapter 21

Jack may have sat down in the club's dining room with the intent of eating a nice dinner, but he was no longer hungry. A good thing since there was not much of a chance to actually put food in his mouth anyway.

He and Cab were photographed and interviewed by both the local papers and national trade magazines. There were reporters from *Billboard, Down Beat,* and *Variety.* Agents were handing him phone numbers; heads of movie studios were interested in him. It was overwhelming. Cab handled the attention very well. At the one brief break they had in the activity, Jack leaned over and asked him, "How are you so calm and collected? These things make me so nervous."

"I actually enjoy it. It's always more fun when I'm talking to regular folks, but talking to people in the biz is part of the gig. Now quick, grab a piece of chicken before more people come this way," Cab said, digging into his meal.

Owney scanned the crowd, "I rather thought Beck would be here tonight."

"Huh?" Jack said, startled.

"Beck Taylor, the entertainment critic from the *New York Age.* He writes some great reviews for the club; he didn't like you much at first. Guess you've grown on him," Owney said with a laugh, "I had Rebecca deliver a press packet and invite him through paper's office. I wonder if he got it. Of course, I wouldn't know the cat if he walked up to me, never actually met him. The man breezes in and out of here as if he were a ghost."

Just then, a gorgeous blonde sauntered up to the table. "Lo, Sugar," she said to Owney as she ruffled his hair, "Evenin' boys."

"Gentleman, this is Mae," Owney said as he stood and put his arm around her waist, "Mae, this is Jack Herman and Cab Calloway."

"Pleasure to meet you both. I wish Owney would lend you out to my club."

"Listen, Dollface, you know it's much too small for anything bigger than a jazz quintet," Owney said.

Mae sighed, "That's the truth. I shoulda asked ya for a bigger club."

"Aw, Baby, you know I'd give you anything you want," Owney cooed.

"Then dance with me," Mae said.

"I'm in the middle of business right now," he said, but as soon as Mae pouted her full red lips. Owney said, "I'll be right back."

Jack and Cab used the opportunity to grab a couple more quick bites from their plates. At the entrance, flashbulbs popped as another group of celebrities and their respective entourages streamed into the club.

Cab looked up from his plate, "Well, I'll be damned if it isn't the Irish Mafia!"

"Uh oh, does that mean trouble? Should we make a run for it?" Jack asked, concerned.

"Ha, ha! No, not that kind of Mafia. These aren't gangsters; they're actors. We've worked at a lot of the same studios in Hollywood. They're some of the best men I know'" Cab stood and waved to the men who were very excited to see him. They made their way over and shook his hand enthusiastically.

He introduced the gentlemen as Pat O'Brien, Frank McHugh, Spencer Tracy, and James Cagney.

Frank removed the cigar from his mouth and sized Jack up. He said, "Hey, you look like one of us."

"Thanks," Jack said. He made his way down the line shaking hands until he came to the tiny redheaded man no taller than Beck. *Oh, Beck, you should be here.* As he shook James' hand, he said, "It's good to meet you. My girl is a huge fan of yours."

"Is that so?" said James with a grin, "She likes the bad boys, eh?"

"She says you're quite the song and dance man, too."

"Oh, ho! I get it. Your dame likes redheaded song and dance men," James said as he smiled and motioned toward Jack's own red curls.

"Too bad she's backstage right now. I know she'd love to meet you," Jack said.

"She's our show director, a very busy lady," Cab explained, "Maybe we can get her out here in a bit."

They posed for a few photos with the Irish Mafia before they were swept off to their own table. Cab and Jack were alone again. Owney had disappeared to his office with the voluptuous Mae, and there were no signs of him resurfacing. The two relaxed once more, knowing that it would be only a matter of minutes before they had to schmooze and pose again.

"Say, where is Miss Rebecca?" Cab asked Jack.

Jack had been dreading this question all night. He tried giving as little info as possible while sticking to the truth. "She's backstage like I said."

"Didn't Owney invite her to dinner?" Cab asked.

"Yes, he did, but she decided that it would be best for her to eat backstage."

"Jack, it's okay. You can tell me the truth. I'm a big boy." Cab sighed, "she didn't want to eat at the same table with a colored person, right?"

"No! That's not it at all. Rebecca doesn't like how Owney has a "Whites Only" policy for the audience. Unless he's hosting a black artist that will help him out professionally, like yourself. She's not eating alone; she's eating with the cast like she does every night. It's her own way of protesting Owney's policy."

"So, now that I know why she's back there. It makes me wonder why are you out here?" Cab leaned forward as if to get a better look at Jack as he waited for an answer. Jack couldn't even look Cab in the eye.

"I see," Cab said. The disappointment hung in the air between them. Cab stood to leave, "I'll be back."

Jack had to handle the next few groups alone. It was exhausting. He spoke with a nightclub owner from the theatre district who was confident he should lead his own orchestra at that club. Another wanted to discuss a recording contract. Finally, an executive from a film studio wanted him to come out to Hollywood to write music for the movies.

There were a few sexy starlets between the businessmen who slipped him their phone numbers and hotel room keys. It was almost time for him to head backstage to get into his makeup and horns.

Leaving the numbers and keys on the table, he shoved the business cards into his pocket. As he did, his fingertips hit Beck's ring. He withdrew his hand from it as though he had touched a flame.

Mending things with Beck would have to wait. Right now, he had a show to do. For that matter, so did Cab. *Where did he go?* Jack wondered. He scanned the room and noticed Cab's bright red zoot suit. He found him with the Irish Mafia; they laughed heartily at a story as Spencer shifted his weight. Jack saw that the animated storyteller was Beck. Standing right next to her, hanging on every word was James Cagney. Jack walked over.

"Rebecca, you've got to write that down. It would make a great picture," James said.

"I'll do it, but only if you play the lead," Beck said.

"Not sure that's one in my wheelhouse, dollface," he said.

"Please, you've done Shakespeare. You can do anything," she said flirtatiously.

"Have you seen our new movie?" Pat asked her.

"Maybe, you guys always have a new picture coming out. Which one is it?" she looked a little uncertain. Jack felt himself hoping she'd mess this up. *No way does she have his movie timeline memorized.*

"Angels with Dirty Faces," Pat answered.

"Yes, as a matter of fact, I have," she said, recovering, "Your performance was heartbreaking Pat. So moving. And James, that was your best role, yet. But, I have a feeling the best is still to come," she said as winked at him.

Did she just wink at him? Jack had had enough. He said a little too gruffly, "Rebecca, we have to get ready for the show."

"I am ready," she said.

"I need you to help me with my make up," Jack insisted.

"You can do it yourself. James asked me to dance, and the preshow music's just started. I'd hate to disappoint him."

"Fine, I'll handle it," he said and turned to leave.

"Jack?" she called after him.

"Yes?" he said, hoping she'd changed her mind.

"You only have one eyebrow, remember? Don't forget to draw the other one on," she said as James took her hands and led her to the dance floor.

Defeated, Jack headed backstage with Cab. As they reached the dressing room, Cab began to chuckle. By the time they reached the door, he was full-on guffawing. "What's so funny?" Jack finally asked.

"You sure took a lot of pictures tonight, Red Devil," Cab managed to say through his laughter, "lots of pictures with only one eyebrow."

Chapter 22

Beck brushed past Jack toward the ladies' dressing room, holding a glass of water from the dining room. Jack followed her to the door in hopes that they could talk. Inside the room, he heard a horrible hacking sound as though someone was coughing up a lung. There were still ladies changing from the final show. Jack didn't want to get too close. But, he was concerned, so he did his best to listen from the hallway.

"Here, Mama, sip on this water instead. It chilled from the kitchen," Beck said with concern in her voice.

"Thank ya, Baby! This tickle just keeps getting worse. I thought it would go away, but it's stubborn." Mrs. Esther said.

"It's more than a tickle. You're burning up. We've got to get you home."

"I'll have to rest up before I can do that," Mrs. Esther said.

"I know. It's no good for you to walk home feeling like this. It's so cold out there, you'll catch your death. We need a car. Who do we know that has a car?" Beck asked.

"Mr. Owney's the only one I know with a car. I'd rather die than ride with that man."

"Mama, shhh. Please don't talk like that. I'll go to talk to Owney," Beck said.

"Don't you dare! I know he's still sore at you for not eating with him tonight."

"How do you know about that?" Beck asked.

"News travels fast around here," Mrs. Esther said.

"I didn't want to upset you."

"I heard you had a squabble with your fella over it."

"I don't want to talk about it, Mama."

"Well, when you do, I'm here," she said as she began hacking again.

"That's it. I'm going to ask Owney if he'll drive us home. I don't care how pissed he gets. You need help. Don't you argue with me. Violet, can you please stay a little longer and watch over Mama for me?"

Beck rounded the corner with a determined look on her face. She ran right into Jack. He had to resist the urge to hug her.

"Oof! Sorry, I didn't see you."

"It's fine. Mrs. Esther sounds terrible. How can I help?" Jack asked.

"We don't need your help," Beck said as she walked past him.

Jack had a feeling that he shouldn't let Beck be alone with Owney. He followed her into the dining area just as Owney emerged from his office.

"I need to talk to you," Beck said.

"I'm busy," Owney said as Mae emerged from behind him.

"Mama Esther is very sick. I need to -" Beck was interrupted by the hacking sound behind her.

"It's okay, Baby. See, I can walk," Mrs. Esther said as she entered the dining room unsteadily, holding the glass in her hand.

Owney's eyes locked on the drinking glass. He angrily marched to over to Mrs. Esther; Jack and Beck were hot on his heels. Owney yanked the glass from Esther's hand as Beck threw her arms protectively around her. Jack moved between Owney and the women to shield them from any further harm.

"Dammit, Rebecca! You know we don't give them the good glasses. I can't use this again," he yelled as he turned and threw the glass against the wall shattering it into many pieces, "Now clean this mess up," he said to Beck. With that, Owney and Mae were off.

Cab emerged from the shadows of the dining room. Putting his arm around Mrs. Esther, he said, "Hey, Beautiful, I hear you want a ride in my big car, huh? You didn't have to go and get sick. All you had to do was ask. Come on, Rebecca, let's get this sweet mama home to her bed where she belongs." Cab and Rebecca helped Mrs. Esther exit the dining room

"I'll clean up the glass," Jack mumbled.

Chapter 23

The pre-dawn colors were just about to overtake the indigo sky. Lowry was softly snoring, but Jack had spent the night lost in thought. He replayed the scene in his head. *I thought I had a firm understanding of the dynamics of black and white relationships. That racism could so be subtle and then suddenly so hostile is shocking. The way Owney lunged at that sweet, old woman as though she was less than human. The terror in Mrs. Esther's eyes, and in Beck's.*

As the sunrise overtook the city outside the tall windows, Jack struggled with what the next steps might be. He had more than enough offers on the table. He could leave the Cotton Club for good. But what if he stayed? Could he do more to help his friends? Not that, he'd done the best job of that so far.

Then there was Beck. She was his friend, his confidant, his love. *She's so angry. Probably even more so after Mama Esther was treated so horribly. I have to fix this.*

The stillness was interrupted by a loud thud at the front door. It was the sound of the newspaper hitting the doorstep. Thankful for any distraction, Jack quietly retrieved the paper from the hall and began skimming the articles. Until he opened the arts and entertainment section and saw himself minus one eyebrow smiling and posing with Cab and the Irish Mafia. The headline read "A Star-Studded turnout for Cab Calloway and His Orchestra at the Cotton Club, by Beck Taylor." She had written, as usual, praise for the musicians. However, she closed her article, saying, " With all of the talent that Mr. Madden's so cleverly recruited, it's a shame that the black citizens of Harlem are not allowed to sit in the dining room and support some of the best artists of their community."

His first thought was, *Oh, Beck. Why poke the bear?* At the same time, he couldn't help but admire her. *I've got your back, Darlin',* Jack promised. As he made his private oath, he reached into his pocket and felt Beck's ring.

Lowry sat up in his bed; he looked surprised to see that his roommate was already awake. "Well, good mornin' sunshine," he said as he stretched. As he crossed to the kitchen to make coffee, he caught a closer look at Jack, "Whoa, I take it back, you look like hell. You sick?"

"No, couldn't sleep," he grumbled.

"You had a good night from what I saw. What happened? Is it girl trouble? Miss Rebecca looked like she was ready to kill last night."

Jack took a deep breath and told Lowry everything from the invite to dine with Cab and Owney all the way up to Owney's angry outburst. He looked at Lowry, waiting for a reaction of shock or anger. Instead, Lowry seemed unimpressed.

"Well?" Jack said, "aren't you going to say something?"

"Was it really news to you that Mr. Madden thinks he's better than us? We know that he and most other white men look at us as little more than trained monkeys. Coming at Mrs. Esther like that is a new low, but it's the type of hatred we see coming," Lowry said thoughtfully. Then, meeting Jack's eyes, he said, "It's the acts of complacency and subtle discrimination that hurt the most."

"You're talking about me, aren't you?" Jack asked.

"You didn't even tell me in person about the dinner. I had to hear about it from Rebecca. She's very disappointed in you, by the way. Good luck fixin' that. Especially after what you just told me."

"I know," Jack said quietly. He felt so ashamed.

"It must be nice. Hangin' with us cats whenever it suits you, then wheelin' dealin' with the white guys whenever you want to get ahead. The color of our skin is not something we can just turn off. I'll always be black, and people will always treat me differently because of it."

"Lowry. I'm so sorry," Jack said as he hung his head, "How can I make this right?"

"I don't know, Man. It's gonna take some time," Lowry said as he leaned against the window, his arms crossed against his body.

"I understand," Jack said as he looked at the floor, "I promise, from now on, I don't eat in the dining room unless we all eat in the dining room." A knock at the door interrupted the men.

"Telegram," the man at the door said, handing the cream-colored paper to Jack.

"Thank you," he said, closing the door. Jack glanced at the paper. "Wait, this is for you, Lowry."

Lowry stared at the paper for a long time. He looked astonished, "It's from the Duke! He's been listening to our broadcasts. He wants me to meet up with him and play with his orchestra in Baltimore next Friday, then continue with the tour from there."

"That's wonderful. You're going, right"? Jack asked.

"Is the Pope Catholic? Course I am. You can stay here if you'd like. You could water my fern for me," Lowry said, indicating a half-dead plant in the corner of the kitchen, "I'm going to go tell the boys in the band."

As Lowry moved to the door, Jack said, "Lowry, about that thing we talked about."

"Give it some time, Jack," Lowry said in a way that let him know that he was not to press any further.

Chapter 24

Later that day, the beautiful morning sun gave way to a gray, gloomy sky. It matched Jack's mood perfectly. He tried to put to paper a tune that was stuck in his head but hadn't made it past the first few bars. He decided to move beyond what he heard, anxious to see where the tune would take him, but it wasn't working. Nothing he tried sounded right. Defeated and lonely, Jack decided to head to work a bit early. Maybe Beck would be there, and they could talk.

As he walked the few blocks from Lowry's to the club, the rain turned from drizzle to downpour. He opened his umbrella and picked up the pace. Once he made it to the alleyway, Jack shook out his umbrella while his back propped open the backstage door. He turned and entered, searching for Beck. In the men's dressing room, he could hear the guys celebrating Lowry's new gig.

"Imagine our own little Lowry on the road with the Duke. Man, I'm so proud of you!" Moses said.

"Couldn't have happened to a better Cat! To Lowry," Leroy said, leading a toast.

Jack really wanted to join them, but he wasn't sure he'd be welcome. He continued down the hall until he reached the ladies' dressing room. It was completely empty as he could see from the open door. *Where is she?* A quick scan of the dining room revealed a lone figure, Pipes.

The man was nearly six and a half feet tall with massive muscular arms and a barrel chest. He was kind enough if things were going his way, but he didn't suffer fools or tolerate rudeness, making him perfect for his job. It also made him intimidating as hell.

"Afternoon, Pipes," Jack said, trying to act nonchalant, "where's Rebecca?"

"She's at the hospital." Pipes said.

"Why? What happened? Is she okay?" Jack's heart began to pound.

"She's fine, it's Esther. Rebecca called and said that she was there with her."

"Oh. I'll go check on them. Be back in a bit," Jack rushed back out into the rain, opening his umbrella and entering a crowd full of others doing the same. He pushed past the bobbing of the group, trying to get to the hospital as fast as he could on the wet sidewalks.

As he reached Harlem Hospital, Jack slowed his pace, wondering what he would do when he arrived. *What if Beck doesn't want me there? She might not want me, but she probably needs someone.* He was determined to be that someone. In the lobby of the hospital was a small gift shop. He bought a small bouquet of yellow daisies and found out from the front desk that Mrs. Esther had been admitted. Her room was on the third floor.

Jack ascended the stairs as quickly as he could. Which left his almost forty-year-old body a little more winded than he cared to admit. He promptly located Mrs. Esther's room and found that it was already full of beautiful bouquets. Mrs. Esther herself, however, had seen better days. Her breathing was labored. Her skin, which was usually a lovely brown shade, had an undeniable bluish undertone to it. Her lips were an even more pronounced blue, adding to her disturbing appearance. Beck looked exhausted as she sat by the bed, holding onto

Mrs. Esther's hand. He'd never seen her without makeup before. She was beautiful to him, but he could tell that she had left home in a hurry. Her clothes were disheveled, and her hair, usually tamed into soft waves, was a wild mess of red curls. *This must be what it would look like to wake up next to her in the morning.*

Beck looked up, and their eyes met. Then she quickly looked back down at Esther's hands. "I don't want your flowers, Jack."

"I didn't bring them for you. I bought them for Mrs. Esther." Jack said as he moved toward the bed, "Mrs. Esther, where may I set these for you?" Ms.Esther pointed to a spot on the windowsill near Beck. As Jack walked over, Beck" s body visibly tensed up.

"How did you know we were here?" Beck asked, pursing her lips.

"Pipes told me, but he didn't mention why Mrs. Esther was here."

"Pneumonia. A pretty bad case of it," Beck said as she took Mrs. Esther's hand.

"It's not that bad." Mrs. Esther protested.

"You didn't know where you were this morning, and even now, you're having so much trouble breathing," Beck said.

"I was just light-headed from all the coughing. I wish they'd send me home. I could rest so much better if I was in my own bed."

"Mama Esther, the doctor said you have to have help breathing right now. Please don't be so stubborn. Here, have some more soup," Beck said as she picked up the bowl and gently spooned some soup into Mrs. Esther's mouth.

"Is there anything I can do?" Jack asked. He carefully placed a hand on Mrs. Esther's shoulder. *She's so frail and helpless. I don't like it. Please get up and argue with me.*

"No, we're fine. The staff's going to kick me out in about 10 minutes when visiting hours are over. I'll run home and change, then I'll be back at the club."

"I wish you wouldn't leave me," Mrs. Esther said, looked up at Beck pleading.

Her words deeply affected Beck. She slowly closed, then opened her eyes while squeezing Mrs. Esther's hand. "Oh Mama, you know I'd stay if I could," she sighed, "I'll be back first thing in the morning. I promise. Can I bring you anything from home? Anything at all?"

"My pink afghan from the end of my bed," Mrs. Esther said, "Hospitals are always so cold."

"You can go on. We're fine," Beck said to Jack, doing her best to avoid his gaze.

"No, let him stay. Nothing like a nice lookin' fella to cheer up a sick old lady," Mrs. Esther said playfully as Beck scowled at her. "A smile from handsome Mr. Herman over there might be just what I need to wake up my appetite." Jack immediately obliged with a flirtatious grin.

"You're too much. Eat your soup." Beck said with a sigh.

"Only if he stays," Mrs. Esther said. For a moment, Jack saw a hint of her signature willfulness flash in her eyes.

"Okay, Mama, "Beck said, rolling her eyes, admitting defeat.

The nursing staff kicked them both out promptly at six. Jack and Beck walked out of the hospital together in silence as they rounded the corner toward Mrs. Esther's house. Beck started to cry. Jack instinctively went to hold her, but Beck wriggled from his grasp.

"Don't!" she said.

"Beck, please let me help you," Jack pleaded. "I don't like seeing you like this. I just want to comfort you."

"I don't want to need you right now. What you did was wrong, and just because I'm scared for Mama Esther right now.

It doesn't mean you can just swoop in," she said as gasped between sobs.

"You win. I won't touch you if it upsets you. I don't want to make things worse. I just want to help. Is there anything I can do?"

"Please let Owney know I'm on my way in. Violet and my other roommates should have handled the backstage stuff for me already."

"Listen, Beck, I am so sorry about last night," Jack said.

"I can't talk about that right now. I can't make *you* feel better. We'll discuss it later."

"Okay. I'll see you at the club," Jack said. He could hear her sobs continue as she walked up the stairs to the front porch. It took every ounce of restraint left in him to keep going toward the club instead of running back to her.

Chapter 25

Backstage was chaotic when Jack arrived for the first show of the evening. Rebecca's roommates had tried hard to pitch in, but they had missed some of the finer points of her job. Mainly the work to be done for the male performers, which was only half completed. Jack grabbed the clean undershirts from the bin and the bucket for Leroy as he headed in. He noticed that the guys were not as talkative with him. He realized it could be worse and decided to keep to the task at hand. As he laid down the stack of undershirts, Cab poked his head in the door. "Jack, Owney wants to see us."

"Alright. Thanks," Jack said. As he turned to go, he could hear the other men murmuring behind him.

"Must be nice," Otis said.

"Well, it was only a matter of time," Isaac said.

"He's going to ask us to dinner again. Isn't he?" Jack asked Cab as they entered the dining room and saw Owney sitting next to Mae. Both of them were dressed to the nines.

"That seems likely, Red Devil," Cab said quietly.

"I'm not doing that again," Jack said.

"Is that so?" Cab asked.

"It was unfair to you and every other black person in our cast. It wasn't clear to me at the time, but it is now," Jack said right before they reached Owney's table.

"Evenin' boys. You remember Mae." Owney said.

"How could we forget such a lovely lady. I didn't get a chance to tell you last night, but I love your movies, Ms. Mae." Cab said.

"Why, thank you, Cab," Mae replied with a smile, "Maybe we'll get to work on a picture together someday."

"It'd be an honor," Cab said with a little bow.

"Listen, why don't you two join us?" Owney said, motioning to two empty seats.

"No, thank you," Jack said, "Things are hectic backstage, and it's close to showtime."

"The Cat's right, we're swamped," Cab said.

"I heard that my assistant was late tonight. I'm sorry she's caused things to run off the rails back there. Rebecca will hear about this from me." Owney said curtly.

"She had a family emergency. Give her a break," Jack shot back.

"See, Sugar?" Owney said to Mae, "I told you Taylor's column would cause me problems. You been reading that crap about the club in the paper?"

"Beck Taylor has a point," Jack said.

"You run a classy joint like this? You don't know the first thing about it. You think you can open the doors and let the negros dine with the regular folks? See how long it takes before there's no more white folks in the dining room." Owney said.

"Uh, I have to go get ready," Cab said uneasily.

"You go ahead, Cab," Owney said as though he were a grade-school teacher, and Cab was his young pupil. It made Jack sick to see his hero dismissed this way.

As Cab left, Rebecca came running into the dining room. To Owney, she said, "I'm so sorry, I'm late. Did Pipes tell you about Mama Esther?"

"Yea, yea, but you have a lot of things to do still, so hop to it. For starters, do your fella's make up." Owney ordered.

"He can do it himself," she said, angrily.

"Obviously, he can't. You shoulda seen the picture in the paper this morning. Humiliating. Make sure he has two eyebrows this time, will ya?" Owney scoffed.

Rebecca worked in silence while Jack sat in the makeup chair. She wouldn't speak, but she was very close to him. There was an intimacy to the work that he had never fully appreciated until now. As he closed his eyes for the eyeshadow application, he relished the feel of her left hand resting on his jaw to steady his face. He breathed in her scent, the ever-present smell of vanilla; it was comforting and alluring all at once. Jack listened to the sound of her breath as she worked quietly on his face. As with all of her sounds, there was music in it. It made him want to compose a melody.

She turned him around to face the mirror as she took her place behind him and ran her hands through his hair. Her fingers made his scalp tingle. He melted as she pushed his hair back to make room for his horns. It was over all too soon. He wanted to take her into his arms and kiss her, but that was out of the question. Jack thought he ought to at least say something clever to her but, "Thanks." was all he managed.

Between shows, he went to Owney's office to speak with her. Beck was alone in the office with her back to the door. "Does that mean I can take her home?... I see...Well, how soon can I come visit?... Visiting hours?... So, ten to six?...I'll be there...Wait!...Can I please speak to her?... Sure, I'll hold," Beck began to pace while she waited. She turned and saw Jack in the doorway, "I called to check on Mama Esther; they said she's doing much better. She can probably go home in a day or two."

"That's wonderful!" Jack said.

Beck raised her hand to request silence, "Yes, I'm here...Mama? How are you?... Good...I'm relieved to hear that, too...No, Mama, they're still saying it will be a couple of days...I know...Anything I can bring you tomorrow?... Yes, I remember that, besides the pink afghan, is there anything you want? I could smuggle in some food...Oh, you need to go to bed?...I'll see you in the morning...Mama? I love you," Beck replaced the receiver in its cradle.

"Mrs. Esther is on the mend," Jack asked. Before he could think, he hugged Beck tight.

"Jack," Beck said as she pushed him away.

He let her go, "I'm sorry. What does she need from home? I can come over and help carry some things," he offered.

"No. I've got it. Mama Esther only wants the afghan from the foot of her bed. She doesn't plan to be in there much longer."

Jack caught a look at the clock on the wall, "We should probably get going. There's a lot to do before the late show."

They entered the dining room at the same time Leroy emerged from backstage looking frantic, "Ms. Rebecca? Ms. Rebecca!" he called from across the seating area.

"Stay where you are, Leroy. I'm coming to you," she said as she and Jack attempted to cross the crowded room.

Leroy didn't hear her over the din of the patrons' voices. He continued walking and loudly explaining what he needed, "You forgot to give me my bucket, Ms. Rebecca. I don't wanna puke all over the backstage. I don't know where we keep 'em, or I'd get it myself."

Worried that Beck's soft voice wasn't carrying Jack projected. "Leroy, stop! We're coming to you." At that moment, a man stood up between Leroy and the pair. It was Owney.

Chapter 26

Jack and Beck weren't able to see Owney's face, but they could tell from the terrified expression that spread across Leroy's that it wasn't good.

"Mr. Madden, I didn't mean to...I was just...," Leroy stuttered.

Jack moved quickly through the maze of tables and chairs toward his friend but was rapidly outpaced by Pipes, who was making long strides toward the center of the room. With a wave of his hand, Owney gave the signal for the house orchestra to start the pre-show music while never taking his eyes off of Leroy, who was frozen in place.

Owney approached him like a lion approaching its frightened prey. Pipes soon made it over and grabbed the man. Beck broke into a run, trying to reach them. Owney slapped Leroy hard across the face. The sound of Owney's open hand meeting the flesh on Leroy's cheek echoed throughout the dining room, even with the orchestra was playing at full volume.

I can let her get in the middle of this. Jack instinctively reached for Beck to keep from her getting any closer. He wrapped his arms around her. While he cared for Leroy, he couldn't risk that Owney would hurt her, too, "No, Beck, you can't," Jack whispered in her ear as she struggled to be free of him.

"Ain't you got no self-control?" Owney said to Leroy, disgusted, "You think these people want to eat with you in here?

They're already afraid you gonna infect them with some Negro disease, and you come in the dining room during their dinner and talk about your bodily functions? You're fired! Get outta here," Leroy didn't move. Instead, he stood there, trembling, "Pipes, take this stupid coon to the curb and put him out with the garbage where he belongs."

As Pipes picked up the small, older man throwing him over his shoulder. He headed for the side door. Jack could see tears of humiliation in his bandmate's eyes. Pipes passed by Beck, who touched Leroy's arm and walked with Pipes, "Leroy, I'm so sorry. Pipes put him down! Please. Let him walk on his own!"

Pipes marched straight on toward the door his pace never slowed, "You have your job, Miss Rebecca, and I have mine. I don't interfere with yours; don't interfere with me."

"Come on, Man. This isn't a decent way to treat another person. At least let him leave on his own," Jack pleaded.

"I'm warning you both," Pipes said as he reached the threshold of the side door. Suddenly, he was interrupted by a horrible belching sound. All attention turned to Leroy; his face was green. Before Pipes could react, Leroy vomited down his back. This further enraged Pipes, who dropped Leroy onto a pile of garbage bags in the alley. Leroy stood up, and Pipes punched him in the belly, causing him to fall back wheezing and coughing. "If I see you around the Cotton Club again, you'll get that and then some," Pipes threatened as he turned to leave. Jack stepped between him and the club, "You don't wanna do that Old Red," Pipes said as he firmly grabbed Jack's shoulders and moved him to the side, "You better get ready, you gotta show to do."

Jack decided that his efforts were best spent helping Beck with Leroy instead of challenging the giant bouncer. Beck kneeled next to Leroy on the sidewalk.

"Are you alright?" she asked.

"They fired me," Leroy said. He dropped his face into his hands and slumped over like a ragdoll.

"I know. I'm so sorry," Beck said as she stood up and offered him her hand.

Jack saw that she couldn't get Leroy up alone, so he helped her stand him up. He said, "We can always help you find another gig, but right now, we need to know if you're okay."

"It hurts, but I can manage. I just need to get home," Leroy said.

"I need to get him home to his wife. Go on back inside. I've got him," Beck said.

"I don't want to leave you," Jack said as the overture started inside the club.

"You're needed on stage," Beck said. He started to argue, but they had Leroy up and moving. *She's right. It's showtime.* Jack sighed and headed to the backstage entrance. *I wish she needed me, at least a little.*

But music always did. Jack walked through the door and sprinted to join his remaining bandmates onstage. Taking the marimba mallets in his hands, he began to strike the rosewood keys. The music sounded sweet to his ears. But the striking of the keys with mallets harder and harder satisfied the anger that demanded release. At least for the moment.

Chapter 27

After the show, Jack told Cab and the rest of the men about Leroy. Otis and Moses both knew people high up at Club Hotcha and the Savoy Ballroom. They were pretty sure that they could get him a new gig. "I don't understand why the first concern is employment. The man was slapped and punched by two other men. Are none of you upset about them hurting your friend? I barely know him, and I'm furious!" Jack said.

"Jack, the problem isn't just two white men at The Cotton Club," Cab explained. "It's an entire system of white people who control the big successful clubs like this one, the broadcast networks, and the recording studios all around the country. We can either cooperate to get our art out there to speak for us, or we can fight back physically and prove to them that we're the 'jungle savages' they think we are."

"That's awful," Jack muttered. He had, of course, read about the nature of racism in 1930s Harlem, but living it, watching people he knew suffer because of it shook him in way that words in a history book never had.

"You're telling me," Cab said, "We're all just doing the best we can."

"Well, what can I do?" Jack asked.

"You're doing it. Stand up for us whenever you possibly can and keep leading people to hear our music."

"Of course," Jack said.

"We don't all agree with that, Mr. Calloway," said Isaac in the back of the room.

"I know, Isaac," Cab said.

"This place is a powder keg, Mr. Herman. If you stay, you best be prepared to choose a side," Isaac said.

"As you can see, Jack. There ain't no easy answers, Cab said.

Jack and Beck made it to the backstage door at the same time.

"Headed home?" Jack asked.

"Yea, I want to get up early and spend some time with Mama Esther before I come in. I hate that I couldn't get her afghan to her before she went to bed, so I'm going to get it there right at ten when visiting hours start," Beck said.

"Mind if I walk you home?"

"I can walk with Violet and the other ladies."

"Beck, are you ever going to give me another chance? You once said that I was the only person here that you could really talk to. You're that person for me, too. I'm lost without you."

"Wow! Leroy was beaten right in front of us tonight, and Mama Esther almost died. But, let's talk about your needs right now," she said as she glared at him.

"That's not fair, Beck. I am trying," Jack said. They were both silent for a moment, looking into each other's eyes. As they looked at one another, Beck's gaze softened slightly, "May I please come visit Mrs. Esther with you in the morning?" Jack asked.

"Okay," she said quietly.

"Was that a yes?" Jack asked as Beck's roommates entered the alley.

"Yes. I've got to go."

"See you in the morning," Jack said with a smile. He knew he would count the hours until he could be with her again.

The next morning Jack wasted no time. He woke up before Lowry and shaved and showered, wanting to look his best for

Beck. He knew this wasn't a date, but at least she was going to let him be in the same room with her. The walk to the hospital seemed to take forever. It was a frigid November morning, so Jack tucked his hands in his pockets. His fingers touched Beck's ring, and he smiled.

Given the cold, Jack wasn't surprised that Beck was not waiting out front for him. In the lobby, he spotted her immediately. Her red curls spilled down onto the back of her purple coat. He walked over and touched her shoulder. "Morning," he said. As Beck turned around, he saw that she was clutching a large, dark pink blanket. Her eyes were red, "Beck, what's wrong?"

"She's gone, Jack. Mama Esther died this morning," Beck said as she began to sob.

"No! She was fine last night," Jack said in disbelief.

"I didn't get to give her the afghan. She must have been so cold," she said, holding out the blanket, "I didn't even get to say goodbye," she sobbed and reached for Jack. As usual, her hands were like ice, Jack took Mrs. Esther's blanket and gently wrapped it around her shoulders, then he pulled her to him. She collapsed into him, sobbing. He managed to get the two of them over to a couch. He pulled her onto his lap and rested her head on his shoulder. Then, with his free arm, he pulled her legs onto the couch, holding her like a small child. People stared, but the two didn't care, isolated in their grief as they were.

After several minutes of holding her and stroking her hair, Jack built up the courage to ask her, "Beck, can you tell me what happened?"

"I came into the lobby this morning, and all of her sons were here. I thought Mama Esther must be delighted to have all of her boys here at once. I told them I was here to give her the afghan, but I could give it to them instead and come back after their visit. That's when they told me she had developed sepsis early this morning, and her organs shut down. They got here just in time to say goodbye."

"Well, at least she wasn't alone."

Beck sat up in his lap to face him and said a bit too loudly, "Don't do that. Don't try and make this okay. I should have been here!"

"You're absolutely right. Nothing about this, okay. But we can't stay here much longer. Let's go back to Mrs. Esther's. I can tuck you back into bed if you like." Jack offered.

"No, two of her sons are back at the house. I don't want them to see me like this. It'll only make them sadder."

"We could go to my place. You could rest there," Beck flashed him a suspicious look to which Jack replied, "Whoa! Nothing like that. Lowry's still asleep. Totally kosher, I could hold you on the couch, or I could sit on the floor while you rest."

"I don't want to wake Lowry. Besides, I'm too angry to sleep. I need to get up and move." Beck declared as she stood and wiped her eyes.

Jack thought for a moment. Suddenly, he knew just what to do, "Hey, do you have your keys to the club with you?"

Beck reached into her coat pocket and felt around until she found them, "Uh-huh."

"Good, no one will be there this early. The walk will help, and I can make you brunch when we get there."

"I'm not hungry," Beck said.

"Mrs. Esther wouldn't want you to starve yourself. Let me do this for you."

"I'll walk with you, but I can't promise I'll eat."

"No woman has ever been able to resist my french toast," Jack said. Beck raised an eyebrow, "I'm just trying to make you smile."

"That's not going to happen again for a long time," Beck said almost in a whisper.

Once they arrived at the club. Beck went into the bathroom to wash her face. The whites of her eyes were bloodshot, making the stare from her olive irises more intense. "Okay. We're alone; let it all out, Beck," Jack said. She began to scream and looked around for something to hit. She grabbed a glass and threw it across the room, smashing it. Jack intervened," We can't break Owney's stuff. We don't want any more trouble," At this, she set down the plate she was going to throw and began to hit herself. Jack stopped her, "Nope, no one hurts the woman I love, not even you," he regarded her for a moment, "You really need to hit something, don't you?"

"I'm not going to hit you, Jack," Beck sighed.

"Well, that's good to hear, because I'm not offering myself up to those fists of fury. Come up here," Jack said, leading her onto the stage. He pointed at the percussion section, "Look, an entire section of things that were designed for hitting."

"But, I don't know how to play them," Beck said, eyeing the instruments.

"It doesn't matter. This is about getting out your rage and your grief. It's the best way I know how because no one gets hurt," Jack took Beck's hand and led her closer, introducing her to some of the options, "You can pick anything you want. The djembe drum can be hit with your bare hands, I can give you the sticks for the big drum kit, or you can use mallets on the marimba. That's the one that looks like a big xylophone."

She approached the marimba at first, striking it hard with the mallets. She seemed to enjoy the feel but stopped abruptly," This sounds too happy," she explained as she went over to the djembe and tentatively struck it with her hands. She began to hit harder and faster. A loud body-racking sob emerged from her as she beat the drum over and over. Her cries continued as she struck the drum for several minutes. Jack was surprised at the energy that came from her pain. As she began to slow her rhythm, he came to stand behind her.

She stopped drumming entirely and collapsed into his arms. Jack sat there with his back against the upstage wall with Beck's head in his lap stroking her hair again. Listening to the terrible sound of her heart breaking.

"I want to go home, Jack. I can't do this anymore. I want to go home. Please," Beck begged as she fell asleep. For the first time in a long time, he started to wish that he could take her back to 1992.

Chapter 28

Two days after Mrs. Esther had passed, Lowry and Jack sat at their table. Lowry looked through the *New York Age* for her obituary, hoping to find the location and time of her funeral. Before he could locate that section of the paper, he found Beck Taylor's article instead. "Woo-wee!" Lowry exclaimed.

"What?" Jack asked.

"Mr. Taylor done called Mr. Madden out," Lowry said, handing the arts and entertainment section of the paper over to Jack, "Check it out."

The headline read "Abuse Rampant at Cotton Club." Beck once again blasted Owney for not allowing black patrons in the club while showcasing black artists. Then, Beck shared the detailed accounts of harassment of the female dancers, the incident with Mrs. Esther, and the attack on Leroy. Citing an "unnamed source" at the club. Jack took a deep breath as he finished reading.

"Mr. Taylor's either brave or crazy," Lowry said.

"I can't believe the paper would print those things," Jack said.

"Yea, Mr. Madden's gonna be after em' now," Lowry said as he continued to look through the paper.

"It's a small newspaper. You think many people will see it?"

"You kidding me? Every black person in Harlem that reads reads the *New York Age*, and them that don't will surely hear about it."

"That's not good," Jack muttered.

"I'll tell ya what's not good, Mrs. Esther's service is in two hours! We gotta get ready."

Jack bought a bouquet of yellow daisies on the way to the chapel. His heart ached at the loss of Mrs. Esther. Not only for how much it had hurt Beck, he too had grown to care for her. In fact, He had grown to care genuinely about so many people here in such a short time. Jack knew that was what Beck had felt when she wrote her article. He understood, but he worried about the repercussions.

People streamed into the chapel. Most of the cast from the Cotton Club and many people from the hospital packed the pews. Beck was seated directly behind Mrs. Esther's family. She stood and motioned Jack forward, "Will you sit with me?" she asked. The service was a loving tribute. The chapel was standing room only, a testament to the life Esther had led.

After Jack and Beck said their goodbyes to the others, he asked her, "Can we take a walk?" Once, he was sure they were a safe distance away. Jack said, "I read your article this morning."

"Good, I hope that lots of people will read it," she said.

"Don't you think Owney will read it?"

"Probably."

"Beck, he's going to be furious with you," Jack warned.

"He doesn't know it's me."

"Have you forgotten how easy it was for me to waltz into the newspaper's office, and find out that you and Beck were connected? The receptionist told me you were his assistant. I'm sure she'd tell Owney."

"I hadn't thought about that... but so what. Maybe it's time I tell Owney it's really me," Beck said. Her eyes blazed with defiance.

"Beck, please don't do that. The man has killed before. You've got to be more careful. You can't go shooting your mouth off whenever you feel like it."

"Watch it, Jack! I'm not your child!" Beck yelled.

"I realize that," he said in a hushed voice.

"Good. Give me a minute," Beck said. She was deep in thought for the next couple of blocks. At last, she said." I can fix this," and she turned right at the corner.

"Where are you going?" Jack asked.

"To the paper. Wanna come?"

I don't want to go anywhere near the newspaper, but I can't let her go alone. Jack followed along. They reached the *New York Age* office right before it closed. As they walked in, the young receptionist jumped and gasped at the sight of Jack.

After she saw Beck was with him, she said, "Oh, it's you. Wait there, Mr. Gellar wants to speak to you," she buzzed into the editor's office, "Virgil? No, I didn't find his contact information, but I'll do you one better. His assistant's in the lobby. Yea, I'll tell her," the receptionist hung up and said, "He'll be right out."

Minutes later, Virgil emerged from his office. Beck and Jack stood to greet him, but he kept his distance. "Rebecca and Mr. Herman? Huh! Never thought I'd see you two together. Look, Rebecca, we have a serious problem. We've trusted Mr. Taylor to the point that I've frequently run his articles without reading them first. Now, that's on me as an editor. Still, your employer submitted a piece which I, unfortunately, ran this morning without proofing.

The piece was more of an op/ed and not really a review. This is not what I pay Mr. Taylor to submit, and it has caused me a lot of trouble with Mr. Madden. I am afraid I have to sever our relationship. Effective immediately, we'll no longer accept any articles of any kind written by Beck Taylor."

"What about freedom of the press? You live in Harlem, Mr. Gellar. You know Beck only said what needed to be said," Beck protested.

"It hasn't been said because it's too dangerous to do so, Rebecca. I'll have you know Mr. Madden was in here not ten minutes ago. He was furious!"

"You didn't tell him that Rebecca's Mr. Taylor's associate did you?" Jack asked, terrified for her.

"Of course not. I don't want to get in the middle of any of this," Virgil replied, "If you ask me, it's incredibly cowardly of Mr. Taylor to hide behind a young woman such as yourself."

"I didn't ask you!" Beck said. She was enraged. Jack knew that the paper had done her a huge favor, and he was afraid she was about to reveal her identity, so he said, "Rebecca, we've got go. Come on. Thanks so much for your discretion, Mr. Gellar, and to you, too, Miss," Jack said as he gently but purposefully moved Beck out the door.

Chapter 29

"What are you doing? I want to go back in there!" Beck said. She pushed against Jack as he moved her down the sidewalk away from the *New York Age*.

"Leave it, Beck. They were nice enough not to spill the beans to Owney."

"But they fired me," she argued.

"Shh! They fired Mr. Taylor." Jack whispered.

"Because they want to censor what needs to be said."

"No, because they wanted reviews from him instead of Op/ed pieces."

"They're just afraid of Owney!"

"You mean, Owney 'The Killer' Madden? Of course, they are, so am I, and you should be, too," Jack insisted.

"You don't understand," she said.

"Yes, I do. This was your way to fight back against all the ugliness we've seen here," Jack said, "Of course, I understand. It's one of the things I love and admire about you."

"They took away my column, my voice," Beck said as she began to cry. She tried hard not to, but her angry tears wouldn't be denied. Beck tried to quickly wipe them away on her coat sleeve.

"Darlin', we just buried Mama Esther. Please let me take you back home to rest before work," Jack said. Beck hung her head, and her shoulders slumped. He could see that for the moment, the fiery redhead felt defeated. He gave her his handkerchief to dry her tears.

"I guess I am pretty tired," she said. Jack took her hand and began to lead her back to Mrs. Esther's place. Beck stopped and said, "I'll go with you on one condition."

"Oh? What's that?" Jack asked. He was willing to do just about anything if she would just rest for a bit.

"Can we go into work a little early?" She asked.

"Why?"

"I need to hit stuff again," she said with a little grin.

"Of course we can," he said, relieved. *That's my girl. She's going to be okay. It will take a while, but we'll get through this.* On the porch, he hugged Beck and gave her a quick kiss on top of her curls. She had not taken care to style her hair into 1930s waves over the past few days, so her hair was wild with curls that looked like she'd spent an afternoon at the beach.

Jack liked this style and mused how it looked a little like his own red hair after a day in Malibu. He remembered that this was how she wore it when he first saw her at the movie studio. He suddenly wished that he could spend a day with her on the coast. Mrs. Esther's son answered the door, which distracted Jack from his daydream. The man invited Jack to sit in the parlor and have a whiskey with him while Beck went up to rest.

"It's a pleasure to finally meet ole' 'Red Devil' Herman," he said.

"Please, call me Jack."

"Will do. I'm Raymond Junior, but most folks just call me Ray," Ray said as he extended his hand to shake Jack's," You know, Mama always spoke highly of you."

"Really? I didn't think she cared for me at all at first."

"That so? If I had to guess, it probably had something to do with you being Rebecca's one and only gentleman caller. She was determined to get that girl married," Ray said with a laugh, "But seriously, Mama always said respect was something to be earned. She never gave it freely. So, if you had hers, then you have mine."

"Thank you," Jack said.

The two men chatted for a while about jazz and the early days of the Cotton Club. When Ray was a little boy. The place had been a speakeasy, and Owney had made quite a bit of dough off the sale of illegal booze. Ray remembered falling asleep in his Mama's dressing room once only to have to make a run for it with her when the police raided. It sounded like an exciting time. Jack almost wished he could have been there, and then he stopped to consider his current predicament and thought better of it.

Suddenly Ray said, "Jack, I need to ask you something kind of personal before Rebecca gets back down here."

"Oh?"

"My brothers and I are planning to sell the house soon. We'd like to put it up for sale in about after Christmas. Half the boarders are nursing students who have planned to graduate by then and move for work. I've talked to the three dancers, and two are getting married. The other one is moving back to Georgia to help her own sick Mama. Do you know if Rebecca has anywhere to go? If not, is a month enough time for her to find a new place? We don't want to leave her without a roof over her head."

"I'm sure we can work something out in a month," Jack said as he touched Beck's ring in his pocket. Hmm, a December wedding might be just the thing to make this Jewish boy finally appreciate Christmas, he mused to himself.

Chapter 30

Upon arriving at the club, Jack and Rebecca spent some quality time with the percussion instruments. He began to teach her to play a short song on the marimba. She was having a hard time picking it up from Jack's spoken instruction. So, he stood behind her with his hands on hers. He was showing her where to strike the mallets when Owney stormed in. He slammed the door hard as he entered the club, which startled the pair. "Get her off the fucking stage." Owney raged at them.

Beck disappeared backstage immediately to Jack's great relief. In the meantime, he decided to play dumb, "You okay, Owney?" he asked innocently.

"No, I'm not okay. I do a lot for this community, and I got some do-gooder taking shots at me in the newspaper," Owney said. As he walked into his office and slammed the door so hard that his nameplate fell off the wall. Jack quickly tended to the instruments he needed to fix and went backstage to check on Beck, who was taking care of the men's dressing room while it was still empty.

"You okay?" he asked.

"Yea, I'm not gonna lie, that was scary. Think it will blow over soon?"

"I do. There won't be any more articles from Beck Taylor. So, he'll find something else to complain about. Just do me a favor and keep a low profile," he said as he pulled her into an embrace, "I couldn't stand it if anything were to happen to you."

"Ahem," Lowry cleared his throat as he entered the room, "y'all need me to leave for a few minutes? Cause I can come back."

Beck blushed and wriggled out of Jack's arms. She said, "No, it's alright. I need to go and um check on that...thing."

As she left, Lowry said, "Okay, Miss Rebecca. Good luck with that," then he looked at Jack and chuckled, "My man, you really are the devil leading that poor girl on like that."

"I'm not leading anyone on, Lowry," Jack said.

"Well, you know Cab's gonna offer you a spot on his tour when he leaves in a few weeks. He's already sore that the Duke stole me out from under him."

"I'm not going on tour," Jack said. He was sure he'd hate touring in the thirties even more than in the nineties.

"You gonna give up all you worked for, cause you're dizzy with that dame?"

"First of all, I hate touring. So, I'm not giving up anything. And, Rebecca's not just another dame. I'm going to give her this," Jack showed Lowry Beck's ring and quickly put it back in his pocket.

"You're crazy! Man, I know you're a lot older than me, but the more famous you get, the more women you're gonna meet. Don't you wanna see what's out there professionally *and* personally speaking?"

"I am older than you, and I've met plenty of women. I know a remarkable one when I see her, and I'm not going to let her get away. I am surprised at you, Lowry. I thought you liked Rebecca. She's always doing whatever she can for all of us."

"Well, sure. Rebecca runs a good crew back here, but that's just homemaker stuff. Any girl can do that. That's how they're raised."

"She is so much more than that. She's our director and a gifted writer. You've read her column. She's not afraid to say the things no one else will say,"

"Wait a minute, Miss Rebecca writes for the newspaper, too? What does she write? Advice or make-up tips? Cause I don't read either of those."

"Neither Lowry. She's not just any columnist. Rebecca is Beck Taylor," Jack said proudly. "The newspaper let her go after her latest column, but she always promoted you cats, and put pressure on Owney to get him to change his policies. She's always pushed for black patrons to be allowed to come in here to support the performers. A lot of people listened to her, you know?"

"No shit? I got this gig with the Duke because of her reviews. That's why he tuned into the broadcast. That's some woman you got there."

"Exactly what I've been trying to tell you," Jack said. At the same time, he realized that Beck wasn't his again. Not officially. But, he was determined to win her back.

"Speaking of my new gig, Jack. The Duke needs me to meet up with the tour tonight ahead of some bad weather. Ms. Gorman says you can take over my place if you want. All I ask is that I can crash on the couch whenever I come through town."

"Of course, Man. I may need bigger digs soon, but there'll always be room for you at my place." Jack said.

"You're a good friend 'Red Devil,' I'm gonna miss you," Lowry said as they shook hands and patted each other on the back.

"You too, Lowry. Don't be a stranger, okay," Jack said. With a sly grin, he added, "Now let's go out there and raise hell together one last time."

Both shows that night were dedicated to the memory of Mrs. Esther. Everyone was at the top of their game, and a few special guests from the old days of the Cotton Club took the stage. They had all come to town to attend her service, and Cab had invited them to join the show for one unforgettable night. Lena Horne was on tour, but even she came back to sing the song Jack had initially written for Mrs. Esther. He was thrilled to hear another jazz legend singing his material. As the show came to a close, Lowry stepped up to say farewell.

"I picked one helluva show to be my last. I will always remember the sound of y'all cheering me on. I'm blessed to have the support of my fellow performers and my dearest friend, Jack Herman, who taught me to pursue my passion for composing. Y'all ain't heard the last of me. I love ya, and I'll miss y'all very much," Lowry said as he blew a kiss to the patrons.

Jack watched backstage as a massive crowd of well-wishers gathered around Lowry to say goodbye. Then, starstruck themselves, most of the performers made a beeline to meet the touring musicians that had come to honor Mrs. Esther. Jack decided it was time to make his way over for one last goodbye when he noticed that Lowry and Violet had their heads together and were gesturing toward Beck. He felt compelled to get closer.

"I just cain't picture it, Honey. She always seems so quiet," Violet said to Lowry.

"Well, you know, it's like they say; still waters run deep," Lowry said.

"That's really cool what she done. I'm going to go over and give her a hug right now," Violet said as she headed toward Beck. Jack stepped in front of her.

"Whoa, please don't do that here," he told her. Then to both of them in a frantic, hushed voice, he said, "I should have said this before, but please button it about Rebecca's articles. If Owney were to find out, she'd really be behind the eight ball."

"Oh. I didn't think about that, Jack. I'm sorry, but I already told Moses and Violet."

"And I done told a buncha people," Violet said.

"I'm sorry, man. I'll go let the cats know to button up about it. Violet, you go spread the word to the ladies. I am really am sorry," Lowry said.

Jack searched the crowd but couldn't find Beck. She wasn't where she had been when he went over to talk Lowry. Panicked, he hurried to the dining room. He was afraid that Owney might have gotten to her before he could. The dining room was empty except for Owney and Pipes.

Chapter 31

Jack hid just beside the door behind a stack of folding chairs. He decided that he had to listen and find what, if anything, Owney knew about Rebecca being Beck.

"What's the problem, Pipes?" Owney asked as he approached his bouncer.

"I found the leak, Boss," Pipes said.

"Now we have plumbing problems? That's capital."

"No, Boss, I know who reported all that stuff to the newspaper."

"Why didn't you just say so? Who is it?" Owney asked.

"It's Rebecca."

"Our Rebecca? The redheaded dame? I don't believe this. Mrs. Esther begged me to give that kid a job when she first turned up in Harlem. It's one thing to have her nag me all the time about how I run my club, but to go to the press?"

"You're not understanding, Boss. She is the press. Beck Taylor and Rebecca are one and the same," Pipe said.

"She's been writing about me in the paper? That little bitch!" Owney began to pace as he talked, "Oh, this is not good. She's been my assistant, she's seen my books, she knows everything about our operation."

"Say no more, Boss. She's outta here. I'll even rough her up a bit to scare her," Pipes assured Owney.

"That's no good. I can't risk her knowing what she knows with that big mouth of hers. I need you to shut her up permanently," Owney said.

"Aw, Boss. Rebecca's so nice. Can't I just teach her a lesson?" Pipes asked.

"No! We're not taking any chances. Get to it," Owney ordered.

"Okay, Boss," Pipes muttered.

Jack's eyes widened with terror. He had opened his big mouth, and just like that, everyone knew about Beck's column. Now, she was in grave danger. He searched frantically for her. She wasn't backstage. He didn't want to enter the dining room from where he eavesdropped and give away his position. Jack stepped quietly but quickly out the rear exit hurrying to the side door. It was locked. Jack ran around to the front doors and tried each one until he finally found one that opened.

He looked all around the dining room. *Where the hell is she?* Just then, she entered the dining room from backstage. She was headed straight for Owney's office, "Rebecca! No!" he managed to say.

"Oh, there you are. Owney needs to see me in his office for a minute. Then, I'm all yours," Beck said, oblivious to the danger.

"This can't wait. Come here," Jack insisted.

"Owney asked for me. I've got to go. Don't want him any angrier than he already is today. I'll keep it short."

Jack crossed quickly to Beck and grabbed her elbow with one hand. He placed the palm of his other hand on the small of her back. "You're coming with me now," he said forcefully. Then, firmly moved her out of the club.

"What the hell?" Why are you being so pushy?" she asked angrily.

"Beck, they know. I'm so sorry, it's all my fault," he said as they walked faster.

"They know I'm Beck Taylor? You told Owney? Why would you do that?"

"No, I'm proud of you so I told Lowry, and the news spread fast. Now, Owney knows, and he told Pipes to kill you," Jack explained.

"Oh, my God!" Beck said her eyes wide with dread, "What am I gonna do?"

"Tonight, we're going to make tracks and lay low."

As they ran through Harlem, the two of them formed a plan. With Lowry gone, Jack would hide her at his place for the night. There they'd plan their next move. Maybe they could travel on the vaudeville circuit. That way, they could stay on the move. He'd stay on tour forever if Beck's life depended on it.

Perhaps, they could make their way out to California. Better yet, figure out how to get the hell back to 1992. That was their preferred plan as it would guarantee that Pipes and Owney couldn't get to her.

Unfortunately, it didn't seem likely that they'd figure out how to time travel worked before the gangsters found them. Jack wondered to himself if he would be able to fight off a big thug like Pipes. He had always worked out regularly, even in Harlem. He might be close to forty, but he was fit.

He exercised at the YMCA doing pull-ups, lifting weights, and he danced on stage every night. *But, this isn't West Side Story. This is a real-life threat to the woman I love. Could I punch a man if I had to? I've never had to hurt or kill someone to save a life. Could I do it?* He wondered. Jack had never been so afraid.

Chapter 32

"I've never been to yours and Lowry's place before," Beck said as they scrambled up the stairs inside the building.

"It's my apartment now that Lowry's left."

"Oh, that's right," Beck said. Jack unlocked the apartment door and turned on the lights. Beck's eyes fell on the one and only bed.

Jack followed her gaze and said, "You can have the bed. I'm used to sleeping on the couch. But before we turn in, we need to talk about what we're going to do."

"I'm about ready to build a time machine," she said with a nervous laugh.

"I know, Darlin'. I'm ready to go home, too. But neither of us knows how to do that. Let's focus on what we can do."

"Okay. If we can't go back to the right year, we could at least go back to the right place. Let's head west," Beck said.

"Back to California? I have some prospects out there as long as they're outside of Owney's sphere of influence." Jack said, thoughtfully.

"Assuming we're stuck in 1938, there's a war coming," she reminded him.

"I'm pretty sure I'm too old to be drafted," he said with a smile.

"I'm not so sure. But what I meant was It's not a safe time to be Jewish, Jack."

"It's not so bad in Hollywood; it's full of Jewish refugees right now. One of my favorite actors, Peter Lorre, just fled from Germany. I'd love to work with him."

"We could take the train and be there in a few days. Are we safe to take the train? Can we afford a train?" Beck asked. As she paced back and forth, the floorboards creaked under her feet.

"I believe, so I've been hoarding the rest of that bonus Owney gave me and saving most of what the Cotton Club paid me. We can buy tickets for as far west as we can get. If we can't get all the way to California, we'll just go as far away as we can. Then, we'll work wherever we end up until we have enough money to get the rest of the way there."

"I have this week's pay in my handbag and the last payment from the paper. I have some savings, but that's all back at Mama Esther's. It's not safe for me to go back there."

"Yea, that's out of the question. That will be the first place they look. We'll rest here for a little while and head out early for the station," Jack said.

"Jack? Do you think we're safe here? Won't they come looking for us?" Beck said as she wrung her hands in her lap.

"I think we have a few hours before they'd come here. I'm pretty sure Pipes knows we're not together anymore," he said, smiling sadly at her.

"Oh, right," she said. Returning the smile.

"It's not ideal, but at least we're not out in the open somewhere. We'll keep our stay short," Jack said as he got up from the couch, "For now, I think we should get some sleep."

Beck looked at her dress thoughtfully then said," This is the only outfit I'll have with me. May I borrow a shirt to sleep in?"

"Of course," Jack grabbed one of his button-down shirts from the closet and handed it to her, "The bathroom is right through that door. Let me know if you need anything else," Beck nodded and went to change.

Jack took his pillow and blanket down from the top shelf of his closet. He placed them on the couch and removed his shirt and shoes. He typically slept in his undershirt and boxers but thought better of taking off his pants.

As he eased off his suspenders to get comfortable, Beck came out of the bathroom. His shirt had never looked better! Backlit by the bathroom light, he could see the silhouette of her body through the fabric. She was standing full-on, and he could see her hourglass shape. He quickly sat down on the couch and threw the blanket over his lap.

"I hung my clothes over the shower curtain rod. I hope that's okay," Beck said as she turned to the side and fussed with her hair in the mirror, affording him a view of her body in profile. She was still standing in the full light of the bathroom, and all Jack could do to answer her was nod.

"Are you alright?" she asked.

"Uh-huh. I mean, the bathroom light is, um, really bright. Could you turn it off, please?"

"Can't I leave it on? I'll pull the door almost all the way closed," Beck asked meekly.

That's when he remembered that she was afraid of the dark. *Poor Beck.* He promptly said, "Of course, whatever you need."

"Thanks for helping me," she said as she climbed into the bed.

"It's the least I can do. After all, it's my fault you're in this mess. Even if it wasn't, I still love you, Beck. I'd do anything for you."

"I can't believe you're leaving Harlem for me," Beck said.

"It has to be done, Darlin'. You're not safe here anymore," he said as he laid his head down on the pillow. All was quiet for a minute until he heard her voice again.

"Jack?"

"Yes?"

"I still love you, too."

"I know. Goodnight."

"Night," she said.

Jack had just dozed off when he heard her voice, almost a whisper call out from across the room.

"Jack?"

"Uh-huh," he said sleepily.

"I'm terrified."

"I know, Darlin'."

"Will you sleep with me? Uh, I mean here in the bed, next to me?"

Is this a good idea? Earlier, he'd gotten excited just looking at her. *Now she wants me to lay next to her? It's a double bed, there's no way to avoid touching each other.* He wanted touch her. *No. Dammit, Jack. You're the reason the poor girl is running for her life. Keep your hormones in check and get in that bed. She deserves to feel as safe as she can now. You're not going to take advantage of the situation.* But all he said to Beck was, "Okay."

Jack crossed the room and crawled carefully into the bed. He laid on his back, corpse-like with his arms crossed over his chest.

Beck giggled, "What's this? Are you a vampire or something? Hold me." She laid her head on his chest, and he put his arm around her. The other arm still crossed over his body, he quickly realized the hand of the arm under her had landed on the curve of her butt. He moved it north to stroke her hair and then placed his hand on her shoulder. He felt her raise her head up; her breath was warm on his neck.

"Would you kiss me, goodnight?" Beck asked. Jack attempted to kiss her as chastely as possible, but Beck pressed her lips firmly against his mouth. As her tongue sought to part his lips, it was clear she wanted a more intimate kiss. The kiss was long and heated. Beck eased her hand under his shirt and ran her fingers through his chest hair.

She began to explore his chest. Which caused his hand that was resting on her shoulder to slip onto the side of her breast. He wondered if he should move it. He didn't want to. After all, Beck hadn't asked him to. Jack wondered if she wanted the same thing he wanted. Then Beck slid her hand down his body and attempted to undo his pants. She fumbled with the button, so he happily helped her. Together they eased them off. Beck kissed him again. He wanted to pull her onto him, but he needed to be sure.

"Beck, are you sure you want to do this?" he whispered.

"Of course I am. I've waited for this for a long time," she said as she climbed on top of him and unbuttoned his shirt. He could just make out the shape of her full breasts and the seductive look in her eyes from the light that came from the crack of the bathroom door. They realized that they would not get as much sleep as they needed, but neither of them cared.

Afterward, they lay there quiet and exhausted, holding one another close. Jack closed his eyes and felt the rhythm of her heart. He had missed her tempo so much! And, this time, his own heart was keeping time with hers. The two hearts beat as one as the reunited lovers rested up for the dangerous journey ahead.

Chapter 33

Jack woke with the sun just a few hours later. He stroked Beck's hair and kissed the top of her head. He couldn't believe she was actually there sleeping on his chest. It felt right; it felt like she had always been there. Jack embraced her, and she stirred. "Mornin', Dollface," he said, grinning at her as she opened her eyes.

It took Beck a second to get her bearings, and then she smiled, kissed him, and rolled over to the other side of the bed. He wanted to lay there with her forever, but they needed to get out of town. Not to mention, his stomach was growling, so he carefully climbed out of bed, determined to let her rest just a little longer. He searched the kitchen and realized that there wasn't much to eat—certainly, nothing resembling breakfast food. Lowry had told him about a good Jewish bakery a few blocks away. So, Jack decided that he would run out and grab fresh bagels for their train trip.

As he crossed back toward the bed, Jack picked his shirt up from the floor and put it on, remembering that it was the shirt he had worn when he first came here from 1992. It no longer smelled of his Malibu home. Instead, it smelled of Beck's vanilla scent. The scent had changed, but it still made Jack feel like he was home. He picked his pants up off the floor, and his foot stepped on something sharp. He sat on the edge of the bed to investigate and saw that It was Beck's ring. It had fallen out of his pocket last night. Thankfully it wasn't damaged.

Jack wished he could say the same for his foot, which had a small but painful gash in the arch. He looked at her sleeping and wondered if now would be the right time to propose. *I don't want to be in a rush when I ask her to be my wife. I'll do it once we're safely on the train.* Jack stashed the ring back in his pocket. Then, gently shook her awake," Beck?" he whispered.

"Uh-huh?" she moaned.

"Time to rise and shine."

Beck sat up slowly, her hair a wild mess, "I'll rise, but I make no promise to shine," she yawned and stretched, then suddenly said, "I'm starving."

"Me too. I'm going to run around the corner and get us some bagels. Have you had bagels before? Do you like bagels?"

Beck laughed," Of course I have. I love bagels and cream cheese."

"Why are you laughing?" Jack asked.

"The first time my mom toasted bagels for us, she made a big deal about it being Jewish food. We didn't have any Jewish people where I grew up, so it was kind of, I don't know, exotic, maybe?"

"I've never been called exotic before," Jack said.

"Not you. Not Jewish people. The food was just new and exciting to us," she said and smiled as she remembered, "The first time that I actually met a Jewish person, I was twelve. I asked the girl sitting next to me in school where she went to church, and she explained that she was Jewish. I got really excited and told her that it was great to meet one of God's chosen people. It was pretty awkward."

"I'm glad I'm not the first Jewish person you met," Jack said, "I'm not even sure how to respond to that."

"Not sure, I'm any less awkward," Beck said.

"Then, we're a matched set. I'm going to go get breakfast. You go ahead and get dressed. We'll head to the station as soon as I get back."

"Please don't be too long. I'm scared to be here alone," Beck said, hugging her knees to her body as she sat in the bed.

"You need a moment to get dressed, and we're both hungry. I'll lock the door and be right back. Don't open it for anyone," Jack said.

"Okay, I'll be ready to leave when you get back."

Jack made it to the bakery quickly as promised, but there was a line around the corner full of hungry people grabbing breakfast on their way to work. He promised himself that he would only wait for ten minutes, not wanting to leave Beck alone any longer than that. But after ten minutes, he was the very next person in line. Jack decided that he could wait a couple of minutes more since he was so close, and he didn't want to return empty-handed. Finally, it was his turn. He ordered quickly and hurried out the door.

As he walked the few blocks back to his apartment, he thought about the adventure that lay before him and Beck. A train trip across the United States in 1938. They would see the architecture of great cities and small towns. Meet people from not only a different era but from so many other places, and there would be so much music to enjoy.

Perhaps he would rediscover styles of music that had been lost to time. He could be like a musical archeologist. Jack chuckled to himself as an image of him dressed as Indiana Jones complete with a bullwhip came to mind.

He opened the worn but beautiful door to the building where he lived and started to go upstairs when two figures burst forth from his doorway. A struggle ensued at the top of the stairs. The door had been ripped from its hinges. Jack quickly realized that the much smaller figure was Beck, and the towering figure was Pipes.

Neighbors emerged from their apartments, but when they saw the gangster, they hid frightened behind their doors. Jack dropped the bagels and sprang up the stairs. Just as Pipes put both hands around Beck's throat, intent on crushing the life out of her. Her face was red as she tried to pry his hands from her neck. Jack took advantage of Pipe's focus and occupied arms to surprise the large man with a hard punch to the nose. He nearly missed Beck, but the move worked. Pipes let go of her as she started to cough and gasp. He turned on Jack hit him in the stomach knocking him back over the threshold of his apartment. Jack fell and hit his head on his broken door.

He was out for a second, he came to and saw that Beck was trying to get to him, but as soon as she turned her back on Pipes, he grabbed her from behind, "JACK!" she screamed. Pipes used his muscular arm to put her in a chokehold and pinned her arms with his other massive arm. Her face was purple, and her eyes were glassy.

Jack scrambled to get up and grabbed a whiskey bottle from the kitchen counter. He ran at the goon intent on smashing him in the head, but Pipes kept turning his body to evade Jack while Beck had hooked her leg behind one of Pipes'. She tried to bring him down with her last bit of strength, but she went limp in Pipes' arms.

Desperate, Jack smashed the full bottle down on Pipes' head, disorienting the large man. Unfortunately, Pipes and Beck were on the edge of the top stair. The man dropped Beck. Before Jack could get around the vast figure to catch her, she crashed down the stairs hitting her head hard against the iron leg of a decorative table in the foyer. While he attempted to grab his girl, Jack bumped the behemoth who toppled over the side of the banister, falling and smashing his head on the marble floor below.

Jack ran to Beck, calling her name, "BECK! BECK!" he reached her and cradled her in his arms. He placed his hand on her neck and felt that she still had a pulse. Jack was determined to get her out of there before Pipes woke up and tried to strangle her again. The elderly black man who lived in the bottom floor apartment peeked out of his door and said, "I'm sorry I couldn't stop him! I called an ambulance for your lady friend. Don't let em take her to Harlem Hospital. Gangsters got too many friends there. Better go now. I'm sure someone has already called the cops," he said as he pointed to Pipes, who had a large pool of blood forming under his head. Jack had been in denial until he looked at him, but he could no longer deny the truth that Pipes would never wake up.

Shaken, he turned his thoughts back to the woman trembling in his arms. He peeked out the door and saw that an ambulance was indeed waiting at the curb. Seeing old automobiles no longer charmed as it had when he first arrived in Harlem. Placing Beck in the antiquated car meant that she was about to receive antiquated medical care.

He was allowed to ride in front as they sped along the perimeter of Central Park headed toward Mount Sinai Hospital. The vehicle had barely pulled into the ambulance bay when the doctors emerged from the building and whisked her away. Jack stood there, terrified in the doorway. *What if I never see her again?*

Chapter 34

A soft-spoken nurse led Jack to the registration desk. "What's your wife's name, sir?" Jack opened his mouth to correct the young woman but thought better of it. People were looking for Beck Taylor, after all. Besides, it would be true soon enough.

"Rebecca Herman," he replied. He liked the way it sounded. There was a melody to it.

"Religion?" she asked.

"Um," Jack wasn't sure, then he remembered Beck saying how happy she was to meet "God's chosen people." He did know the answer. "Christian," he said.

The older nurse looked down her glasses at him and sighed, "See Ruthie? Another cute Jewish man married to a shiksa! What's wrong with finding a nice Jewish girl like Ruthie here?"

"Shut your head, Hazel. His wife's hurt bad. Sorry about my colleague, Mr. Herman. You can take a seat in the waiting area, and the doctor will let you know when you can see your wife."

As Jack walked to his seat, he heard the nurses behind him still chatting.

"All I'm saying is that's one cute redhead. If his wife's hurt that bad, he could be back on the market soon."

"Hazel, please! You should be ashamed of yourself."

"Oh please, I'm too old for shame!" Hazel said.

Though a bit tasteless, the banter reminded Jack of holiday dinners with his mom and his aunts. *If I have to sit and worry about Beck, at least I can do it in a place where the people feel like family.* He wished that his mom could meet Beck. She wouldn't care that she wasn't Jewish. She'd just be happy he'd found love. *Is it pathetic to be almost forty and still want your mom?* Jack didn't care. He wanted her to hug him and tell him that everything would be okay. Like Beck, his mother was a writer. She always knew just the right words to say.

"Heya, Jack," said a man's voice from behind. Jack jumped, fearing it was another one of Owney's goons," Whoa there, remember me?" It was then Jack turned and realized that he was face to face with mobster Tony Firelli.

"Yes, we met at Patsy's," Jack said as he shook Tony's hand and asked, "Are you here to see someone, too?"

"Yea, you. My cousin Sal works here with the financials, and he called me up to say that my favorite musician just came in with his dame. I heard your tomato was pretty bruised up. So, I did a little digging and found out about the scramble at your place this morning."

"You did? That was fast," Jack was worried. *If the news has already reached the other side of Harlem, how long will I be able to hide Beck here?*

"I got connections, my friend. Nothing' happens in Harlem that I can't find out about. I'm a fan of yours, as you know. I wanna help. Let me pick up your girl's tab for her stay. Don't worry, I told Sal to keep her location under wraps. Owney's connected, too, ya know?"

"Does this mean I owe you a favor?" Jack asked nervously.

"You catch on quick. I was gonna let ya owe me one, but then I heard that Pipes McGee ain't gonna be a problem for me no more. So the way I see it, we're square," Tony said with a nod.

"Thank you, Mr. Firelli."

"Take care, Jack. Here's my card, in case you decide you wanna change careers after today. That was a big man ya brought down. Much respect," Tony said as he grabbed Jack's shoulders and gave him a big kiss on the cheek.

While he was relieved that Beck would stay hidden, the conversation with Tony caused him to reflect on what happened to Pipes. *I actually caused the death of another human being! Of course, it was an accident, and I was trying to save the woman I loved, but a man is dead because of me.* No matter how justified, it sickened him.

After two very long hours, a man in a white coat approached Jack, "Mr. Herman?"

Jack stood up and realized he was a little shaky on his feet. "Yes?"

"Dr. Nacht, I'm the doctor in charge of your wife's care. I just wanted to brief you on her condition, and then you can go back and see her. Mrs. Herman has suffered a concussion from her fall. As you mentioned to the ambulance driver, she suffered another concussion about three months ago. Our main concern with this type of injury is swelling of the brain, which can be fatal and is more likely to happen when the brain has sustained a prior injury. We're giving her drugs to try to prevent the swelling. We'll carefully monitor her blood pressure to make sure we don't cause a problem with her heart. She's receiving pure oxygen through a cannula, which will help with her recovery. The good news is that she's awake and asking for you."

When he heard that, Jack attempted to move past the doctor. He wanted to see Beck and let her know he was there. The doctor, however, blocked his way.

"Wait, I know you're anxious to be with her. Just let me finish, and I'll have a nurse take you right to her. Mrs. Herman is also receiving pain medication for the severe headache she has and some medicine to relax her body to keep her head in the ideal recovery position. Please don't move her or her bed. Expect that she'll be a bit groggy and confused from both the accident and the treatment. She's young and otherwise in excellent health, so I am cautiously optimistic. Still, the next twenty-four hours will be critical."

Ruth suddenly rushed up to Dr. Nacht from the wing of rooms behind him.

"Excuse me, Dr. Nacht. I need to speak with you right away," she said.

The two stepped just out of earshot, but Jack could see that Ruth was gesturing toward the wing Dr. Nacht had come from. He tried hard to make out what they were saying. He was alarmed when the two left to go back to the wing of rooms. It seemed like forever, but the doctor returned after ten minutes.

"Mr. Herman, the nurse called me to examine your wife. She is experiencing some vision loss, which could be from the injury or from the medication."

"She's blind?" Jack asked.

"I've requested a consult with the ophthalmologist, to be sure. But, in my experience, most patients eventually recover their vision," Dr. Nacht said.

"You have to let me go to her. Please, Beck's afraid of the dark. She must be terrified," Jack pleaded.

"Ruth will take you to see her now, but your wife needs you to be calm. Can you do that for her, Mr. Herman?" Dr. Nacht asked.

"Of course," Jack said as he slowed his breath, controlling it the way he had learned to do for playing the trombone.

"Ready?" Ruth asked. Satisfied that Jack, at least looked calm, she said, "Follow me."

Jack saw Beck laying flat on her back with pillows to keep her head still. He was surprised to see that her eyes had been bandaged. There was a chair at her bedside that he pulled as close as possible to her bed. Her poor face was bruised, and her body was frail.

"Beck?" he asked softly, not sure if she was awake.

"Jack," she said as she tried to move and reach out to him.

"No, don't move. I'll come to you," he said, remembering the doctor's orders. Jack took her hand, which was so cold that it was purple despite the warm blanket covering her body. He covered her hand with his other hand to warm it.

"I can't see anything. I'm scared," Beck said.

"The doctor says it's only temporary. You'll see again soon," Jack said, not wanting to tell her that she might always be in darkness. He looked at the bandages again and asked, "Did they say why they bandaged your eyes?"

"They said my eyes needed to rest to heal," Beck shuddered and moaned, "Uhh, My head really hurts."

"I'm sure it does, Darlin'. That was some fall!"

"I don't want to talk about it," she said. After several moments of silence, Jack began to wonder if Beck had fallen asleep when she suddenly said, "We missed our train."

"It doesn't matter. We'll go to California as soon as you're better," Jack said, he kissed her hand.

"I don't think I'm going to get better, Jack."

"Don't talk like that. You're very strong, and already doing better than the doctor expected. You're gonna beat this."

"Not this time. It feels like I'm disconnecting. I don't know if that makes any sense."

"You can't leave me alone, Beck," Jack said. He couldn't imagine his life without her.

"You're going to be fine. You're going to do great things. You'll reinvent yourself again and keep them all guessing. I know you will," Beck said as she smiled.

"I want to do all that, but I want to do it with you."

She squeezed his hand, "I will always be there, Jack."

"Not in the way I want," Jack argued as tears began to form in his eyes.

"I need you to do something for me, please," she asked.

"Anything," Jack said, desperate to help her.

"Sing to me," Beck asked.

"I can't do that, right now," he said, his voice quivering with emotion.

"I can't see Jack. I'm scared. Your voice is my favorite sound. Please sing for me," she pleaded.

Jack knew he couldn't refuse her. He took a deep breath and said, "Any requests?"

"Saint James Infirmary," she said.

"No, that's way too morbid, Beck."

"I like the way you sing it. Besides, isn't morbid kind of your thing?"

She had him there. Jack took another deep breath and sang:

"I went down to St. James infirmary, I saw my baby there,

She was stretched out on a long white table, so sweet, so cold, so fair,

Let her go, let her go, Oh bless her, wherever she may be

She may search this whole wide world over,

But she'll never find another sweet...man..."

Jack stopped, "I can't, Beck. I'm so sorry," Tears rolled silently down his cheeks. He wiped them away, and though she couldn't see them see he was sure she'd heard the tears in his voice.

"Okay, it's okay. You pick this time," Beck said gently.

Jack put his hand on her heart and felt the tempo he loved. He closed his eyes and concentrated. The obvious song choice came to him. She had told him that "Don't You Go" was her favorite song of his. So, Jack sang it to her. His heart in every word, while Beck smiled and squeezed his hand.

"That was perfect. Thank you," Beck said, suddenly her expression changed.

"Are you alright?" he asked.

"I'm exhausted. I just need a little rest. Stay with me?"

"Of course, I will. I love you, Beck."

"I love you, Jack."

He leaned over and put his head on her chest listening to the rhythm of her heart. He was exhausted, too. Just as he started to doze, he noticed the tempo had slowed. Then, he lost it altogether.

Chapter 35

When Jack realized that he had lost Beck's heartbeat, he sat straight up, intent on alerting the nurses. But, as he looked around, he saw walls full of vinyl records and palm trees swaying in the breeze outside the window. Someone was banging on the front door and calling out for him. Rufus was barking and scratching at the jazz room door.

Jack got up from his bed and felt a twinge of pain from the small cut in the arch of his foot. His mouth and eyes were dry, his head throbbed. He opened the door and greeted his furry companion, then made his way slowly to the front entry. The voice was familiar. As he moved closer, he realized it was Barry.

"Where the hell have you been, man? We've been in the studio for an hour. You didn't answer your phone. What wrong with you, Jack?"

Jack was relieved to see his dog and Barry. At least he wasn't stuck in 1938 running from Irish gangsters. But, Beck was gone. He'd lost her. Jack fell to his knees, sobbing.

"Uh, Jack, it's okay. If you're not feeling well, I'll go. Don't worry, I'll smooth things over with the other guys," Barry said as he awkwardly attempted to soothe Jack by patting him on his head.

"She's dead, Barry. I lost her," Jack cried and grabbed Barry's legs.

Barry attempted to calm Jack and figure out who was dead. Jack tried to explain what happened, but none of what he managed to say through his sobs made any sense. Barry finally said, "Jack, you're sick. I'm going to get you some help. Okay? I'll be right back." He went to the phone in the kitchen and called for an ambulance. Jack heard the sirens as he passed out on the tile entry. He awoke hours later in a hospital room of his own. His mother and Robert were by his bedside. He pretended to sleep while he listened to them.

"Well, what did Barry say?" Miriam asked.

"He said that Jack has lost his damn mind. He was going on and on about some girl that died. It creeped Barry out, and he's known Jack forever. He doesn't spook easily," Robert said.

"There's nothing wrong with Jack's mind, Robert. The doctor said that he was admitted for dehydration and exhaustion. As usual, he's just trying to do too much. We'll be able to take him home in a couple of days."

"Have you talked to him yet?" Robert asked.

"No, they just let me come back a few minutes ago," she explained.

Robert noticed that Jack's eyes were open. "Hey faker, if you wanted to see us, you could have just invited us over for dinner or something," he said as he ruffled Jack's curls.

"I'll try and remember that next time," Jack said. He had always looked up to his big brother, so he tried to act brave during Robert's visit. As soon as his brother left, he was grateful for some time alone with his mom. She watched as her eldest son left, then turned to Jack.

"What's really going on?" she asked gently.

"Mom, I met the sweetest girl," he said.

"You did?" Miriam asked, hopefully.

"Yes, and we loved each other. I was going to ask her to marry me, but something terrible happened, and now she's dead," Jack started to cry again.

"I just saw you on Sunday, Sweetie. You didn't mention any girl then. Was she someone new cause this seems a little fast."

There's no way to explain this to her. Wait, did she say that she saw me this week? I've been gone for three months.

"Mom, what day is it?" Jack asked.

"Wednesday, why?"

He had gone to bed Tuesday night and woke up in Harlem the next day. It all made sense now. The whole thing had to have been a dream. He wasn't sure which was more devastating, that Beck had died or that she had never existed. His body recovered, but his heart was broken. Two days later, it was time to return home.

"I brought you some clean clothes from home, Sweetie," his mom said, handing over shorts and a T-shirt.

"Thanks, Mom," Jack mumbled. She picked up the bag with his 1930s outfit inside and left him alone to dress. It felt foreign to wear a T-shirt and shorts after being dressed up every day for so long. *But, that never happened,* he reminded himself as he slipped on his flip flops and joined Miriam in the hall.

As they arrived at the house, Jack noted that it had been thoroughly cleaned. His mom must have had the housekeepers in while he was in the hospital. The place that once felt like home was now vast and empty. Jack slid out of his flip flops and onto the couch. His mom was hovering with a worried look on her face.

"I spoke to Barry and the boys. They'd love to come over and play some music with you," she said.

"I'll call them when I'm ready," Jack said as he picked the TV remote and began to scroll through the TV guide.

"Your manager called, too. He said to remind you that Howard something or other, is coming over on Monday to hear the new music for his picture."

"Howard? Howard Fritz is coming here in two days?"

"Uh-huh, is that bad?" his mom asked.

"It's terrible! I haven't written anything new for him," Jack said in a panic.

"Well, you have tonight, Saturday, and Sunday to come up with something. Why don't you head downstairs and whip some up music for this guy?"

"It's not that simple, Mom," Jack was offended. Did she actually think his job was that easy?

"I know, and it's even more difficult if you just lay around."

"I was just released from the hospital, where I was treated for exhaustion. Now, If you don't mind, I'm gonna rest on my couch for the rest of the day," Jack said.

"That's not how you were raised to speak to your mom. I'm going home now," Miriam said, wounded. As she passed the kitchen counter, she reminded Jack, "The anti-depressants the doctor prescribed are right here on the bar. I'll hope you'll take them. It might help."

"I don't need drugs, Mom," Jack replied.

"Where do you want the bag of clothes from the hospital?"

"Just leave them by the bar," Jack said a little too brusquely. His mom left in a huff, but he was too tired to go after her. One of the first quirky comedy films he had scored was on the TV, and he quickly changed the channel just as the main titles began to play. It bothered him to listen to his work once it was finished. Today, he found himself more easily annoyed than usual.

The next channel was in the middle of a black and white movie complete with a shoot out. When the main character appeared on the screen, it was James Cagney walking into a 1930s music hall. Jack said, "No!" which caused Rufus to startle and wake from his nap. Jack finally settled on a classic horror movie marathon. The Bride of Frankenstein was first up. It was one of his favorites, so he let it play.

Several hours of monster movies later, Jack had budged from his couch twice. Once to feed himself and the dog and once more to use the bathroom and let Rufus out. As Jack stared at the TV, Rufus lay next to him, licking the cheese dust off Jack's fingers. The processed food offended his senses at first. He reminded himself that he had only dreamed of being in the 1930s; he hadn't really been there. His stomach, however, disagreed, and Jack had to return to the bathroom.

He laid back down on the couch and watched The Blob. He found the monstrous ooze unflatteringly relatable. "I've got to get up," he said to Rufus, who seemed content to remain on the couch. Jack worked his way out from underneath his stubborn dog and drug his body slowly downstairs to the studio.

Propped up in front of his bay, he stared at the monitor as it played one of Howard's scenes. The one where the hero first met the love of his life. It hurt too bad to watch as memories of Beck came flooding back to him. Given that it was a romance, almost every scene was an image of the main characters madly in love. It sickened him.

I need to hit something. In the percussion section, he banged on the timpani drums. It felt good. The sound that emerged from the skins was anything but romantic. Once he was sweaty and a little less peeved, Jack approached the film backward from its final scene.

The story did not end happily. The two lovers had to say goodbye as an impending war sent the man away. The final images were close-ups of their faces as the woman stood on the train platform with tears rolling down her cheeks, the man reaching his hand out to her through the train's open window. *This is too much.* Jack crossed to the couch and fell asleep.

It was already Saturday afternoon when he woke. At the bay, he tried to watch the scene again. He stared at the end credits as they scrolled by. *Maybe I could start here. It's just names and a black background. Nothing romantic.* He had been in the industry long enough to recognize about half of the names that scrolled by. Suddenly, the name Beck Taylor appeared on the screen. "Wait," he said. He backed it up to the screen that listed a Beck Taylor under the list of Production Assistants.

His heart skipped a beat. Impulsively, he picked up the phone and called Howard. His answering machine took the call. "Howard, this is Jack Herman. I need a favor. Tom is looking to hire a production assistant for his next project. He heard good things about your PA, Beck Taylor. Since Tom's in London, he asked me to set up a meeting with Beck. Could you please help us out with that? Anytime this week works, I'm flexible. See you Monday."

Well, that was dumb. Now someone named Beck Taylor will be counting on a job with Tom Price. But I have to try what if it's her? There was that pretty redhead at the studio, after all. But what are the odds that she's a PA named Beck Taylor? I've seen these credits so many times before. Probably where I came up with the name in my dream.

His heart-hurting again, Jack pushed on for a few more hours, writing a couple cues, but nothing he was satisfied with. He fell into a dreamless sleep on his keyboard.

The phone rang early Sunday, waking Jack. He'd left the door from the stairway open, so he decided to screen the phone call. After his outgoing message had played, Tom Price's voice came over the answering machine, "Hey Jack, I'm sorry. I'm in London, and I just realized the time back there. Listen, I wanted to remind you that I'm coming into town next week to work on the Halloween musical. We really need to get to work; the stop motion animators are ready to go. They need a script. The problem is there's not one! I was hoping we could start with the songs, maybe. It would give them something to work on. I'll call you when I land to set up a schedule. Later."

Jack felt like an elephant was sitting on his chest. The band wanted to record, Howard wanted a score, and Tom needed musical numbers. Once again, he stalked over to his percussion instruments and beat the djembe until he was a sweaty mess.

He hadn't showered since before his hospital stay. Maybe that would help.

After his shower, he reached for the cheesy puffs bag he'd left on the couch. Rufus had finished it off while Jack was downstairs. He thought to scold the dog but remembered how sick they'd made him. *Rufus did me a favor. I'll grab an apple instead.* Jack was at the top of the stairs when he noticed it didn't feel right. He'd picked up a tomato by mistake. Jack looked at the fruit and saw where he was standing. Beck's fall replayed in his mind, and tears came again, "Great! Now I'm the weird guy who cries at tomatoes," he muttered to himself.

He heard Beck giggle in his head and say, "Sure, you collect bones, shrunken heads, and creepy dolls, but crying over tomatoes is the one thing that makes you 'the weird guy,'" He smiled, but his heart ached to hear her voice. How could she still seem so real to him?

Back at the bay, Jack had an idea. Beck's theme could play over the last scene. The challenge was to remember it. He had dreamt music many times, but it typically disappeared right when he woke up or as soon as he heard any other piece. Hell! He had almost lost that superhero theme when the melody came to him on a noisy plane ride. He had to run to the bathroom and hum it loudly over the roar of the plane's engines into his portable tape player. It was the only way he'd saved it from being wiped from his memory by the landing music.

He had no portable tape player in his dream of 1938. But, it was less than twenty fours until Howard Fritz would be there. Desperate, Jack picked up the tape player and tried to hum what he could remember of the theme.

It took hours, but Jack did it. He had managed to piece together the song he wrote for Beck. He played the piece first on the keyboard and then moved over to play the melody on the violin as he had initially done in his dream. Hearing the notes emerge from his violin reminded him of her dressed as Persephone being led away by Mama Esther in the revue. Her fiery red curls, the longing look she gave him over her shoulder. *She looked like an angel. Pull it together, Jack.* He wondered if this was what insanity felt like.

By the time Howard Fritz knocked on his door on Monday afternoon, Jack felt a little better. He was nervous, but he'd managed to clean up and eat a little something. He didn't feel like putting on his signature suspenders yet. Instead, he had settled on a black T-shirt and jeans.

"Hello, Jack," Howard said curtly. He walked right into the studio without waiting for an invitation, "I got your message. Beck Taylor will meet you at the coffee shop across from the studio tomorrow at noon," Howard sat down at the bay and looked at Jack, "Now, what do you have for me?"

"Well, I'm not as far along as I'd liked to be," Jack said apologetically.

Howard replied with a disgruntled, "Uh-huh."

"But I think I've nailed the tone of the film. What's important is the longing that these two lovers have for one another. They're a perfect match, but these external forces keep pulling them apart."

"Agreed. The story is all about love and longing. The characters overcome some smaller obstacles early on, but when the war comes...well, it's just bigger than both of them. Bigger than everyone, really."

"Exactly. You have some great moments in there where I can tell that they're devoted to one another. But, she still gives him hell when she needs to."

"I wouldn't say that," Howard said.

"Um, what I mean is that they're great together, but they're not the same. The lovers complement each other nicely," Jack tried hard to show Howard that he understood his vision for the film, but it was a struggle. He was barely able to watch the movie, much less talk about it.

Jack had always excelled at reading body language. As he looked at Howard's face and posture, he could tell that he'd had just about enough of Jack.

"Jack? Have you actually written anything new for my movie?" Howard asked, narrowing his eyes at him.

"Well, I have this love theme that I think will underscore the point when they can no longer be together. It's a jazz violin piece. I plan to compose the entire score in that 1930s jazz style."

"Fine. Just play it already," Howard said as he glanced at his watch.

Jack had the sudden urge to hit Howard, but logic prevailed. He kept his clenched fists on his lap. He took a deep breath and even managed to grin at Howard. Then, he said through his teeth, "Of course."

Jack closed his eyes as he began to play his violin. There was Beck standing in front of him. He swayed as he kept time. Jack felt the tempo of her heartbeat. Instead of his violin, he imagined he was holding her once more close against him. Swaying to the music at the Halloween party in Harlem, looking into her eyes, and then it happened. Jack stopped playing. He fell to his knees, sobbing. Howard stood but stayed next to the bay. From across the room, he said stiffly, "Um, Jack? Can I help you?"

Jack attempted to speak but only managed to sob.

"Can I call someone for you?" Howard offered. When Jack failed to answer after several moments of silence occasionally punctuated by sobs, Howard grabbed his coat. He said, "I'm going to go now. I hope you feel better soon."

My composing career is over. He managed to put his violin away and climbed upstairs to the main house. After sleeping in the studio or on the couch, Jack decided to finally spend the night in his own bed. He made his way through the familiar space in the dark to soothe his swollen, red eyes. As he crossed in front of the bar on his way to the bedroom, he tripped over something plastic—the plastic bag from the hospital. The antiseptic smell was unmistakable.

I'll deal with it later. He lumbered into his bedroom, dragging the bag behind him like a sleepy child lugs his blanket. Rufus followed closely behind. Jack sat it next to the bed and climbed in. *It's so good to finally be back in my own bed. It's only been a few days, but it seemed like forever.*

Chapter 36

Jack woke up to the sound of his phone ringing. He looked at the clock and realized he had slept for fifteen hours. Still groggy, he reached for the phone and tried to clear his throat so the caller on the other end would not realize he was sleeping well into the afternoon.

"Hello," he said, his voice gruff, his mouth was dry.

"Hey, Jack, did I wake you?" asked the caller. It was his manager, Ronald.

"No, I just haven't talked to anyone today," Jack said, and then he quickly cleared his throat.

"You probably know why I'm calling," Ronald said gently.

"Howard Fritz?" Jack asked. Cradling his head in his hand.

"Yea, it's just not going to work out, Jack. He's going in another direction," Ronald explained. "In light of what happened, he and I agreed that it would be best if he found a new composer, which means you're free to do what you need to do."

"You mean compose another movie?" Jack asked.

There was a long sigh from the other end of the line. Jack had been Ronald's first client and a good friend. He could tell that this was hard for him, "Howard told me everything, Jack. I'm worried that you've been burning the candle at both ends with the band and the film composing work. Take some time off. Do something fun. Go see someone if you need to. I can help you find a counselor if you want. Whatever you need to do to; just feel better."

"Do you think another director will ever hire me?" Jack said, his cheeks burning with embarrassment.

"Yes, Howard promised to keep this quiet. But, if you go back to work before you're ready, I'm afraid the next director might not be so discrete."

"Okay. But Tom will be here next week to work on the musical."

"Then take a week and do what you need to do. If you're still not well, I can talk to Tom."

"That won't be necessary," Jack assured him.

"Had you written much for Howard?"

"Nothing he was interested in, just some short 1930s jazz pieces. The love theme was the only thing fully formed."

"Well, at least you weren't too far into the work. I've got to go, but please call me if I can help. Okay?"

"I will," Jack said as he put down the phone. He felt ashamed that he'd put Ronald in this awkward spot. He wanted to bury himself in his sheets and never come out. But, Rufus insisted he move.

Jack sat on the deck while Rufus sniffed around the bushes in the garden below. Determined to clear his calendar for the week, he opened his date planner. Jack expected his week to be wide open as he'd initially planned to work on Howard's score. So, he was quite startled when he saw that in a few hours, he was to meet with Beck Taylor!

Things had turned out so badly during his session with Howard that Jack had forgotten all about the appointment. As he got ready to leave, he told himself that there was no way this could be the same woman. He wanted so badly to call and cancel, but he didn't have her contact information. His contact was Howard. *No way in hell I am going to call and ask him for her number.*

Since there was no way to cancel, Jack felt compelled to go. As he made the long drive down from Malibu, his emotions ran the gamut. *This could be the cute girl from the studio. Couldn't it? Not likely.* Besides, if against all odds, her name was Beck Taylor, there was no way she could measure up to the angel of his dreams.

Moreover, he was meeting with someone who was hoping for a job with Tom Price, something Jack didn't have the authority to give. Unless this was his Beck, Jack and the person he was meeting were both in for a disappointment. Ever the dreamer, he clung to the one small shred of hope that he would walk into the coffee shop and see her waiting for him.

To his astonishment, Jack was a few minutes early, even with the ever-present LA traffic. As he entered the cafe, his heart skipped a beat. There was a woman with a head full of red curls at the counter. He hurried across the room and touched her shoulder, "Beck?" he asked as she paid for her order. The woman turned to him and sneered, offended by his touch. Her face looked nothing like Beck's, "I'm sorry," he muttered.

He skulked over to a table near the window and waited. Studying each woman who walked in the door. Hopefully, Beck Taylor would recognize him since he was a public figure, and he had no idea what she looked like. This proved tricky as more than one woman in the shop seemed to recognize him, but being true citizens of Hollywood, they didn't approach him.

Right at noon, a tall young man with blonde surfer hair bounded into the cafe. He made a beeline for Jack's table. "Dude! I'm a huge fan," he bellowed as he walked over.

"Are you...?" Jack stopped. *Surely not.*

"Beck Taylor at your service, "he said as he gave Jack a firm handshake," I can't believe it's you, man. Your Halloween show was rad last year."

"Um, thanks," he said. There was an ache in the pit of his stomach. He needed to leave. After a moment, he finally brought himself to say, "Look, I'm sorry, but I heard back from

Tom this morning. He had to fill the job with someone who was - the nephew of a studio exec."

"That's some gnarly nepotism," Beck said as he studied Jack's face, "Hey, it's chill. It's not your fault. Here, sign my CD. We'll call it good."

"Thanks for understanding," Jack managed to say as he reached for the man's Sharpie and CD.

"Make it out to Beckham, please?" the young man added.

Chapter 37

Jack slammed his front door behind him. He was furious with himself and Beckham Taylor, who certainly wasn't his Beck. As Jack marched down the hall, he removed his shoes and threw them. He stormed into his bedroom and collided with his dresser, which caused an antique doll in a bell jar to fall to the floor. In a blind rage, he swept both the dresser and his nightstand clear of everything. Then he stripped his mattress clean of its bedding. He paused only once to pummel a pillow before hurling it across the room. His screams pierced the quiet canyon as he destroyed his bedroom.

He searched wildly for something, anything else to throw or smash, when his eyes landed on the bag from the hospital leaning against the bed. He wrestled with it until it finally ripped open. His shoes and outfit tumbled onto the bed. Each shoe was thrown hard across the room. Next, he set about tossing the pile of clothes. As he picked up the slacks, something fell out of the front pocket. Something small and shiny that hit the mattress and bounced onto the floor. Jack bent over and picked it up. It was a heart-shaped opal ring with two tiny diamonds.

He slid onto the floor and stared at it in disbelief. Caught between his back and the mattress, the dress shirt slid down and fell onto his head. There it was, the scent of vanilla mixing in with the sterile smell of the hospital. The fragrance was faint but unmistakable. She was real. That meant that all of it was real.

Jack's heart was racing. He felt so many things all at once. Knowing she had existed meant that he hadn't had some epic dream followed by a breakdown. He wasn't insane, only grieving. The loss felt real because Beck was real. As he sat there holding her ring, the ring he had never been able to give her, he allowed all of his memories of her to come flooding back into his consciousness.

The first time he saw her at the club, dancing awkwardly together at the Savoy, and how small her hand felt in his when he walked her home after work. It all played out like a movie in front of him, except that he remembered her touch and the way she smelled. He removed his shirt from his head, took it into his hands, he inhaled deeply. Closing his eyes, he tried to imagine that he was her once again resting his head near her heart.

This image, combined with the antiseptic smell, reminded him of their last moments together. The pain hit him, and he felt as though he had lost her all over again. He remembered what she'd said, "You're going to do great things. You'll reinvent yourself, and keep them all guessing. I know you will," then she had squeezed his hand and promised, "I will always be there, Jack."

For the first time since he had returned to 1992, he began to feel like maybe he could reinvent himself. Beck wasn't there the way he wanted her to be, but he could feel her all around him. He could hear the music of her voice and sense the tempo of her heartbeat. He smiled at the way her red curls used to tickle his chin as her head fit neatly beneath his when they embraced; the weight of her body pressed against his chest as he had held her close on their last night together.

The sound of the telephone startled him. He didn't want to break the spell, so he let the call go to his answering machine.

He tried to ignore it, so he could be alone with Beck's memory a little longer. It was Tom letting him know that he had made it to LA and would see him in a couple of days. It was time to get to work on the Halloween musical. The one Beck had been so excited for, "I'll make you proud, Darlin'," he whispered.

Chapter 38

"Do you want a drink? I could mix up something," Jack asked Tom as they sat at the bay. He had spent the Fall finishing the songs for the musical. It had helped him to stay busy. Jack knew he would never be the same after loving and losing Beck, but at least he could write again. In fact, he found he felt closer to the red-headed heroine of their project and surer of her voice than he ever had before. Beck would have loved the musical, he was sure.

As usual, he felt very proud of what he had written until it was time to play it for the director. Tom was more than a director. He was one of Jack's closest friends. However, that old stage fright would creep in every time no matter who was sitting in the director's chair. After what had happened with Howard, Jack was especially apprehensive.

"Nice try, No distractions," Tom said as he smiled at his friend, "Just play the music." Tom was all too familiar with Jack's attempts at distraction. Jack knew better than to try again; it would only make Tom cranky. Pushing play, he leaned back in his chair, he touched Beck's ring, which now hung on a chain around his neck hidden under his shirt.

The men listened carefully. Tom leaned closer to the bay and closed his eyes. He laughed out loud and nodded at the villain's song. When it came to the heroine's songs, he said, "Yes, there she is. That's what I was looking for," Jack was relieved. He played the rest of the songs. When Tom heard the finale, he turned to Jack and said, " Okay. I think we've really got something here."

"Yeah, I think it turned out okay," Jack agreed, which was the highest compliment he'd dare pay his work.

"This is more than okay. I can't wait to get this over to the screenwriter and the animators. We have a movie," Tom said as he high fived Jack.

"Tom..about the main character."

"Yeah?"

"I feel really close to him. I know we talked in the beginning, but we never set anything in stone. I feel like he's - me. Please let me sing for him in the movie?"

"I always assumed you would. I can't imagine anyone else in that role. Speaking of feeling close to him...what's going on?".

"What do you mean?" Jack asked.

"The love story there at the end. It's beautiful. It feels so real. So, when do I get to meet her?" Tom asked with a grin.

"It didn't work out," Jack said, looking at his feet.

"I'm sorry, man," Tom said.

Jack was desperate to tell someone his story. He looked at Tom and thought hard about what would happen if he dared.

"Hey, Tom. Now that we're done, would you like that cocktail? We could go out on the deck and watch the sunset."

"Now that I know you're not stalling, I'm down," Tom said.

The men relaxed on Jack's deck overlooking the canyon, it was a crisp December night, and there was a peek of the Pacific in between the mountains. Jack poured Tom a second cocktail while they watched the sunset. As the light faded, he summoned up the courage to tell Tom the whole story.

"Hey Tom, can I tell you about the craziest thing that ever happened to me?"Jack asked.

"I love crazy. Go for it!"

"Okay. I'm telling you this because you're like a second brother to me. I can't tell Robert because he'll just tease me. I'm afraid my mom would have me committed. But, you tell bizarre stories all the time so..."

"You're stalling again. Lay it on me," Tom said.

Jack set about explaining what had happened over the past three months. As soon as he uttered the final words, "Then I landed back here." He was met by Tom's stunned face and several minutes of awful silence.

"Are you sure it wasn't a dream?" Tom asked when he had finished.

"I thought so at first, but she seemed so real to me. Then, I found this in the pocket of the pants I was wearing," Jack said as he pulled the chain out of his shirt to show Tom Beck's ring. Tom turned back to the view beyond the deck, and Jack could see his wheels turning.

"That's one outlandish story, man," Tom finally said.

"I know, I lived it," Jack said, "I haven't been able to talk to anyone about Beck or what happened. You're the only person I know who might believe me." Tom avoided his gaze and said nothing.

"Tom? You do believe me, don't you?" Jack asked.

Tom stood up and turned toward Jack, "Sorry, man. I don't think I can. I want to, but it's too - out there. I've gotta go. I'll be in touch soon about the musical."

With that, one of his closest friends walked out the door. He turned his face toward the ocean and tucked Beck's ring back into his shirt. He kept his hand on the jewelry pressing it gently against his heart.

Tomorrow, he would meet with the band to tell them the truth about his hearing and prepare for the group's end. He hummed Beck's theme to himself and felt her presence. Bracing for another challenging day.

Chapter 39

Just as Jack was about to head down to the studio, his phone rang. He assumed one of the guys was running late, so he picked up the phone. "Hello?"

"Jack, it's Ronald; how ya feeling?"

"Better. I was just headed downstairs to meet with the band. Can I call you back?"

"I just wanted to let you know that I heard from the producers of Tom's musical. They love the songs. I had them send over the demos. I'll use them to see what I can do to drum up some more projects for you."

"Sounds good," Jack said.

"We might have to start with a smaller project and work our way back up." Ronald cautioned him.

"I'm okay with that. After today, I'll have plenty of time."

"Making the big leap, huh?"

"Yeah. It's time," Jack said.

"Well, I'll let you get to it. Take care," Ronald said as he hung up.

And now I'm late, not good, especially for this meeting. Jack came quickly downstairs and saw that his bandmates were waiting for him in the studio. The tension was thick, and he couldn't blame them. He'd been at worst an absent leader and, at best, a distracted one for the past couple of years.

All eight members were present. Most of them had grown up with him. Two were high school friends, three had stuck with him when the theatre troupe morphed into a rock band. Jack couldn't look them in the eye. *I don't want to lose my friends, but things have to change.* Choosing his words carefully, Jack started to speak, but he didn't get a chance.

"Hey Hollywood, you said two o'clock. We all made up here in traffic. You just had to walk down the stairs. Why are you late?" Andrew asked, bluntly.

"I'm sorry. The phone rang, and I thought it was one of you. It was my manager. I got off as soon as I could," Jack explained.

"So, even when you're supposed to be with us, you're working on your side gig? Nice," Andrew snarled.

Barry stood up. His imposing height drew all the focus to him. He said, "Listen, fighting won't get us anywhere. We came here today to see where we stand as a group and to decide whether or not we're moving forward. We've all put our hearts and souls into this band. Let's just try to hear each other out. Okay?"

"Thanks, Barry," Jack said, "I've called all of you here today to let you know that I will not be continuing with the band."

"It fucking figures," Andrew said, "Hollywood calls, and you're outta here."

"This wasn't an easy a decision to make. I plan to pursue film composing full time, but that's not the only reason I'm doing this. Last time we met, you pointed out how you all have families, and I don't. I can't manage two careers and a private life. I barely have time to see my mom and my brother as much as I work," Jack explained.

"I understand having one career at a time, but why choose film scoring over the band," their drummer Vito asked.

"I don't like repeating myself. In the band, I have to sing the same things over and over. When I write, it's always something new. Then there's the touring, you all know how I feel about that. Besides, I found out at my last check-up that I can't tour anymore."

"Jack, are you sick?" Barry asked.

"No, nothing like that. But, I've damaged my hearing. The doctor said that if I continue playing in front of a rock band, I could lose it all." Jack explained.

"Shit! That's the worst thing that can happen to a musician," Vito said.

"So, the question of whether or not to continue has already been decided. Now, we need to talk about how we wrap this up." Andrew said a little more calmly.

"We're pretty close to finishing the album. It would be a shame for those songs to go unpublished," Barry said, "Are you able to finish the album with us, Jack?"

"I'd love to finish it. I have a bit of time before my next project starts up," Jack said, not wanting to tell them that he had no idea when another film would come his way.

"Maybe we could do a short tour?" Andrew asked.

"We're gonna have to get your hearing checked. Did you not hear the man say that he can't perform in front of the band no more?" Vito said.

"I'm afraid that even a short tour is out of the question," Jack said apologetically.

"What about a farewell concert? Would that be okay?" Barry asked.

Jack took a moment to think. *I'm pretty sure that one concert wouldn't hurt, but I really don't want to get up in front of a huge crowd again. The last time I enjoyed performing was at the Cotton Club on Halloween. That's it, Halloween. Ah Ooga is known for its Halloween concerts, and it's the one performance I look forward to every year.*

"Let's do it," he said finally. And with an impish grin, he added, "On Halloween."

"That's ten months from now," Andrew protested.

"I know. That's gives us enough time to release and market the album and the concert," Jack explained.

"We have a lot of good material here. With that timeline, we can record it all and give the fans a double album," Barry suggested.

"Yeah, the album could drop in the summer, we promote the shit out of it, and throw one hell of a goodbye party on Halloween. I dig it," Vito said.

They all looked to Andrew, who looked up from tuning his bass and said, "It's kind of a long timeline, but we end on a high note. Plus, it'll give Hollywood here some breathing space. Okay, I'm in."

With the matter settled, the rest of the day felt like old times. They went through the list of songs for the album and noted which ones still needed work.

"I have one I'd like to add to the list. I wrote it last week," Jack said.

He played it for them on his old acoustic guitar. It was the most personal song he had ever written, all about the grief he felt at the loss of Beck. Writing it had helped Jack feel better, but when he finished playing, he looked up to a bunch of concerned faces.

"Uh, are you alright, Jack? That song sounds like you've been through some stuff!" Andrew asked.

"Yeah, I have been, but I'm working through it," Jack said.

"That was beautiful, but I didn't hear a horn part in it," said the saxophone player who Jack suddenly realized he had never seen before.

"Yeah... there's really not one for this song," Jack said, still staring curiously at the sax player, a well dressed black man in his thirties,

"Well, why don't we come back tomorrow ready to work on one of the other tracks, and you three can record this song now," the sax player suggested.

"Sounds good," Jack said, still staring at the stranger.

As the horn players packed up their instruments, Jack made his way over to Barry and whispered: "Um, who's the new sax player?"

Barry looked over at the horn players and said, "Marvin Ringold? He's not new. He's been with us for the past five years."

"Are you sure? What happened to Patrick?" Jack asked.

"We've never had a horn player named Patrick. Are you sure you're okay, Jack?"

Jack could picture Patrick clearly in his mind. He was a brawny guy with brown hair and freckles who used to call his saxophone a gobble pipe. It had been the first time Jack had heard it referred to by that name. Patrick had told him that his grandpa worked in a jazz club and taught him all the lingo. That's when he remembered Patrick's last name was McGee...just like Pipes McGee. A dark cloud settled over Jack as he remembered that morning on the stairs.

"You okay, Jack?" Marvin asked as Jack became aware that he had been staring at Marvin this entire time.

"Yea, I was just thinking something through. Got lost in thought," he said. *I wonder what else I altered. Beck's gone too soon, and Patrick has never been born. It's too much.* He would take refuge in the music. Jack turned to Barry and said, "I'm good to go on the new song if you are."

That night, he lay awake alone on the studio couch listening to the recording. He was holding Beck's ring, thinking about all of the music she'd inspired. Most of it, she would never get to hear. *I would trade it all to have you here with me, Beck.*

Chapter 40

It was a late June morning. Jack was sitting in the studio listening to the songs slated for the new album when someone knocked on the outside studio door. He paused the playback, hoping it was the clips he was waiting for from Tom's project. He opened the door, expecting to see a courier. To his surprise, Tom was standing there with the reels.

"Waiting for these?" he asked.

"Tom? I didn't know you were back from London," Jack said.

"We have to start promoting the movie tomorrow. Where else would I be?"

"I thought we were doing separate interviews," Jack said as he looked down at the floor.

"Why?" Tom asked.

"Well, things with us have been sort of..."

"Weird. Yeah, I gotta be honest. I thought you had gone off the edge, man."

"And now?" Jack asked.

"Well, I made a side trip to New York on my way here. I went to the library to do some research for a new project. I couldn't get your story off my mind. I searched through the microfiche copies of the *New York Age* from 1938, and I found these." Tom handed Jack a folder and explained, "This is every article Beck Taylor wrote for the paper. My favorite is the one with the picture. It's a little blurry, but there you are with only one eyebrow," Tom said with a chuckle as he helped Jack locate the blurry photo in the stack of papers.

"You brought me her words. I can't thank you enough," Jack said, staring at Beck's articles.

"I still don't understand how it happened, Jack. That does look like you, but I don't understand how you did it." Tom said as they stared at Jack's picture in the paper.

"I wish I knew. That was the scariest part. We had no understanding of how we came to be there. No control over when or if we'd ever come home."

"You were in the Jazz Age. Tell me you at least had some fun. I know how much you're into that stuff."

"Absolutely. I jammed with some incredibly talented musicians and fell in love with Beck. I felt so free to try new things. There were no expectations."

"Okay, now I'm jealous. I wouldn't mind starting over and having that kind of freedom," Tom said.

"But we don't have to travel back in time. We just have to take risks and stick to our guns," Jack said.

"I'm sorry I doubted you. You have to admit that was a pretty crazy story," Tom said as he gave Jack a playful jab on the arm. Until this moment, Jack hadn't understood just how much he needed someone to believe him.

After Tom left, Jack sat down to read Beck's words. He was halfway through her first article when the phone rang.

"Hey, Jack, it's Ronald. Do you have a minute?"

"Of course."

"First, I wanted to check and make sure that you got the clips from the musical and the promo schedule."

"Yeah, everything's here. Tom brought it by this afternoon," Jack said, "We're doing as many interviews as we can together before he has to go back to London. He's cool with me mentioning the new album."

"Great. Listen, Jack, remember when I said I'd shop that jazz score around? Well, I got a call today from Figment Films."

"Who's that?" Jack asked.

"They're a small, independent studio. They've had some success with finding new directors and taking their films to the major festivals. They said that they have a new director who's interested in the jazz score."

"Well, it's not really finished. I'd have to work on it and make sure it sets the right tone for their film," Jack reminded Ronald.

"I know, and they're small-time so -"

"There's no money, right?" Jack interrupted. He knew the drill.

"Yeah. It would be one of your silver dollar scores," Ronald said.

"Well, what do you think?" Jack asked.

"They got a pretty good reception with their films at Sundance and Cannes last year. It could be good exposure for you. Why don't I set up a meeting with the director, and if you don't like him, I can let em down easy for you later."

"I guess it couldn't hurt," Jack said, trying to sound casual. It had been months since he'd been asked to work on a film. He was excited and relieved.

"Good, I'll set it up. Do you want me there in case you need to bail early?" Ronald asked.

"I can handle it. Thanks, Ron," Jack said as he ended the call.

He sat Beck's articles on his nightstand and went down to the studio. He spent a little time playing around as he tried to jog his memory of the music that he had written in 1938. It might be viewed as a step back going from a Grammy-winning blockbuster to a small indie film, but he missed composing.

Chapter 41

Jack was skeptical as he drove past two major studios and pulled into the industrial part of Culver City. He found the large warehouse Figment Films was leasing and parked his car. This was not the way he usually started a project. Typically, he received a cut of the movie nearly finished, and he'd set up a meeting with the director.

Manning the front desk was a teenager in a Guns N Roses T-shirt reading Metal Edge magazine. She looked annoyed as Jack approached, "Hi, I'm Jack Herman. I have an appointment with Thomas Platt," he said.

"Dad! Someone's here to see you," she called over her shoulder. A man emerged from the makeshift soundstage in shorts and a T-shirt holding a cordless drill. He noticed Jack and looked embarrassed.

"Steph, why didn't you tell me Mr. Herman was here?" the man said through clenched teeth and a forced smile. He set down the drill and extended his hand to Jack. As they shook, the man said, "I'm Thomas Platt, one of the producers of *Lovers in A Dangerous Time*. We can't thank you enough for considering our film."

"I'm excited to hear more about it," Jack said. He looked past Thomas in an attempt to locate the director. He was anxious to meet the person he'd work most closely with on the production. His comfort level with the director would be a key factor in whether or not Jack moved forward with the film.

"Let me show you the sets," Thomas said as he and Steph led Jack through the large double doors onto the soundstage, "We're a small company, so we all wear many hats. I'm a producer, but I also build the sets. Jim, our other producer, is a master electrician, so naturally, he does the lights. His wife does costumes, and my wife, Elizabeth, is a cosmetologist. Our director's also the writer. That's just how we roll here."

Jack was stunned at the recreation of the interior of the Cotton Club. It was a very faithful replica. He carefully explored the set and said," The detail work is incredible. Who was your consultant?"

"Our director had a very clear vision of how it should look. Speaking of, Steph? Do you know where she is?"

"I don't know," Steph said with a shrug.

"Go find her, please," Thomas instructed. Steph rolled her eyes, "Go now," Thomas insisted.

Jack walked onto the stage and wished he could play with Lowry again. He longed to put on his devil horns and play the trombone. Of course, what he wanted most was to take Beck into his arms and dance with her one last time. As he looked around the stage, he heard footsteps behind him.

"Hello Jack," a soft familiar voice said. Jack turned around, and his heart began to race as he met with a shining pair of olive green eyes and that unforgettable smile.

"Beck? Is it really you?" he said as he jumped off the stage and ran to embrace her.

Thomas looked confused. He said, "I was going to say this is our director Beck Taylor, but I guess you've met."

"It was long time ago," Beck said with a smile. Jack held her tight, afraid he would lose her again, "Um, Thomas, could you give us a minute?" she asked.

Thomas said, "Uh, huh. I'm just going to let you fill him in on the project," as he started to leave; he noticed that Steph was still standing next to the couple staring at them, "Steph. Let's go."

"Fine," Steph said as she followed her dad back to the front office.

"Where have you been?" Jack asked as he stepped back to look at her keeping both of his hands on her shoulders. Afraid to let go.

"I've been here in LA. I fell asleep with your head on my chest and woke up in the hospital here."

"Are you okay? You can see me, right?" Jack asked, suddenly remembering her vision loss.

"Yes. My sight came back after a few days, but my memory was fuzzy for a while. The doctor suggested that I write my memories down, so I started writing our story. I finished the script about four months ago, and I was telling Elizabeth about it while we were working on another film. She's Thomas' wife. She liked the story, so she pitched it to Thomas and Jim. They're the producers."

"Can we go somewhere and talk? Can I take you to dinner?" he asked.

Beck beamed, "I'd love that. But, I'm supposed to be pitching you the movie. Can we go after?"

"I'm not so easy to work with, you know," Jack said with a grin, "You sure you want me for this project?"

"You're the only man for the job. Besides, you don't scare me. I've worked with you before."

"Well, then I'm all yours," he said as he looked at her. Seeing her again in what was now 1993. He noticed her untamed red curls and appreciated the way her fitted teal T-shirt accentuated the green in her eyes. The way her blue jeans curved to fit her shape.

"What's wrong. Am I not dressed up enough for dinner? I could stop by my apartment and change," Beck offered as she followed his gaze.

"You look beautiful. I just can't believe you're really here," Tears began to form in his eyes as he said quietly," I thought you were dead."

"Oh, Jack, I'm so sorry. Is that why you didn't come and find me?" Beck asked as she put her arms around his neck.

"For a while, I thought it was all a dream or that I'd had a psychotic break. I actually tried to find you once, but it was a disaster."

"I thought it was a dream or the head injury, but then I found something that proved it was real. Hold on," Beck said as she headed back toward the make-up area.

Jack didn't like being away from her, "Where are you going?" he asked anxiously.

"I have some things for you. Just a sec," Beck said as she disappeared into the back.

He realized he still had something for her, too. Her ring was still around his neck. Jack used this moment alone to quickly put it in his pocket. Beck returned with a record album tucked under her arm.

"After I got out of the hospital, I went back to the same used record store where I found my Ah Ooga music. I wandered into the jazz section. This was mixed in with some of Duke Ellington and Cab Calloway's records," Beck showed him the album.

It was titled *The Original Cotton Club Revue: featuring Cab Calloway, Lowry Ringold, and Jack "the Red Devil" Herrmann.* There on the cover was the entire cast of the show, including Mrs. Esther, Leroy, and Jack with Beck by his side. He leaned in to get a closer look.

"Finally. A picture where I have both eyebrows," Jack said.

Beck laughed then said, "This is how I knew that all of it really happened," she offered him a marker, "Will you sign my album, Mr. Herman?"

He took the marker from Beck and signed her album. When he looked up, she was covering each of her eyes with a silver dollar.

"What are you doing?" Jack asked, somewhat disturbed.

"It's your payment for the score," she said. Beck saw that he was upset and said, "I'm sorry. I guess it's not funny considering; here you take them," she handed Jack the two silver dollars.

"You know I only charge one silver dollar, right?"

"Look at them," Beck said. Jack saw that one was a shiny 1992 silver dollar, and the other was a well-loved silver dollar from 1938, "You need both of them."

"I need you," Jack said as he kissed Beck passionately.

"Haven't you learned your lesson about kissing me at work?" she said with a flirty smile, "C'mon, let's go eat."

"Sounds good. On our way out, we can let Thomas know that you have your composer."

"Where are you taking me for dinner?" Beck asked.

"Guess," Jack said, planning to take her wherever she wanted to go.

"A pizza place not run by the mob," she said playfully.

"Hmmm, Most pizza places are run by the mob. The only way to be certain we don't run into trouble is to have pizza delivered to my place," he said, not wanting to share her with the rest of the world just yet.

"Why? Jack Herman, you'd lead them right to us," she said with a laugh.

"I'm willing to risk it if you'll come home with me. Please, I want to show you my place," Jack said, hoping that it would soon be her place, too.

Chapter 42

"This place is huge," Beck said as they walked into Jack's house, "I hope I don't get lost in here," As Rufus bounded up to her, she smiled and bent down to scratch between his ears, "Well, hello there."

"Don't worry, I'll find you," Jack said, "That's Rufus," he told her as he went to order the pizza. While on the phone, he watched her explore the house and grinned. After he'd returned from 1938, the large house had seemed so empty, but with Beck standing in his living room, the place felt like home again. She moved around like a curious child as she looked at his collections of bones and voodoo artifacts.

"This reminds me of the Halloween party in Harlem. The Días de Los Muertos skulls are actually quite pretty," Beck said. She continued to explore, poring over the artwork, and reading the spines of the books on his shelf. She stopped at a glass case that contained a mummified finger.

"Is that real?" she asked.

"Yes, welcome to the Underworld, Persephone.", Jack said in a low voice and winked at her, "The shrunken heads real, too. You're not going to run away, are you?"

"I don't think I can, your hell hound might catch me, and I'd end up on your wall," she said indicating Rufus, who lounged on the living room rug.

Jack chuckled at the thought of his old dog chasing any-thing. *But is she actually scared?* "You're here for five minutes, and I've already scared you away?" he asked.

"No way. You're stuck with me. Now, where's my pomegran-ate?" Beck said as she ran to Jack and threw her arms around him.

"You're what?"

"To get Persephone to stay, Hades tricked her into eating a pomegranate seed. Apparently, once you eat in the Under-world, you're stuck there forever," She informed him.

"I don't have a pomegranate; pizza will have to do," Jack de-clared as he tightened his embrace.

"You know I can't resist pizza," she said. They held each other tight for a moment, then Beck asked suddenly, "Can I see your studio?"

"Of course, right this way," He led Beck down the stairs, de-lighted in her enthusiasm. She paused at the bottom of the stairs when she saw his sizeable creepy doll collection. Some dolls had eerie fixed expressions, some were missing their eyes, and some were just heads.

"Oh my!" she said as she slowly looked over the dolls. Jack could see that Beck looked a little unnerved, so he explained, "When I was a little boy, I was afraid of a movie poster, it had a picture of a doll's head. Robert found the picture in a magazine and used it to scare me. So, one day I taped it to the edge of my bed and made sure that it was the last thing I saw at night and the first thing I saw in the morning."

"Why would you do that?" Beck asked.

"So, I'd get used to it. Once I was desensitized to that image, my brother lost a bit of his power over me. Anytime I'd get scared of something new, I'd force myself to be near it. With the dolls, I went from being afraid to eventually being drawn into the history they possess after being passed down from one person to the next. Most of these are antiques, so they've seen a lot. Each one has a story. I'll tell you'll all of them eventually."

Beck stepped in for a closer look. She stopped at one of the dolls who had its face in the corner as though it were in trouble. Beck asked, "Why is this one in the corner?"

"She knows what she did," Jack said with a grin as he walked past her. Desperate to distract her, he turned on the lights over his percussion section, "Check this out."

"Look at all those instruments," Beck rushed over and looked at Jack's balafon, "Is this one of the ones you built yourself?"

"Yea, that's one of the balafons we use in concert," Jack said.

"I remember you said that they're usually on a bamboo frame, but you made a metal frame for yours."

"That's right, it's much stronger than bamboo, and it folds up so I can take it with me to the shows," he said, happy to see her interest, "I'll teach you to play it sometime if you'd like." Beck beamed at him, then she saw the monitors one had music notation on the screen, and the other screen had movie clips from Tom's Halloween musical.

"What's this?" she asked as she moved in for a closer look.

"Have a seat, Madame Director. You and I will be spending quite a bit of time here," he smiled. Then, he said, "Want a sneak peek at the Halloween musical?"

"Yes," Beck said, her eyes wide with excitement.

Jack showed her a couple of clips, one of a song that he sang as the skeleton and another of the female lead's song. Beck looked so happy that Jack didn't mind listening to his own work for once.

"I love it so much! Especially the Frankengirl. I get her," Beck said.

"You do?" he asked.

"I know what it's like to come apart at the seams and have to put yourself back together again," she explained.

"I know you do, Darlin'," Jack said as he kissed her gently on the forehead.

"I see so much of you in that skeleton man. I know how tired you are of being in the band, but you're so brilliant at it that everyone wants you to keep doing it," she said as she squeezed his hand, "I heard the new album. It's different."

"Different meaning bad?" Jack asked.

"No, I liked it. I think it's probably the most personal writing you've ever done, but I didn't know you when you were recording the other albums. Maybe your feelings have just changed over time?"

"I wrote most of it before we met, and I was working through some frustration. The ballad I wrote when I thought I'd lost you. Beck, I'm pretty well known. It's a lot easier to find me than it is to find you. Why didn't you come to me sooner?" Jack asked, hurt at all the grief he'd suffered and the time they'd lost.

"You might be more visible, but you're not as approachable, Jack. What was I supposed to do? Call your manager and tell him we met in 1938? Storm the guard hut at the bottom of your gated community? I didn't want to do that. I wanted to recover from my injuries and show you that I was pursuing my dreams. I wanted you to be with someone you could be proud of."

"I thought you were dead, Beck," Jack said quietly.

"I didn't know that. If I'd known you were grieving, maybe things would have been different. For all I knew, you had written the whole thing off as a dream. You said you did at first, and so did I. I'm sorry you had to go through that. I'm sorry that I had to recover without you. Loving someone comes at a cost sometimes."

"I would have been there for you," Jack said.

"I know you would have. Listen, we've both had a tough time, but we're together right here, right now. I'll stay as long as you'll put up with me."

"Ha! I'm the one you'll have to put up with," Jack scoffed.

"Speaking of 'putting up with you,' I read that this is the last album for Ah Ooga. How did the guys take the news that you're leaving?" Beck asked.

"Not well at first, but they get it. No one wants me to go deaf. We're getting ready for a farewell concert on Halloween, and the musical premieres the week before. It's going to be busy for a bit."

"Sound like I won't see you very much," she said with a frown.

"You will. I'd like you to come with me to the musical's premiere, and I'm composing the music for your movie so we'll see a lot of each other. You'll probably get sick of me."

"Never. I'd love to go to the premiere with you. Now, if only I can buy a ticket to the concert before it sells out this time," Beck said with a grin.

"Darlin', I'll give you one of the best seats in the house as long as you promise to wear ear protection."

"It's a deal," she said. She looked over the equipment again and asked, "How does this work?"

"Film scoring?"

"Yes, I'm not a musician, so this is the part I'm nervous about. I'm afraid I don't know enough about music to tell you what I want."

"You don't have to be a musician. I'm actually glad you're not a musician. It's harder for me when the director wants to talk about music. That's not the best way to go about this. Instead, you'll show me a scene and talk to me about the emotions behind it. Just speak to me in terms of feelings, and I'll compose that into music to set the right tone for your story," he explained.

The doorbell rang upstairs, "Pizza!" they both said at once, realizing how hungry they were.

As they finished their dinner, Jack caught a glimpse of the sunset out the window. The sky was brilliant full of purples, pinks, and oranges. "Come with me," he said, pulling her onto the deck. The sun was just beginning to dip into the ocean.

"Oh my gosh! The view is breathtaking from up here," Beck said.

"Yes, it is," he said, looking at Beck, "the sunset and the ocean are nice, too. Come sit with me." Jack led her over to his outdoor loveseat. As the sky grew darker, the temperature started to drop, so he turned on the patio heater. Beck was lost in thought. "What are you thinking about so hard?" he asked.

"When we were talking at the movie studio, I told you that I thought our time in 1938 was a dream until I found that album. You said that you thought it was a dream, too. I was wondering, what finally convinced you that it really happened?"

Jack put his hand in his pocket and felt the ring he had always intended to put on her finger. *Will she think it's too soon? I could tell her that I found the articles Tom brought me, but I don't want to lie to her. Besides, I already tried twice to propose, and wasn't that was fifty-five years ago? It's time, dammit!*

"Well, I had been carrying something around in my pocket since Halloween night. When I got back to the present, I spent a couple of days in the hospital for dehydration and exhaustion. They sent my suit home with me in a bag. When I finally dumped out the clothes I'd been wearing onto my bed, I found something I'd put in my pocket in 1938 was still there."

"What was it?" she asked.

Jack got down on one knee and pulled the ring from his pocket. Beck gasped when she saw it. Jack took a deep breath and said, "Rebecca Taylor, the three months we spent in 1938 meant so much to me. You were the one thing in my life. I didn't know I was missing. When I lost you, it almost killed me.

Now that I've found you, I don't ever want to lose you again. Will you marry me?"

Beck beamed at Jack, "I've eaten in the underworld, so I guess there's no turning back."

"Is that a yes?" Jack asked.

"Yes!" Beck tackled him with a big hug and breathed into his ear, "yes, yes, yes!"

Chapter 43

The sound of the marimba woke Jack from his nap. He smiled, then checked his watch. It was just after three, and they had a busy night ahead of them. It was time to start getting ready. As he headed down the hall to the studio, the doorbell rang. He diverted to the front of the door along with Rufus. Elizabeth Platt, Thomas' wife, stood at the door with two women who looked to be about Beck's age. Jack opened up the door, and Elizabeth gave him a huge hug.

"So, good to see you again. Melissa and Jennifer meet Jack Herman," Elizabeth said.

The girls looked at Jack starstruck and blushed. Melissa hugged him and said, "We know, we were at your wedding. You might not remember us; it was a busy day."

Jennifer also gave him a big squeeze, "Yeah, we've worked with Beck and Elizabeth a few times. Also, we're big Ah Ooga fans," she said as her cheeks turned even redder.

"Enough fawning ladies, we've got work to do," Elizabeth said as she dragged in a massive makeup case, The other ladies grabbed additional bags of supplies.

"Can I give you a hand with those?" Jack asked.

"No, just point me in the direction of the master bath, and I'll get set up. Your mission is to retrieve your lovely wife so I can make her even lovelier," Elizabeth said.

Jack pointed her down the hall towards the master suite. She had reminded of his original mission. Downstairs he found

Beck sitting in the percussion section under the balafon looking at the gourds. Her damp hair was piled up on her head in a
clip, and she was wearing a fuzzy lavender bathrobe. Rufus ran
over and crawled into her lap.

"Hey, Darlin'. There's a team of hair and makeup people
waiting for you upstairs," he said.

"I know I heard the doorbell," she said. Then she explained,
"I wanted to compare how a song sounded on the marimba ver-
sus the balafon, but I think I've cracked one of your gourds. I'm
so sorry."

"Beck, they get old and dry out. It's okay. I'll get a new one.
You need to get upstairs," Jack said.

"But I'm so nervous. Can't I just hide down here and hit
things?"

"No, you're going to Oscars, young lady, and that's final. Besides, If you stay down here, you're just going to break more of
my stuff," Jack said in jest as he moved Rufus, then took her
hand and helped her up off the floor.

"Hey! I said I was sorry," Beck said, kissing him on the cheek.

"I'm just teasing, but seriously you need to get ready. Your
friends are waiting upstairs to help you," he said, leading her
out of the studio.

"I'm so scared. I know it's a long shot. Most people don't win
their first time nominated, but you won the first time you were
nominated for a Grammy. Then again, most people don't get
nominated for their first screenplay either. Oh my Gosh! This
could happen. I'm freaking out!" Beck said.

They had reached the top of the stairs. Jack embraced her.
"Beck, take a few deep breaths for me," As he felt her comply,
he stood back and put his hand over her heart. After several
deep breaths, the familiar tempo that he loved so much had returned, "Listen, we're going to get all dolled up and go to this
entertaining and glamorous event. We're probably both going
to lose, but just being nominated is an honor. Afterward, we'll

come home, put on our PJs, and have a loser party for two. Now go get ready," he said as he kissed her.

He didn't want to tell her, but he was nervous, too. Jack hated public speaking more than performing. The category for Best Original Music Score was full of worthy nominees and big scores that were written for large orchestras. Those were usually the sorts of scores that earned awards. Their movie had had a tiny budget.

Unable to afford an orchestra, Jack wrote for an eight-piece jazz ensemble. He had called in every favor he had to fill the scenes where the entire band was featured. He was pretty sure that he wouldn't be taking home the statue. If he was honest, Beck wouldn't be either. Her screenplay was up against movies that had bigger budgets and did better at the box office. They were a pair of underdogs for sure.

Giggles floated down the hall from Jack's bedroom. He had thought about putting in some time downstairs. He needed to get to work. The offers had been pouring in now that he was an Oscar contender. He had three projects slated for this 1994 alone. He checked his watch and realized he only had half an hour before he needed to get ready. He decided to watch a re-run of Twilight Zone instead. His thoughts drifted to the night he went to the Grammys. How it was just Rufus and him in the house. No one had to show up hours ahead of time to help him get ready. *Things are different now, in the best possible way.*

Jack drifted down the hall to the jazz room and put on one of his vintage suits. Beck's favorite was black with pinstripes, single-breasted with a double-breasted vest and high-waisted trousers. "It's an English drape to show off your muscular shoulders and small waist," Beck had explained to him at the tailors.

It has been a long time since someone else dressed me. One less thing to worry about. He remembered how much she loved suspenders and put on a pair under his vest. A sly little grin came to his lips when he thought about surprising her later. *She can never resist suspenders.*

There was a knock at the door. "Jack? Can I come in?" Beck asked.

"Of course, Darlin'," Jack said. He opened the door, and there was Beck all dolled up for the ceremony. She was draped in royal purple, satin from the flutter sleeves at her shoulders all the way to the floor. The satin looked as though it had been poured on, highlighting each of her curves. Her red hair was styled in elegant waves and parted so that her right eye peeked out from her under the S curve of her hair. "Wow! Veronica Lake, what have you done with my wife?"

"Do I look alright?"

"You look gorgeous, he said as he pulled Beck to him. To his surprise, his hands touched bare skin. "Let me see the back."

Beck turned around to show Jack the plunging back of her dress. "I've never worn anything like this. It feels a little strange. It took three women and most of the roll of fashion tape to strap me in here. I don't know if we'll be able to get it off. I might be stuck in here forever."

"I'm always up for a challenge. When we get home, I'll be happy to rescue you from the satin," Jack said with a wink.

"I have something for you," she said. Beck handed him a small gift box. There was a gold pocket watch inside. The inscription said, "We are untethered to time, yet strongly tethered to one another. No matter the shifting sands of the hourglass, may we always cling to each other. Love, Beck".

"Oh, Beck," Jack said as he smiled at his bride.

"It's what the voodoo lady said to us at the Halloween party." she reminded him.

"I remember," Jack said as he embraced her once again.

"A dapper suit like that needs a nice watch and chain to go with it," she said, smiling up at him.

The doorbell rang as Elizabeth and the other ladies headed down the hall.

"Looks like your limo's here. Do us proud tonight, you two," Elizabeth said over her shoulder as she headed for the door.

"Shall we?" Jack asked as he offered Beck his arm.

Miriam was waiting for them in the limo. "Hello, you two," she said, hugging both of them.

"Miriam," Beck said as she returned her mother in law's hug, "You look so beautiful!"

"Well, we might be on TV, so I had to fix up a bit," Miriam smiled as she showed off her adorable gold, satin gown.

"Only the winners are on TV, Mom," Jack said gently.

"You're both winners to me. Besides, we all have to walk the red carpet," she said.

"Oh no! I'd kind of put that part out of my head. Now, I'm nervous again," Beck said with a moan.

"You handled the red carpet just fine at the movie premieres," Jack reassured her.

"This is different. It's a much bigger audience, and they're all expecting something from us. The crowd is staring us down and wondering if we'll win or lose," Beck said, fidgeting with her wedding ring.

"Speaking of expecting any news for me on that front?" Miriam said with a grin.

"Mom. Stop it! We haven't even been married a year, and we both have very full schedules," Jack said, his cheeks turning red.

"I can't help it. You're not getting any younger. Besides, you and Beck would make such cute redheaded babies," Miriam said.

"Sorry, it's just not on our radar right now. Maybe someday," Beck said, squeezing Miriam's hand, "Now, can we please talk about something else?"

Jack was relieved that Beck was not in a hurry to start a family; they were very busy people. He hoped her attempt to distract his mom would work. There was already enough for them to be nervous about.

"Okay, tell me again how you two met?" Miriam asked.

"Mom, we've told you. We met in a jazz club in 1938," Jack said with a devilish grin. He could never think of a decent lie, and with the way he had joked with people in the past, this tactic worked for him.

"Ha, ha! Very funny. I asked Beck," she said, staring over her glasses at her daughter in law.

"Like the man said, we both worked at the jazz club together," Beck said nonchalantly as she winked at Jack.

"Ugh! Not you, too. You're a matched set," Miriam said, shaking her head as they pulled up to the red carpet.

Chapter 44

As they made their way down the red carpet, the ladies fielded most of the questions. Jack was grateful. These things made him feel like a mole that had been dragged into the sunlight, desperate to go back into his hole. His mother and brother had always been the outgoing ones in the family. Now that Beck was part of his family, he felt he had another ally in these situations. He loved watching how easily she engaged the reporters—another glimpse of her in her element.

They were shown to their table, and Miriam set out in search of the restroom. As Jack and Beck sat down, he leaned over and whispered in her ear, "You handled that beautifully. If you win, you're going to be fine."

Beck looked panicked. She was checking for the nearest exit. She said, "You promised me I wouldn't win,"

"I did not. I didn't promise you. I said it's unlikely. Besides, you handled all the red carpet stuff like a pro. What gives?"

"I love talking to people one at a time or in even small groups. If they'd let me go table to table thanking everyone, I'd be fine. It's the huge auditorium full of people and the world-wide audience that's freaking me out."

"I see," Jack said as he squeezed her trembling hand, "You poor thing. You really are nervous. Too bad Leroy's not here to bring you a bucket, huh?"

Beck could not help but smile at the mention of their old pal from the Cotton Club, "If only. I miss them all so much."

"Me too, Darlin'. Win or lose, let's make them proud," Jack said as he kissed her cheek.

As the opening music swelled, they turned their attention to the stage. Jack's mom finally returned from the ladies' room, "I just met Meryl Streep! She's so pretty in person. So nice, too," Miriam said in a loud whisper. Jack smiled and squeezed his mom's hand. It was so much fun to see the Academy Awards through her eyes.

Thirty minutes into the show, they introduced the Award for Best Original Music Score. Beck and Miriam each squeezed one of Jack's hands, which made him feel more trapped than comforted. When it was announced that the top-grossing animated film had won, Jack wasn't a bit surprised. He reclaimed his hands from the ladies and clapped for his colleagues.

His mom whispered, "Hmph! What do they know? You'll get em' next time."

He smiled at his mom and then whispered to his wife, "See, what did I tell you?"

Unfortunately for Beck, her category was toward the very end of the ceremony. When Meryl won for Best Actress, Jack's mom jumped up and cheered. Meryl gave her a little wave on her way up to the stage. "I can die happy now," Miriam said with a sigh.

The next category was Best Original Screenplay, Beck's category. The favorite to win was a crime movie based on old pulp fiction comics. Jack was rooting for his wife, but he knew her chances were slim. Lost in thought about her odds, he missed the announcement of the winner. He only realized it when his mom nudged him, "Oh my goodness, she did it! Why isn't she moving? Jack, you have to tell Beck to get up there."

He looked at his wife, who was paler than usual. She was stunned. He stood up and pressed his hand gently on her back, "You did it, Dollface! Get up there." he said as he helped her to her feet.

Beck managed through a slightly shaky voice to thank the people involved with the movie. She thanked Mama Esther and the others from the Club, and her family. "Most of all, I want to thank my husband and inspiration Jack Herman. Without you, there is no story," Beck said as tears rolled down her cheeks. Leaving the stage, she blew him a kiss.

Jack was about to speak to his mom when one of the officials approached. She leaned over and whispered, "Mr. Herman, Mrs. Herman would like you to join her in the press area."

"Of course," he said," Mom? Would you like to join us in the press room?"

"No, I want to see who wins Best Picture," Miriam said as she waved Jack on.

"Okay, just wait here for us if we're not back by the end of the ceremony," he said. The woman led him back to the press area. He searched the room and finally located Beck's red wavy locks. He came up from behind and hugged her, "I am so proud of you."

"I'm so glad you're here," she said, turning around to hug him again, "I am so freaked out right now!"

"The hard parts over, Darlin'. You won."

"No, it's not! Will you please go up there with me?" Beck pleaded.

He remembered the night he won the Grammy. And how rude that one reporter had been. *I would have loved an ally at that moment. They'd better not be ugly to Beck.* "Of course, I will," he said as the butterflies started fluttering in his own stomach.

"Will you hold Oscar for me a minute? He's heavier than I thought he'd be," Beck said, handing him the statuette. Just then, the announcer escorted them to the side of the stage.

"Wait here, and I'll introduce you. Are you coming up, too, Mr. Herman?" the announcer asked. Jack and Beck nodded. The announcer said, "Ladies and Gentlemen of the press. It is my honor to introduce tonight's winner for Best Original Screenplay Rebecca Herman and nominee for Best Original Score Jack Herman."

They crossed the stage together, and Jack handed Beck her award once she reached the mic so she could be photographed with it. The first reporter of the evening stood up and asked, "Mr. Herman, how do you feel about leaving empty-handed tonight?"

Jack started to feel annoyed, and then he put his arm around Beck's waist. He grinned one of his devilish grins and said, "Who says I'm leaving empty-handed?" Beck smiled up at him as the crowd chuckled. Then he said," Seriously, it was an honor to be nominated, but tonight is about the winners. I'm just here as moral support and arm candy at this point."

A young woman stood up in the back. She asked, "Mrs. Herman, I really enjoyed your movie. Will we see more projects from you soon?"

"Thank you. I'm writing a film right now that's a thriller, and I'm in talks to direct a quirky comedy for Fox. Both are early in development, so I can't reveal much more than that," Beck said.

An older woman from People magazine stood up next, "Congratulations on your recent marriage. With such a busy husband and your new career, how will you find time to spend together?"

Beck tilted her head and cut her eyes at Jack then she looked at the reporter and said, "That's kind of personal. Are you married?"

"Yes, I am. But -" the lady said with a stammer.

"Your job's very busy. How do you stay connected?" Beck asked.

"We just make time for each other." the reporter said, embarrassed at the personal nature of Beck's question.

"Exactly. That's what Jack and I do," Beck said, "Next question, please."

A younger lady stood up from E! Network, "Yours was a whirlwind courtship. How did you two meet again?"

"I've known Jack since 1938. We met when we worked at the same jazz club," Beck said matter of factly.

"How did you two really meet?" the reporter pressed.

"Like Beck said, we met way back in 1938," Jack said as he shrugged his shoulders.

"Just like you met Barry Stephens back in 1926, huh?" the reporter from MTV said.

"No," Jack said slyly, "Barry and I started playing together in 1926. I met him the year before."

The next reporter was an older man from Variety, "Mrs. Herman, someone as young as you rarely writes an Oscar-winning screenplay. Especially on their first try. Are sure that your husband didn't help doctor it just a little?"

"Excuse me?" Beck asked.

"The script is very much about music. You've said you're not a musician. Are you sure he didn't offer some edits?"

Beck's cheeks burned red. Then, she leaned back into Jack and said. "Oh sure, my husband works his ass off twelve hours a day, but he's absolutely thrilled to come out of his studio and whip my script into shape. Better yet, he loves for me to interrupt one of those twelve-hour sessions just to help me finish a scene. Come on, give me a break," Beck said sarcastically.

Jack was fuming. It was one thing to treat him that way, but it really pissed him off to see how rude most of the reporters had been to Beck. He leaned forward and whispered in her ear, "Want me to jump in?" She shook her head.

"I believe we're done here. Goodnight," Beck said cooly as she left the stage with Jack walking behind her, "Let's go find your mom," she said as she squeezed his hand.

In the limo, they told Miriam about the press conference. "Oh Beck, I'm so sorry that they pooped all over your big night that way," she said as she patted Beck's knee.

"I was about to lose it when I remembered that when Jack won his Grammy, lots of people doubted that he wrote his own music. And, when Mary Shelley wrote Frankenstein, everyone said it had to be her husband's work since he was an established poet. So, I figured I would just appreciate that I was in good company," Beck explained.

"I'm so proud of you, Beck," Jack said as he cradled her in his arms on the backbench of the limo. Her back resting against his chest.

"I'm proud of you, too, Love. I know I screwed up by winning but, can we still have our Pj party?"

"Of course we can," Jack said.

"Well, kids, we're almost to my house. Does Oscar live at your place or mine?" Miriam asked, joking with them.

"He's going to live with us because I need all the encouragement I can get," Beck said, "I've been meaning to ask if a couple of Jack's awards could come back to our place. Is that okay?" Beck asked.

"That's up to him. Jack?" Miriam asked.

"Maybe it's time to take a few to the house. We don't want Oscar to be lonely." Jack said.

"I know, Miriam. Why don't you take Oscar home with you this week so he can meet your friends in the book club, then we can pick him and some of his friends up next Sunday when we come over for dinner." Beck suggested.

"That works for me. I'm so proud of you two. I'm so glad that Jack found you. Goodnight, Sweeties," she said as she exited the limo with Oscar, "Oh, he is heavy!" they heard her say to the driver as she stepped out of the car holding Beck's award.

As they rode back to Malibu, Beck relaxed in Jack's arms, and her breathing became steady. The tempo of her heartbeat matching his own. As he rested his chin on her head, he thought about how proud he was of her. He honestly didn't mind that he hadn't won. It felt so good to be able to finally focus on composing full time. It was all he had ever wanted. Well, not all. He thought as he held his dozing wife in his arms. Life was indeed richer now that he had someone to share it with. He hadn't taken home the trophy, but he certainly hadn't left empty-handed.

Acknowledgements

There are so many people who have helped me bring this story to print, I want to thank them all. Elijah Herrick for helping with the research for 1930s Harlem. Emily Zaas for your honest critique and editing. You are a great friend and my story is stronger because of you. Michael Ingram for beta-reading, copy editing, and making sure I didn't forget about Tony. Brendan Kelso for being a constant source of information and motivation for bringing this book (and the ones to follow) to the masses. I am so grateful for your insight and friendship. To 100Covers.com for the beautiful cover design.

To my mom, Barbi Taylor Ingram, for the much needed encouragement today and always. To my dad and stepmother, Steve and Twilla Robinson, for your understanding and patience when I wrote constantly during my visit.

To my fellow writers at Stage Write in Santa Maria, CA, Dixie, Brian, Nakia, Nitana, Candyce, Dan, and Wiley Charles for being a great sounding board and cheering me on in all of my writing endeavors. Teri Bayus and everyone else at the Central Coast Writers Conference for being an incredible resource. I have learned so much from your events.

To the staff at the Nipomo, CA Starbucks for the Sea Salt Caramel Hot Chocolates, a peaceful place to write, and for always asking me about the book even when I came through the drive thru. To Steve Anderson for reminding me that a well lived life is research and that it's never too late to pursue a dream.

To all of my friends who have shown enthusiasm for this story along the way, including my fellow eighties music fans Makena, Leah, Ashley, Jennifer, Linda, Jim, and Ruth. To my children Devin, Cagney, Elijah, Meah, and Natalie who called me an author before I had the confidence to call myself one. I hope I make you as proud of me as I am of all of you. And finally, to Jay Herrick, for your unwavering support, patience, and love. Thank you for living an epic love story with me.

Angela has always had a passion for storytelling which led to work as an actress, director, drama teacher, and writer. She has adapted classic literature into plays for children which are available through Playing with Plays. Angela loves music (especially Eighties music), movies, and reading. She lives with her husband Jay, three of their five children, and their three cats Gatsby, Chaplin, and Keaton. Devil's Chord is her debut novel.